The Gossip Columnist's Daughter

Also by Peter Orner

Fiction

Last Car Over the Sagamore Bridge

Love and Shame and Love

The Second Coming of Mavala Shikongo

Esther Stories

Maggie Brown & Others

Nonfiction

Still No Word from You: Notes in the Margin

Am I Alone Here?

As Editor

The Four Deportations of Jean Marseille

Lavil: Life, Love, and Death in Port-au-Prince

Hope Deferred: Narratives of Zimbabwean Lives

Underground America

THE GOSSIP COLUMNIST'S DAUGHTER

A Novel

PETER ORNER

LITTLE, BROWN AND COMPANY
New York Boston London

This is a book of fiction. Names, characters, places, and incidents are either the product of the author's imagination or, if real, are used fictitiously.

Copyright © 2025 by Peter Orner

Hachette Book Group supports the right to free expression and the value of copyright. The purpose of copyright is to encourage writers and artists to produce the creative works that enrich our culture.

The scanning, uploading, and distribution of this book without permission is a theft of the author's intellectual property. If you would like permission to use material from the book (other than for review purposes), please contact permissions@hbgusa.com. Thank you for your support of the author's rights.

Little, Brown and Company
Hachette Book Group
1290 Avenue of the Americas, New York, NY 10104
littlebrown.com

First Edition: August 2025

Little, Brown and Company is a division of Hachette Book Group, Inc. The Little, Brown name and logo are trademarks of Hachette Book Group, Inc.

The publisher is not responsible for websites (or their content) that are not owned by the publisher.

The Hachette Speakers Bureau provides a wide range of authors for speaking events. To find out more, go to hachettespeakersbureau.com or email hachettespeakers@hbgusa.com.

Little, Brown and Company books may be purchased in bulk for business, educational, or promotional use. For information, please contact your local bookseller or the Hachette Book Group Special Markets Department at special.markets@hbgusa.com.

Book interior design by Marie Mundaca

ISBN 9780316224659
LCCN 2024949996

Printing 1, 2025

LSC-C

Printed in the United States of America

For Katie, Phoebe, and Roscoe

The most intolerable people are provincial celebrities.
— *Chekhov*

I.

Kupcinets and Rosenthals

LOS ANGELES
DECEMBER 1963

THREE MEN DROP into Los Angeles out of a Chicago November. Outside the terminal, waiting by the curb, much as they try to refuse it, the men can't help but enjoy the heat of the morning sun on their faces. They've begun to sweat in their heavy charcoal suits and overcoats.

You don't wear a lightweight suit on an occasion like this.

Two of the men stand so close their thighs touch. Irv Kupcinet, the *Chicago Sun-Times* columnist, and his pal, my grandfather Lou Rosenthal. Both are in their early fifties. Irv is bulky, and at the same time compact, an ex–college quarterback (plus a half season with the Philadelphia Eagles). His meaty face is dominated by a long, bluntly angled nose that surges ahead of him like a ship's prow. His blood-soaked eyes are hidden by the brim of his fedora, pulled low.

Irv Kupcinet has legions of friends — the freshly dead president was one of them — but nobody on earth is more devoted to him than Lou Rosenthal.

Lou's short, rotund, and bald as a newborn. A lawyer

specializing in wills and trusts, he's not here in his professional capacity. Even so, my grandfather's expertise at handling the property of the dead will be useful over the next two days. As he stands beside Irv, Lou stares at the sidewalk as if he's trying to read it. Scattered across each concrete square are specks of glass that wink in the sun.

The third man, standing alone, is my grandfather's brother, Solly. He's sixteen years younger than Lou, closer in age to my father, his nephew, than to his older brother. And he's as hulking as Lou is squat. To my knowledge, no Rosenthal male before or since has ever cleared five feet six on a good day. My father used to say that Great-grandmother Willamina must have had an assignation with the Jolly Green Giant.

At more than a foot taller, Solly not only dwarfs Lou, but he's also got a few inches on the columnist.

In his massive hands, Solly holds Irv's and Lou's suitcases. He has yet to set them down. His face is unevenly shaved and pocked with small patches of beard. Solly made the trip without a change of clothes. When my grandfather summoned him to the airport, he had no time to pack a bag. It was sleeting when they left Chicago. He's still wearing his galoshes.

A friend of mine, a novelist, once said that minor characters don't know they're minor. Doesn't this apply to us all? Those of us who are minor characters have no idea. We all think we're the star of our own show. But Solly Rosenthal, standing on the sidewalk in front of an airport, holding two suitcases, neither of which is his, is well aware he's an afterthought.

My grandfather shrugs off his overcoat and hands it, wordlessly, to his brother. Solly sets down one of the cases and drapes the coat over his shoulder.

"Irv?" Lou says.

No answer.

"Irv?"

Still no response.

"Why don't you take your coat off and give it to Solly?"

The columnist's gaze is fixed beyond the car park in front of them. He's motionless but for a nearly imperceptible rocking motion, slightly forward, slightly back — forward, back, forward, back — an ancient movement only his body remembers. Lou thinks of his own father, who used to rock on his heels like that in the old synagogue on Twenty-Sixth Street. So slightly you had to watch him closely in order to know he was moving at all.

THREE CHICAGOANS WAIT. Is *wait* the right word when there's only dread of what's to come? What does time have to do with it? A worst possible thing has already happened. We're not waiting, Lou thinks. Do sitting ducks wait?

Solly grips the suitcases.

My brother's hands, Lou thinks, when was the last time I touched my brother's hands?

Outside the terminal there's the usual bustle of people on their way somewhere or coming back from somewhere else. Taxis bleat. Doors slam. Laughter, goodbyes. Somebody shouts, "Wait, you forgot..."

We leave, Lou thinks, we come back. We leave again. If this is living, then dying only amounts to staying put.

Meanwhile, there's luggage. An apt word. *Lug... lug... luggage.* Lou takes another look at his brother. We play our parts. One of us grieves. One of us worries. The third, he schleps.

The columnist stands impervious.

A young couple a few feet away ram their mouths together so hard you'd think they'd do permanent damage to their teeth. Like they're welded together. Such a public spectacle. Did a war end somewhere? He can't see the girl's face, hidden as it is by the fall of her hair. He wishes they'd knock it off. If only for Irv's sake, though Irv wouldn't notice if these two started to hump right here on the sidewalk.

"Irv," Lou repeats, "why don't you give Solly your coat?"

DEERFIELD, ILLINOIS
SEPTEMBER 2019

THE NURSING HOME on Waukegan Road, next to the old Sara Lee cake factory. The place is called Sunshine or Sunrise. I can't keep it straight. They shut down the plant years ago. All that's left are broken windows, smokestacks, and a vast parking lot. Yet the sugary reek of industrial cake still permeates these windows that are otherwise screwed shut. Babs calls the place Joliet.

She's stopped eating.

One of my earliest memories is of Babs feeding me family cars. We're in what they call the dayroom. I dip a plastic spoon into a carton of Yoplait.

"Open wide for Lou's cherry-red Lincoln Continental Coupe, doors as big as Rhode Island!"

"Why are you shouting?" Babs says.

It all reverses. History repeats itself backward.

With disgust, she accepts the spoonful. Again, I dip the spoon in the carton.

"Vroom, vroom! It's your own '83 Seville. Two-tone paint

job and that weird hump of a trunk, remember? Like you could stuff a body in it? Open, Babs, open..."

We're surrounded by strangers in wheelchairs haphazardly parked like bumper cars. It's midmorning. Some doze. Some slurp cold coffee. Others stare at the wall. At a table in the corner, they're playing cards. That serious murmuring. Nobody here is waiting around to die. They're waiting on lunch. Except Babs. For her, lunch can come and go and come and go. Next time, on my way here, I'll pick up canned peaches. She always had a thing for canned peaches.

I'd take a canned peach over a peach peach.

Lou always said that was the Depression talking. And for the same reason, he said, he wouldn't touch a canned anything anything.

Babs and Lou. Lou and Babs.

We called them by their first names.

Eyes closed, her head droops. She's sitting in a plastic chair. She says she wouldn't be caught dead in a wheelchair. I'd said, At Sunrise or Sunshine, that makes you immortal. She'd nearly laughed. That was months ago.

"Babs. Don't sleep."

She's become frail. Years she worried her mind would go before her body. A former dancer, she's always taken such good care of her body. Now her mind's intact and her body's so weak...

Eyes still clamped, she says, "And you know something?"

"What?"

"There's not a single soul here I like."

"What about Sylvia Weinstein? Did you two get over that thing?"

"Weinberg. What thing?"

"Didn't you have a tiff with Sylvia Weinstein?"

"Don't you listen?"

"But you like Sylvia, am I right?"

"Sylvia's dead."

"Sylvia Weinstein's dead?"

"Weinberg!"

"When?"

"Two days ago. Two months ago. What's it matter?"

I heap the spoon again.

"Open up for Solly's Gremlin."

"Solly's what?"

"You don't remember Solly's blue Gremlin? Like a Pinto but even worse. Huge man, itty-bitty car. Lucy said Solly didn't drive his car, he wore it."

She opens her eyes.

"Your teeth are yellow," she says.

"It's the stress."

"What?"

"The discoloration is caused by stress."

"That's absurd," she says.

I cram the spoon between my grandmother's lips.

"Couple more. What about Aunt Judith's VW Bug? Didn't she have a convertible Bug? Didn't she once drive all the way to Chicago from Seattle with the top down because the mechanism was broken? She said it only rained on her in Nebraska."

Babs bats the spoon out of my hand. Yogurt scatters across the parquet. The card players look up, briefly, from their game.

"Don't talk about Judy."

Her eyes lucid, furious.

I leave her and go into the men's room in the hallway. A bathroom in a nursing home. Disinfectant. That little red string you pull if you need help. We all end up here, one way or another. I yank some paper towels from the dispenser. When I come back, she's looking out the window at the remains of the defunct plant.

"It's like a crematorium," she says.

I stoop and wipe up the yogurt.

"Look, I just want you to eat a little more. Nurse Tabitha said you need more protein and more — "

"Who are you anyway?" She shields her eyes with her hand as if there's a glare.

"Babs."

"Oh, what difference does it make? You could be anybody."

She leans forward and squints at my face as if she's suddenly taken an interest in something else she sees in it.

"Jed."

"Yeah?"

"Don't you have a wife?"

"We never married."

"Where is she?"

"Around."

"Around? What does that mean?"

"It means she's around. Shouting distance. Just a little more, will you?"

I'm running out of cars. My father's Mercedes 280SE with the bloodred seats, the one we called his Nazi staff car. My own crap-ass Civic that's in the shop...

"Shouting distance?" Babs says.

"I don't want to talk about it."

"It's like you speak some other language."

"Please, Babs, Nurse Tab —"

"She dropped you."

"Nurse Tabitha?"

"Your wife."

"I didn't say that."

"Gave you your walking papers."

Those deep-set eyes and that nose, not so much big as prominent. First thing you noticed about her. Fleshy, bulbous, direct. Babs always said she had her father's nose, a Hodash nose. Her tailor father had a little shop on Plymouth Court, near Dearborn Park. He died when Babs was eleven. She said one of her few contributions to the Rosenthal family was the introduction of the Hodash nose into our gene pool. Lucy and I both have her father's nose.

"Hanna and I are separated. But nobody dropped anybody — I've got an apartment a few blocks away. It's a trial separation."

"Trial is right. I know that Hanna without the *h*."

"It's just an alternative spelling."

"That's what you say. Isn't there a baby?"

"We're co-parenting."

"What?"

"Parenting alone, together."

"I'm starting to feel woozy," she says.

"Times change. People evolve."

"You think I don't get it?" she says. "You think I don't know what it's like?"

"What what's like?"

"To be dropped!"

I've basically been dropped, but why go into it with my grandmother.

"The separation was a mutual, informed decision on both sides, which is why we're sharing responsi — "

"It's in your eyes."

"What?"

"Dropped. Right there in your sky-blue eyes. Nobody in the family has such eyes. I've always found it suspicious on the part of your mother. Irises like yours don't just appear" — she takes a look around the room, lowers her voice — "and they've never been very Jewish-looking."

"Babs."

"And you know what else?"

"Tell me but open up for Lucy's new Mini Cooper."

"She dropped us like old shoes."

"Who did?"

"Who?" She turns her face toward the saloon doors of the dayroom like she expects whoever she's talking about to saunter right through them. "You're asking me who?"

"Who?" I say. "Who?"

"Who who? Everybody knows who who. And who who would take one whiff of this place and swish away to the Arts Club or the Union League or the Cliff Dwellers or the

Alliance Française even though that woman couldn't speak a word of —"

"Essee?"

My grandmother flinches. The name alone still jabs.

"Visit? Out here? Lower herself? And you know she hated the suburbs with a venom only she — "

"Essee's dead, Babs."

"You think I don't know?"

"At least fifteen years."

"Longer."

And she clenches her eyes as if she can't shut them tight enough, out of sorrow, out of rage, it's hard to tell. And there it is, the old wound.

"Babs?"

She shakes her head. No, no more talking.

I remember thinking, not then, later, after Babs died, about the fact that she'd used the word *us*. Dropped us like old shoes. Babs and Lou? The two of them had always led such entirely disconnected lives. I thought about my grandparents' separate twin beds. Rock-hard mattresses. Jumping from one to the other was like jumping from concrete to concrete. Stub your toe if you landed the wrong way.

Us?

Not that us.

Essee and Babs, Babs and Essee. The idea of them. The two once-inseparable friends. Two friends joined at the hip for decades. In their teens Babs and Essee danced together around the city as chorus girls in shows and theaters and movie palaces like the Oriental, McVicker's, the Illinois, the Chicago, the Selwyn, the Edgewater Beach Hotel...They high-kicked side by side together at the Century of Progress in '33. Maid of honor at each other's weddings. And their husbands, too, weren't they the buddiest of buddies?

In the dayroom, the card players murmur, the sleepers sleep. When I finally stand and zip my jacket, Babs, eyes still closed, reaches up with her long fingers, claws my chin. And her voice like a claw, too, clawing at the air between us.

"When Judy died that bitch didn't send a card."

That was a Tuesday. A week and a half later she was gone. She was one hundred and one and four months.

WHEN WE WERE kids, Babs rarely laughed. But we could tell from her face that she once had. As if she was laughed out. As if the remains of the laughs were there in the bags beneath her large oval eyes.

I'm losing her face.

I stare at the old publicity photos. Babs posing before, I imagine, some letch gaping at her from under a black shroud. She's sixteen or seventeen. In one, she balances on her left toe, her right leg raised high over her head. Both arms reach upward. Those legs, those arms, her hands, beautiful hands, but her face, her Hodash nose, her big eyes, I stare and still I can't see her.

Lucy used to say that Babs would have made a powerful-looking man. That she was handsome in profile, like FDR on a dime.

The Oriental, McVicker's, the Illinois, the Chicago, the Selwyn, the Edgewater Beach. I repeat the names of old theaters like prayers for the dead. She danced on those stages.

After rehearsal her feet would bleed, and she'd sleep standing up on the streetcar ride home.

She had talent. Her teacher, Miss Merriel Abbott, told her she had fluidity. You can't teach it. Teach water to be water?

Miss Merriel once took her aside. "Leave. Go to New York. You're too short, but it might not matter. You'd get spotted out of any line." And after that, who knew?

But as much as she bled for it, she never gave New York a first thought, much less a second.

For many Chicagoans, and my grandmother was one of them, New York doesn't seduce. You can't have two promised lands.

Anyway, it was impossible. Go off and dance without Essee? If she didn't dance with Essee, she didn't dance.

It was that simple.

Plus, her mother wanted her to go to college.

And yes, there was also the fact, more incidental but true, that she'd promised Lou Rosenthal she'd marry him.

"Marry? Marry?" Miss Merriel Abbott had shouted. "With legs like yours?"

I'd walk over to Babs and Lou's after school and watch the Cubs on WGN. She rarely cooked anything at all but sometimes she'd fry me a grilled cheese sandwich in a buttered pan. She'd ask if I wanted sliced tomato with my Velveeta. When I'd say no, she'd say: *You'll get scurvy.*

The two of us in the kitchen of the old house on Waverly Road. She wasn't that kind of grandmother. She didn't dote on us or fret or run around whipping snapshots sheathed in plastic out of her wallet. She was Babs, never once was she Grandma Anybody. Grandkids, Lucy and I, were just something that happened to her in the normal course of a long life.

She was usually on her way somewhere else. To dance class, exercise class, bridge club, the hairdresser. A lipstick smooch and hello and goodbye in the same breath. I can't fish a dime out of my pocket without thinking of her. She had places to be even when she didn't. I realize this now. She wasn't always late for a class or an appointment. Often she left the house just to leave.

I READ *Light in August* in college and I'm not sure I finished it. But I remember a character, a disgraced reverend named Hightower who tells himself (he's a recluse who never leaves his house) that the most important event in his life happened years before he was born — when a Union sniper shot his grandfather off a horse during the Civil War.

I don't remember what Hightower did to get himself disgraced. Does it matter? Aren't there infinite ways to disgrace yourself? Faulkner knew plenty of them. But Hightower's grandfather, shouting the glories of defeat as he drops out of his saddle — this the reverend conjures nightly. It makes perverse sense. *The* pivotal episode of our lives happens before we even exist.

In our family, nobody got shot off any horse. To my knowledge, no Rosenthal has even ridden a horse since we fled the tatters of the Austro-Hungarian Empire and washed up in Chicago in the first decade of the last century.

No, in my case, it's less dramatic. A friendship ended. In November of 1963, seven years before I was born, a friendship between two couples abruptly severed. Though it would be more accurate to say that these were two entirely separate friendships. One day the friendships were in place, the next they weren't. And to this day nobody, not even my mother, who has firsthand knowledge, can say precisely why. Not that anybody else wonders about this. My mother certainly doesn't.

The four friends, of course, are all long dead.

I'm digging up the rift again. Maybe our old stories are all I've ever had. By now I've aired enough of my family's dirty laundry to open a chain of dry cleaners. Why stop now? After the rift, the drop, the breakup, the estrangement, the schism, the excommunication, whatever we want to call it, neither of my grandparents breathed a single word about any of this, and an unofficial rule took hold in my family (honored by everyone except my father, who never followed rules, official or unofficial) that barred us from even uttering the names Irv and Essee Kupcinet out loud in my grandparents' presence, let alone discussing any of the particulars of their friendship in public.

The betrayal I've already begun to commit cuts deeper than simply naming names. But don't all families have their myths? The ones we cling to in the dead of night, as Reverend Hightower clung to his, if only to explain ourselves to ourselves?

We can't hurt our dead, can we?

I'M CHASING A theory that the events of late November and early December 1963 threw my family off, diminished us, hobbled our development. That we became the sum of our limitations, as Rosenthals, as Chicagoans, and that these limitations, I conjecture, have extended across the generations, and that the roots of our family's failures, both major and minor — among them laziness and overambition (these first two not canceling each other out), vanity, stubbornness, greed, covetousness, occasional criminality (blue- and white-collar), ordinariness, envy, inability to love, excessive lust* — can be traced to an obscure episode in a now-distant time.

---

* Incomplete list

DIMINISHED US? DIMINISHED who? Because Babs and Lou were once friends with a justly forgotten gasbag — and Essee? Don't even get me started on Essee — we failed? At what exactly?

At life. I'm not saying all of us. A majority.

You don't fail at life, Jed. Nobody fails at life. You fail at one thing. You pick yourself up and you give it another shot. Or you try something else. You don't wallow.

To wallow is to live.

You're wasting my billable hours.

Lucy. Anybody with a sister knows you don't need a sister's physical presence in order to have a conversation.

I can play both parts.

And ordinary? Who the fuck is ordinary?

Not that I'm not proud. All hail average Chicagoans: if everybody on earth was an average Chicagoan, the world would be a hell of a lot more, I don't know, basically decent? But take the Rosenthals in the aggregate. If I'm below average and you're above average and Mom's above average (not that she's really included, having dumped the name and this family altogether) and Dad was way below average (loss of points for being unnecessarily angry all the time), and Babs and Lou, well, you know, in the end, they clocked in as pretty much average if you deduct Lou's troubles with the law from his stately lawyer reputation and Babs being aloof and preoccupied and always running from one place to another —

The whole premise is so bonkers it doesn't warrant a response. But let's say, for the sake of argument, that this idiocy applies to certain members of this family, notably you and Dad, what's any of it got to do with the Kupcinets?

Like old shoes, Lucy, they dropped us. Don't you get it?

Lucy? Luce? Voices vanish. Even when you're only yacking in your head, there's no theatrical click anymore when somebody hangs up, no yawning dial tone.

FIRST, LUCY:

My sister's difficult birth was the first of the three events that rocked our family in the second half of November 1963. On the nineteenth at three o'clock in the morning, Lucy joined the Rosenthals. She was born at Michael Reese on the South Side. Like any baby, Lucy preferred the womb, but she didn't cry when she emerged into the artificial light of the delivery room. In fact, hard as it is for me to believe, my sister, who could now make her presence known from the most remote depths of a black hole, made no sound whatsoever.

She refused to even breathe.

My mother, who's in her eighties, still talks about the way the attending nurse held up her newborn by the neck like a chicken she was about to wring and began to flick the bottoms of Lucy's feet with her index finger. I imagine Lucy's tiny fist of a face. I imagine her training her eyes on the offending nurse and those eyes doing what they've done to me throughout my life, and that's drilling pin-sized holes in that nurse's skull.

Then they put my sister in a glass box and wheeled her away to the NICU.

My mother, dazed and sprawled, lay there on the bed thinking, Flicked her feet? This is the state-of-the-art Jewish hospital everybody brags about?

THREE DAYS LATER, my father sank to his knees in the corridor outside the neonatal unit. He'd vote for Ronald Reagan twice in the eighties, but at that time, like any other Young Turk in Chicago, he worshipped JFK. *Tricky Dick never got anybody laid.*

Friday, November 22. 12:45 Central Time.

My mother, who was inside the unit and hadn't heard the news, happened to be looking toward the plate-glass window when my father dropped out of sight. Now you see him. Now you don't. She left the side of my sister's box and stepped closer to the window. She peered down at my father on his knees and thought, overcome by emotion, he'd begun to pray for his daughter's life. He wasn't one to pray for anything. She'd never seen him on his knees. She never would again.

My young parents, these two people I never knew.

My father, a shaggy mophead in a collegiate sweater.

My mother, wearing a hospital gown over her clothes and a surgical mask. On her head a plastic hat like Babs used to wear in the shower. Exhausted and frightened, my mother watched my father on his knees. The president hadn't been pronounced dead yet. Behind my mother, tubes in her nose she'd have torn out if she could have, my sister lay prone in a glass box. It's a kind of still life, a family diorama — minus me. I've always wondered, Did my mother love my father in that moment she misunderstood why he was on his knees? It's something else I missed by being born seven years too late.

LUCY REMAINED AT Michael Reese for three and a half weeks. At the beginning, the doctors said that it was touch and go whether she'd make it. *Touch and go?* my mother says. *What does that even mean? Touch what? Go where?* They also told her that if the baby did survive, whatever damage Lucy might have suffered due to lack of oxygen to the brain might not be known for years to come. This terrified my mother. Lucy did, eventually, begin to breathe on her own. They released her from the glass box and sent her home wrapped in a Michael Reese blanket my mother still keeps folded in her closet. Apparently she hadn't needed that oxygen. Lucy became, in time, an early talker. An extraordinarily early talker. At twelve months she was completing sentences. At sixteen months, she was correcting the nanny's grammar.

Like Lou and my father before her, Lucy's now a Loop attorney, a junior partner at Hurwitz, Ford, Randall, Fortin, and Bunker with an office in the River Point Tower in the West Loop. Forty-second floor with a lake view.

Hang on. I adored Agatha, and even at sixteen months understood that her melodious patois made the King's English sound pompous and idiotic, so you know what you can do? Stick your total fiction up your ass, okay?

ON NOVEMBER 24, a strip club owner, while surrounded by police and the press in the basement of Dallas police headquarters, shoots the suspect, Lee Harvey Oswald, in the stomach at point-blank range on live television.

Oswald's wincing, blanched face lit up by the flashes of the camera bulbs.

A Chicagoan. Jack Ruby was born Jacob Rubenstein. In the Jewish ghetto off Maxwell Street they'd called him Sparky.

All roads, one way or another, lead to Chicago.

Jack Ruby: a lovable fuckup, a ham, an attention craver. After failing in Chicago, he moved to Dallas to fail there. Ruby had a habit of helping people out. Whether you wanted any help or not, Jack Ruby would help you. Beg him, No, please, I don't need any help, Jack, please go away, and he wouldn't take no for answer. He'd be there for you. One of his strippers filed what they used to call a peace bond against him with the court to get him to stay away and stop helping her.

After his arrest, one friend said: Jack always had to be at the openings and closings of shows.

He hit the right closing. Jack Ruby took one easy potshot at immortality and nailed it. He never denied he shot that smirking commie smartass. Whatever it takes to be remembered.

The Gossip Columnist's Daughter

It's odd how certain facts and images remain static. While we'll always know his name, the man himself will be forever locked in a photograph where you only see him from behind. A squat man in a dark suit and fedora thrusting out his arm. It's Oswald's face we remember. Ruby? He's faceless, though his booking photo is easy enough to find. Ruby has a doughy look. He's everyman and so he's nobody. Jack Ruby is my high school algebra teacher, Mr. McCord. He's the guy behind the counter at Manny's Deli on South Jefferson. He's the toll taker on the Tristate whose face you never look at.

In jail, he told investigators that he did it for Jackie. That he'd wanted to help Jackie. To spare her and little Caroline and John-John the trauma of having to return to Dallas for Oswald's trial.

Ruby also said he wanted to let the world know that Jews have gumption.

He loved dogs. He called them his children. A few hours after the shooting, the cops found a couple of dachshunds in Ruby's Oldsmobile 88, along with a bowl of food on the back seat.

SIX DAYS LATER, Saturday, November 30, a young woman is found dead in her apartment in West Hollywood. Her name is Karyn Kupcinet. Home in Chicago she's known as Cookie.

All roads — always, always — lead back to Chicago.

She was twenty-two, an actress, and the daughter of my grandparents' dearest friends, Irv and Essee.

She wasn't well known. Her career had only just begun. And at the time, the country was convulsing. Yet Cookie's death, even coming as it did amid all that chaos, became, if only briefly, a national story because of the relative fame of Cookie's father, a Chicago gossip columnist, Irv Kupcinet. Everybody called him Kup.

He called himself "Mr. Chicago."

Like Marilyn Monroe, Cookie Kupcinet was found nude. Though the two had little in common aside from what they weren't wearing when they were found, the press played up the echoes of Monroe, who'd died the previous August. Cookie was arguably a rising star. Thanks to a degree of talent and her father's connections, she'd appeared in guest spots on *Hawaiian Eye, The Red Skelton Hour, Mrs. G. Goes to College, Wide Country,* and *The Donna Reed Show.* She also had a bit part in a Jerry Lewis movie called *The Ladies Man,* released in July of 1961. Cookie plays a boardinghouse girl in a house full of boardinghouse girls. Jerry's character, Herbert Heebert, is hired as the new live-in handyman. Uproarious comedy ensues. In one scene Cookie announces to the matron of the house that Herbie — that's *Herbert,* Lewis corrects her; *H-e-r-b-e-r-t is Herbert!* — will have his breakfast now.

She also appeared in an episode of *Perry Mason,* which aired posthumously in January of 1964.

IN ONE OF those unimportant coincidences you only stumble across when you're trying to tell a true story, on the evening of November 30, 1963, Irv and Essee Kupcinet were attending a gala to celebrate the grand opening of a Sara Lee cake facility in Deerfield, next door to the nursing home where my grandmother died fifty-six years later. Touted as the world's largest bakery, the plant was capable of producing nine thousand butter cakes an hour. Naturally, there had to be celebrities on hand to celebrate the occasion.

    Call Kupcinet. There's not a ribbon that man won't snip...

    Someone from the Los Angeles County Sheriff's Department contacted Russ Stewart, Kup's editor at the *Sun-Times,* and it was Stewart who, after calling all over the city, finally managed to locate Kup way the hell out in the suburbs. The secretary to the plant manager called the columnist to the phone.

    Irv, listen. I've got — Cookie, it's about Cookie.

    Decades later, in his second memoir, *Kup: A Man, an Era, a City,** Kup writes that when he approached Essee after the call, he hadn't needed to say anything. Essee immediately read the news in his eyes.

---

* Cowritten with Paul Neimark (Chicago: Bonus Books, 1988).

Irv and Essee fled the grand opening without a word to anyone and headed back to the city. In 1963, if it was a night without traffic, this would have taken about thirty-five minutes. At a certain point one or the other must have broken the silence and said something — anything.

The city rising into view as they move south on the expressway.

We left her to the wolves. Our own wolves.

AS SOON AS the Kupcinets returned to the apartment at 257 East Lake Shore at around nine o'clock, Essee called the switchboard at Michael Reese and had Babs Rosenthal paged. And that's when Babs, who'd spent the previous three days at Michael Reese, where my sister still resided in a glass box, sprinted out of the hospital. By jumping up and down on the corner outside Michael Reese, she managed to hail a cab. "Yellow! Checker yellow! Yellow!" Once in the back seat, she bellowed at the cabbie: "Two fifty-seven East Lake Shore! Take the Drive! No, construction, take Michigan! No, State! Oh, please!"

At East Lake Shore, my grandmother, having left the fare, a five-dollar bill, on the back seat, leapt out of the cab while it was still in motion. She fell and, for a moment, from the pavement, looked up at Irv and Essee's building. Two fifty-seven had been built in the twenties to look like a mock castle. Two turrets rose up either side of the building, topped by battlements. Defensive architecture. Warriors had a place to hide behind while they fought off enemies. Babs had almost expected the place to be in ruins, but there it was. Serenely, comically lording over the street, as it always had. A minor tourist attraction in the neighborhood. She got up and hobbled through the front doors on a now-sprained ankle. Puck, the old doorman, waved her past his marble desk and Babs staggered into the Kupcinets' private elevator. It was one of those methodical, patient elevators that takes its sweet time, and my grandmother wanted to scream. When the doors finally opened on the fifth floor, directly into the foyer of the apartment, the cook, Johnetta, was waiting, eyes bloated from weeping. Johnetta collapsed into my grandmother's arms, almost knocking her over.

"I know, Johnny. I know."

"She couldn't tie her own shoes. On TV...didn't matter. That baby, that child. No, she couldn't tie her own—"

"It's all right, honey." Babs rubbed Johnetta's back. "It's all right, all right."

Johnetta released my grandmother and for a moment the two of them stared at each other. Allies, up to a point. Just get through this moment. Later, after the rift, Johnetta wouldn't speak to Babs, either.

"Where is she?"

"In the bedroom. She won't eat. She's on the floor. She won't get off the floor."

IRV AND LOU missed the last plane out of O'Hare for Los Angeles. They'd been joined at the airport by my uncle Solly, who was there to serve as a body man to protect Irv from the scrum of reporters that had already been assigned to the breaking story of his daughter's death. The fact that Solly had previous experience with this sort of work wasn't something the family ever boasted about. Lou had called him earlier. "Sol, listen, grab a cab out to O'Hare. We're going to need you for a couple of days, okay?"

Rather than going home, the three men slept, or didn't sleep, at O'Hare.

On the flight, Lou rested his hand on Irv's sleeve as Irv nodded off in fits and starts. He'd wake up and remember and curse himself. "Sleep? How can a father sleep?" Then his head would droop, and he'd nod off before waking up again. "Sleep? How can any father — "

"Easy, Irv, easy."

BABS SENT THE new and very frightened young Japanese maid home. The girl scuttled out of the living room where she'd been pretending to dust and practically threw herself into the little elevator, still wearing her rubber gloves. Johnetta, though, wouldn't budge. She stood in the front foyer in her apron and white nurse's shoes and wouldn't budge.

"What will she eat?"

"You think I can't cook?"

"I know you can't," Johnetta said.

"I'll call, Johnny. If she needs anything, I'll call."

"What happened to your ankle?"

"It's nothing."

"Why are you hopping?"

"It's nothing."

"You need some ice."

"What about Cleopatra?"

"I'll feed Cleopatra. And I'll call, Johnny. If she needs anything at all, I'll call."

Johnetta stood in the foyer. Twenty-one years with the Kupcinets. She'd raised the child. Who did people think raised the child? She crossed her arms to steady herself. When Babs reached out to her, Johnetta stepped backward and jerked her head in the direction of the bedroom down the hall.

"She needs Jesus is who she needs."

"Tell Puck not to let a single person up here. Okay?"

Almost at once, before the elevator had even delivered Johnetta to the lobby, the phones began to ring. Kup and his phones. He'd had nine lines installed at 257 East Lake Shore. The most in any private residence in the city. Nine phones in a row along a table in the foyer. Two teletype machines. Essee used to say it was like living in a police station. Before Babs entered the bedroom, she took each of them off the hook and wrapped the receivers in towels, muffling the voices.

She spent the next three days holed up in the apartment with Essee and the Pekingese.

Lou was with Irv, Babs was with Essee.

Who else but the Rosenthals would have dropped everything? And with their first grandchild in a glass box in the neonatal at Michael Reese?

But Johnetta hadn't been kidding. My grandmother couldn't boil a hot dog.

After a day and a half, Babs summoned her daughter — my aunt, then a graduate student at UW. Judith took a Greyhound from Madison and arrived at 257 on Monday afternoon, December 2. Babs popped out of the bedroom for a moment to give Judith a hug but otherwise she remained behind the bedroom door.

Essee herself wouldn't emerge from the bedroom. Not until it was time for the funeral, on Tuesday. Judith made a couple of tuna sandwiches but mostly she brewed pot after pot of coffee. She'd leave the cups on a tray outside the bedroom door. Then she'd knock gently to let her mother know they were there before making herself scarce. In middle school she and Cookie would steal chocolate bars from the small grocery on Clark across from Francis Parker. Her first best friend. Cookie had always been flighty and distractible. A nonstop talker, she'd chatter about one thing and then another and then get so caught up in her own laughter she'd lose track of what she'd been trying to say. The only time she ever concentrated in high school was onstage, but even then her eyes sometimes seemed to wander away from the scene. Judith sat on the immaculate white couch in the Kupcinets' sunken living room, the little dog asleep in her lap, and watched the lake. She hadn't spoken to Cookie in years. Now the distance between them was bewildering.

A short day, windless, cold. The lake a darkening green, flat, waveless. No sound from the bedroom.

ROGERS PARK, CHICAGO
APRIL 2023

ALL MY DEAD sleep in Skokie. The family plot at Memorial Cemetery. Section A-12, the Jewish neighborhood. Plot 48. Babs and Lou. Uncle Solly. My father and Aunt Judith. I'm awake in an apartment on West Pratt in Rogers Park. Hanna lives on Jarvis with Snook in the house the three of us lived in together. Alive or dead you've got to lie down someplace. From here, 711 West Pratt, Apt. 5D (the corner of West Pratt and North Greenview), 1739 Jarvis is nine blocks north (Farwell, Morse, Lunt, Greenleaf, Estes, Touhy, Chase, Sherwin, Jarvis) and two and a half blocks west (Ashland, Paulina). If I hustle, half run, half walk, I can get there in just under sixteen minutes. If I stop for a takeaway coffee at The Common Cup, tack on another three to eleven minutes, depending on the length of the line. At night, I take pills. So much sleep exhausts me. They advertised this as a garden apartment. There are some shrubs outside, no garden. The windows are eye level with the sidewalk. Rudy and I watch the shoes go by, some fast, others slow. The feet inside the slow shoes have no place to go. Why hurry to get there? Rudy's a cat. Five years ago, just before Snook was born, Hanna picked him out of a lineup at the shelter on Western Avenue. A runt of a white cat with coffee-stained fur and eerie pink eyes. That one, Hanna said. The one that doesn't blink. Turned out Hanna's allergic. Or she says she's allergic. I think everybody's allergic to cats and only the people who don't like cats say so. Rudy sleeps a lot, too. When he's awake, he ignores me, languidly. Other times he stares at me with his scrunched little face (he really doesn't ever blink), his body still, like he's about to spring and go for my eyes. *How did I end up in this place with you? I had sunlight, treats, her, clean kitty litter, toys I never played with, a child I couldn't stand, but still it was home.*

I HUNKER IN my windowless cube at Loyola. The psychology professors have offices that face the lake. I think the chemists do also, though I've never met one. But maybe at this point an English department is lucky to be housed at all. Our enrollments are in the toilet. This office has a Soviet Brezhnev-era feel. A solid cement kind of nowhere. It's very quiet. Aside from the medievalist across the hall, who turns up every once in a while, nobody comes in to work anymore. Coming in to work is a relic, an abandoned social practice.

The cat's here. I chauffeur Rudy to work with me in his carrier. He likes the cube and this interrogation-room lighting. The silence of the English department beats the silence of the apartment on West Pratt. There's more reliable heat. He dozes by the radiator.

These pale yellow walls. I've covered nearly every available space with photocopies of newspaper clippings, mostly from November and December 1963. I'm working, see? I'm on a crushing deadline. I need to be left alone.

I'm on a deadline, steer clear! Can't you see I'm on a deadline?

Rudy, without bothering to raise his head: Nobody seeks you, least of all a publisher. *Fourteen years since his unheralded and nearly simultaneously remaindered second novel,* Montrose Beach, Winter, *Jedidiah Rosenthal has at last broken his weighty...*

At the shelter you seemed like such a nice cat.

Pet me and die.

For a living, I sit at the head of a long seminar table and serve up pre-cooked wisdom. *You have to kill your darlings, you have to smother them in their infancy. As Virginia Woolf once wrote to Vita Sackville-West, lovely phrases are only just that...* And the creative writing students around the table nod. They're very generous with their nodding.

I've grown a beard. I leave potato chip crumbs in it.

It doesn't hurt to be a Jew at a Jesuit university. Not much is expected of me, as if the powers that be recognize that the foundational mistake of my life, the rejection of Christ as the Son of God, was baked in at birth. And sure, the Jews murdered Him, but we Jesuits let bygones be bygones. (For the record, my mother used to say that it's not as if we believe Jesus was a bad person. No, no. In fact, we believe he was a very nice man, just delusional. Maybe he hit his head as a child or something?) I've always been made to feel welcome at Loyola, like a wayward son myself, maybe a little too welcome. After eleven or so years on the faculty, I'm still being greeted as if I've always just arrived at the party.

"Good morning, Monsignor Flanagan."

"Ah, Professor Rosenthal! Welcome! Welcome!"

* * *

A wayward son who never went anywhere. Who's been here all along. Like my father before me, I've never left Chicago.

I call my sister, this time with a phone.

"How's it going?"

"Fine," she says. "You?"

"Not bad. You?"

"We just covered that."

"That was perfunctory. Now I'm asking."

"What's up, Jed? Nobody uses the phone to talk anymore."

"What's up? I'm on a deadline!"

"Is it fiction or nonfiction? What's auto-fiction? Somebody said the other day that's what you — "

"I don't want to talk about my singular art. Wait — "

"Don't get a hard-on. It was Mom."

"Great."

"Still the thing about Kup and Essee?"

"They preoccupy me. What can I say? And I'm still out of other ideas."

"I don't want to be cruel, Jeddy, but those two weren't even news when they were news. Kup and those columns, how many years of those insipid columns? And Essee? You know what Mom says about Essee don't you?"

"That she wouldn't have pissed on you if you were on fire, but if Frank Sinatra was on fire — "

"Right. Love that. Use that. Are you actually writing the thing now?"

"I write emails."

"When's this deadline?"

"Seven years ago."

"That's not a deadline, that's a corpse. Do they even remember?"

"I doubt it."

"They pay you?"

"Not much."

"They'll remember. Okay, Jed, listen, I have to get back to—"

"They dropped us. Like old shoes, Luce, they—"

"Please stop."

"They cut us out of the party."

"Not us—Babs and Lou."

"Babs and Lou are us, Lucy."

She does that sputtery thing with her lips she used to do as a kid when she was exasperated. And she could ventriloquize to make it sound like someone across the room was farting. Used to amaze me.

"You're bananas. Sixty fucking years ago."

"Luce, I miss your voice—"

"I'm right here."

"Talk to me."

"How's Snook?"

"Last weekend I took her to Lambs Farm."

"Isn't she getting a little old for Lambs Farm?"

"She humored me. She rode a pony shorter than she is. Her feet dragged on the ground."

"And Hanna? You know Rachel thinks you both ought to be commended for sticking to co-parenting so long. She says that in her practice, most couples give it up after a few months and retreat to traditional gender imbalances, but you two, what, you made it through a pandemic, the worst of it anyway, and now it's been, what, three years?"

"Getting on four. Listen, Luce, I've got a horde of students outside the door clamoring for knowledge."

"Fare thee well, Professor."

A WEALTHY JEWISH land speculator named Michael Reese, a man who'd never lived a day in Chicago — he'd made a mint in the silver mines of Nevada — left all his money to some family he had in Chicago. When Chicago's first Jewish hospital burned down in the Great Chicago Fire, the family used the money to help build a new hospital for Jews, and anybody else who needed one, a novel concept at the time. Over the years the hospital gained fame as a research institution as well as the first hospital to implement widespread use of incubators in the children's ward. Buildings stretched from Bronzeville to the lakefront. After 129 years, Michael Reese closed for good in 2009. Then they knocked the entire complex down. Chicago is giddy for knocking buildings down. Historic hospital? Forget it. Where's the money in history? The money's in erecting something new, anything at all, so long as it's new. And so, a mighty hospital, where a nurse whose name is lost to history once flicked my sister's feet, has vanished. Yet Michael Reese lives on, at least in part because of how many illustrious Jews were born there. CEOs, senior partners, ophthalmologists, bank presidents, senators... A chosen hospital for a chosen people. And others not so chosen.

Among those born at Michael Reese are the following: Jack Ruby, born 1911. Lou Rosenthal, born 1912. Babs Rosenthal née Tucker, born 1918. Solly Rosenthal, born 1928. Aubrey Rosenthal, born 1939. Judith Rosenthal, born 1941. Lucy Rosenthal, born 1963. Jed Rosenthal, born 1970. I suspect (but can't prove) that Cookie Kupcinet (1941) and her brother Jerry (1944)[*] were also born at Michael Reese. It's where Jewish women like Essee, Babs, and my mother went to have their babies.

You think I'm not chosen?
You're chosen, Luce. You're chosen.

---

[*] Like his sister, Jerry Kupcinet moved out to Hollywood from Chicago. An Emmy-nominated director, he worked on *Judge Judy*, *That's Incredible!*, and *The Richard Simmons Show*. He died in 2019.

HIGHLAND PARK, ILLINOIS
NOVEMBER 2023

MY MOTHER SPECIALIZES in inviting people who have no place to go on Thanksgiving. The mute widower down the block. Our right-wing second cousins from Kenosha. A clerk from the Citgo in Highwood who she befriended earlier that day while buying a carton of Benson and Hedges. My second-grade teacher, Mrs. Gerstad, is present this year. She used to make us tie our shoes only to the left side of our desks. Tie your shoes to the right of your desk and you'd disorder the universe. Where did my mother find Mrs. Gerstad and how's it possible the woman is still alive? My mother's table always has space, though everybody scatters throughout the house with paper plates. My stepfather, in a Bears jersey (Singletary, 50), roams around refilling drinks. "Refill? Who needs a refill?"

Lucy, who's been pre-drinking in preparation for this holiday since 9 a.m., holds forth in the den about the upcoming Republican primaries. "No, I mean this seriously, and with all respect. Are you all electing a candidate or reelecting an ape?" The Wisconsin cousins grin and bear it. They want to be invited back next year. They like my mother's parties.

Lucy's wife, Rachel, tries to shush her.

"Let's just get through this," Rachel says. "It's Thanksgiving."

"That's the answer? Call some artificial truce in honor of cranberry sauce? Pretend this whole deal isn't propaganda? Because the pilgrims wore funny hats with buckles they weren't mass murderers? Where are our Pottawatomie sisters and brothers?"

"Gonna be a long night," Rachel says.

In the kitchen, my mother sips her second martini; I can always get her talking after a second martini. In our house, Thanksgiving runs on martinis. Turkey's incidental.

I ask her again, as I do any chance I get lately, about Cookie Kupcinet.

"What more needs to be said?" my mother says. "The kid was in over her head. It's not like she was the last. There's always another girl in the wings. Probably last week, some girl who'd gone out to Hollywood to pursue her wildest — But why go all the way to Hollywood? It happens in Winnetka, in DeKalb, in Waukegan. Some kid only trying to make her life, any life, big life, small life, but she can't make it, takes pills — but in Cookie's case, I'm not saying it wasn't glamorous, maybe a lot glamorous. Found naked and strangled in Hollywood? At the time I remember being jealous. What's more glamorous than being found naked and strangled in Hollywood?"

"Except you say she wasn't strangled."

"Everybody knew she wasn't strangled."

"You're not making sense."

"Why are we still talking about this?"

"You're contradicting yourself."

"Jed, she took pills."

"But how did you know for sure? The papers, the coroner's report, all said strangled. Even today, Wikipedia and every true-crime—"

"We knew because we knew. There was a wink, wink. Don't you get it?"

"But people get strangled, Mom."

"You want to know what I thought at the time? What we all thought? It's the kind of girl she was. Today she'd be called highly emotional. Anxiety disorder. Manic. She had three or four plastic surgeries. And she was how old? Every time I saw her she was slightly someone else. Effusive, dramatic. Your father always said she was dumb as rocks, but it's not true. She was smart, read a lot. And sweet, yes. Hugs, Cookie always would hug you and kiss you. And then she'd hug and kiss you again. She was like that. She liked to pull you close and then closer. She needed people around all the time. So when the boyfriend dumped her, I'm forgetting his name—"

"Prine."

"Right, Prine. Andy Prine! Tall lug of a guy, very good-looking. Strong jaw. He was on some cowboy show. I wonder what happened to him."

"They ravaged him in the press. He couldn't get work. Laid low for years. He was never a star again. Worked his way back to small parts in movies and guest spots on shows. *One*

Day at a Time, Matlock, Hart to Hart, The Dukes of Hazzard, Deep Space Nine. Recurring role on *Murder, She Wrote.* Had a career. Toward the end of his life he sold paintings on his website. He died on vacation in Paris a few years ago."

"God, I love *Murder, She Wrote.* How were the paintings?"

"Not bad."

"Sounds like he did all right."

"Still, he never lived it down, he'll always be associated with Cookie. Prine tried to get away from her when she was alive, but after she was dead, forget about it. They were together for good, which is what Cookie wanted. She never wanted to let him go."

My mother takes a swig of her martini, which she drinks dry, very dry. When she orders a drink in a restaurant, my mother always sounds like a suburban James Bond. *I like it dry, very dry. With just a smidge of vermouth. Do we understand each other?*

"I'm not sure this obsession is healthy," my mother says.

"Not an obsession. This is research."

"Talking to me is research?"

"Absolutely."

"Where are Hanna and Snook spending the holiday?" my mother says.

"I don't want to talk about it."

"I miss Snook."

"They're at her brother's house in Duluth."

"Where?"

"Duluth. Duluth, Minnesota."

"You think I don't know where Duluth is?"

My stepfather swoops by with a pitcher.

"I see you're low, darling." To me, he says, "Fran's a hoot. Dirty stories. I mean she's got a whole repertoire of real smutty—"

"Who's Fran?"

"Your beloved teacher."

"Mrs. Gerstad?"

"Give me a smidge," my mother says. "No—a bigger smidge. Thank you, honey. Leave us, will you?"

Over the lip of her glass my mother says, "You'll bring Snook to Christmas?"

"Yes, I've got Christmas. But Hanna asks that we, for once, emphasize Chanukah."

"Oh, for Christ's sake, we're Midwestern Jews who celebrate Christmas. Tell her to get over it. Chanukah is for chumps."

"She'll never get over it. She also asks that we start calling Snook Leah."

"Any other offenses we commit?"

"Her name's Leah, Mom."

"I never said Leah wasn't a beautiful name. Old Testament. She's in Genesis. Take that, Hanna. And somewhere else, too. I forget. Leviticus? What is the thing you two are doing again?"

"Who?"

"You and Hanna."

"You mean co-parenting?"

"Right, but how do you define it, again?"

"Parenting apart, together."

"That's it!"

"Get it?"

"Not really. When I dumped your father, I dumped your father."

"It's best for Snook."

"Yes."

"It's about logistics."

"Isn't it always?"

"It's not pure co-parenting. She stays at my place on Wednesdays and Saturdays. We thought it was too much back and forth if Snook had to —"

"Makes sense."

"But I pick her up, I drop her off, I, you know —"

"I do know."

"Essee," I said. "Tell me more about Essee."

"She's not worth it."

"I'm collecting whatever I can get my hands on."

"Lemme think."

My mother looks up at the kitchen ceiling as if she's trying to run out the clock on this conversation.

"What about she wouldn't piss on you if you were on fire, but she would have pissed on Frank Sin —"

"I don't know where Lucy got that vulgar — but true, Essee would certainly have used whatever means necessary to put out Frank Sinatra if he happened to be on —"

"Tell me something else, Mom. Throw me a bone."

She fiddles in her pockets for her cigarettes before realizing she has no pockets.

"Hal, where are my — All right. When Cookie was in high school, Essee force-fed her diet pills. How's that for a bone? I'd call that a femur."

"How do you know?"
"Judith told me."
"When?"
"What do you mean when? When she was alive. Judith told me when she was alive. She's been dead since — how long?"
"Late nineties."
"That's all I've got. Go spar with Lucy in the living room? She's getting bored of the cousins. They won't fight back. You know she doesn't like to hold forth unless somebody fights back. And she's drinking too much. Rachel doesn't like it when she drinks too much."

Whenever I'm downtown, I cross the Chicago River and head north on Michigan Avenue, past the Tribune Tower, past all the new stores, past the old Walgreens, which is somehow still there, to the Drake Hotel, where I use the bathroom. As a kid I always used to get such a kick out of pissing at the Drake. Then I leave the hotel out the north door and take a right and walk down East Lake Shore, a brief street perpendicular to the Outer Drive, just where it makes that crazy dogleg — as if to plunge straight into Lake Michigan — and walk to the end of the block to where Kup and Essee Kupcinet used to live, at 257. Any farther east and that goofy mock castle would have been in the lake. It's gone. There is no 257 East Lake Shore anymore. An address that no longer exists. A coordinate of no place. I couldn't get enough of the little fortress as a kid. My father, ignoring the prohibition against mentioning the Kupcinets, used to walk me over from the Drake to look at it. *See the fifth-floor windows? That's where Irv and Essee...* Even now, when I stand in front of the dull brick building that replaced it, I close my eyes and imagine Essee up there at the top of the tower, behind the battlements, with a bow and arrow pointing down at Babs, who's pleading to her from the sidewalk with open arms.

"Scram," Essee shouts. "Or I'll fire."

In Bed, Nude

FIND KUP'S DAUGHTER DEAD

I've been staring at this headline for years. It's on the wall. The grammar has always puzzled me. *Find*? Who's supposed to do the finding? Why the imperative? It's as if we're being ordered to find Cookie dead ourselves.

Thanks to the medievalist across the hall, Professor O'Connor, who possesses esoteric knowledge beyond his own field of esoteric knowledge, I now know that it used to be common for newspapers to use the imperative. It gave a jolt of immediacy to headlines. And it was true. I hadn't noticed that on the very same *Chicago Tribune* front page, just beneath the story about Cookie, there was another:

CALL OSWALD 'LONER'

All these shocks were happening in real time. My mother says that Cookie's death, coming as it did so fast on the heels of the assassination, nearly took her breath away. My mother, camping out in the hallway at Michael Reese, her own daughter's fate still uncertain, remembers thinking after first hearing the news about Cookie, *The madness, it's getting closer.*

Hollywood. Nov. 30 AP — Actress Karyn Kupcinet was found murdered in her Hollywood home today, police reported. The twenty-three-year-old brunette beauty was the daughter of Irv Kupcinet, Chicago columnist. Police said she was found in bed, nude. She had been beaten about the head and there were indications she had been strangled.

[The Los Angeles Times reported that police were considering the possibility that the death was a suicide. Police found a spoon, a coffee cup, and an empty brandy snifter in the room. They theorized that Ms. Kupcinet might have taken an overdose of pills.]

The scene of Miss Kupcinet's murder was a modest apartment on the South Side of Hollywood.

Miss Kupcinet went to Wellesley College. She once told a reporter she put on twenty-five pounds in one semester. "I was Miss Five-by-Five," she said. But seeking an entertainment career, she went on a stringent diet. She was five feet three and a half inches tall and weighed one hundred and five pounds in recent years...

COOKIE WAS TWENTY-TWO when she died, not twenty-three. She didn't attend Wellesley. She attended, for a year, Pine Manor Junior College, also located in Wellesley, Massachusetts.

It's understandable that, in the rush to cover a breaking story, early Associated Press reporting might get certain facts — big and small — wrong.

She wasn't found nude in bed. She was found nude on the couch in her living room. There turned out to be no physical evidence that she'd been beaten.

Yet, to me, the most curious aspect of this initial story as it appeared on Sunday morning, December 1, is the inclusion of the bracketed (and italicized) paragraph floating the police theory that Cookie might have committed suicide.

Chicagoans must have suffered whiplash.
Good Lord, Kup's daughter was strangled!
No! She's on TV, right?
Wait. Now they're saying she took pills.
No!
Hold it, murdered, now it's back to murdered...

* * *

The Gossip Columnist's Daughter

I have no way of knowing whether or not the bracketed paragraph was part of the original AP wire story, but I suspect it was typed up by someone at the *Tribune* and wedged, at the last minute, between the first and second paragraphs. In 1963, Kup had massive clout in Chicago. Even the *Trib* might not have wanted to get on his bad side by running with an insinuation that hadn't been proven. Yet they must have felt they had to hedge their bets. This way, if it turned out to be wrong, they could always blame it on the *Los Angeles Times*.

…Jerry Lewis, with whom Miss Kupcinet had recently appeared, said, "She was a vibrant young kid. She had a great dramatic future. I've known her since she was a baby. Her father and I are very fast friends."

Lieutenant George Walsh, sheriff's deputy in charge of the investigation, described Andrew Prine, twenty-six, the lanky, six-foot-two television actor seen as a costarring rodeo rider in NBC's *Wide Country,* as her boyfriend. "He says he doesn't know anything about what happened," Walsh said.

Detectives are questioning Miss Kupcinet's "tremendous" number of friends, acquaintances, and associates in the television, acting, and writing worlds. "This girl had more friends than anybody I ever heard of," Lieutenant Walsh said. "And not a knocker in the bunch. They all loved her."

Kupcinet was "deeply interested" in philosophy and anthropology and had become an avid reader of "existentialist literature."

Meanwhile, Irv Kupcinet, *Chicago Sun-Times* columnist, arrived by plane early today from Chicago, where he is known in nightclub and television circles as "Mr. Chicago." Kupcinet was accompanied by an attorney, Louis B. Rosenthal, also of Chicago, and a third man who was not identified.

THE FOLLOWING DAY, Monday, December 2, newspapers as far-flung as the Toronto *Globe and Mail*, the *Cedar Rapids Gazette*, and the *Baton Rouge Advocate* all covered the release of the coroner's autopsy.

Signed by assistant chief Los Angeles County autopsy surgeon Dr. Harold Kade, the report stated that Karyn Kupcinet's death was the result of "asphyxiation due to manual strangulation" and that she'd been choked with such force that a bone in her neck was broken.

No other wounds were discovered on the body.

Given decomposition, she'd been dead since late Wednesday or early Thursday.

Had she lived, she'd be eighty-two.

There are still Chicagoans who remember. Some claim, like my mother, that autopsy report or no autopsy report, there was never any doubt. Cookie overdosed, intentionally or unintentionally.

Yet, even now, sixty years later, there remain loyalists who uphold the official version, the one that Irv and Essee Kupcinet clung to with all their strength — and clout — to the end of their lives.

Someone strangled their daughter.

My grandparents Babs and Lou Rosenthal, of course, were loyalists, the most loyal of loyalists, until they weren't anybody.

PART OF A note found on a memo pad in Cookie's kitchen:

I'm no good. I'm not really that pretty. My figure's fat and will never be the way my mother wants it. I won't let it be what she wants. How stupid. I want to be slim and she loves me and wants me to be slim — intellectualization doesn't mark. Why must I be so alone. Have I fallen that short of my ideal? Why does my image of me have to be so aesthetic and perfect? What's the use of living with nothing to believe in? Have faith in? Where's the security or habit or order — oh shit — what good is that going to do? What happens to me — or my Andy? Why doesn't he want me? Why? There's no GOD. There's nothing but phony motives, fatheads, and drunks and I want out. I like President Kennedy, Bertrand Russell, Theodor Reiks, Peter O'Toole, Sydney J. Harris, Albert Finney. I just care about now. Who gives a shit about 10 years from now?

I LIKE THAT she calls people fatheads. It makes me think she laughed, even on her lowest days. But did she think that Hollywood wouldn't be full of phonies and fatheads, egoists and drunks? She'd grown up around these people. Stars were in and out of the apartment at 257 East Lake Shore day and night. Cookie would come home from sixth grade and Robert Mitchum would be passed out beneath the dining room table. His legs went on for miles.

She'd open a bathroom door and Shirley MacLaine would be on the toilet.

Gimme a sec, cutie.

What she says about her mother. Out on her own and still she's tethered to Essee's demands and yet she agrees with them. "Intellectualization doesn't mark." What does this even mean? That thinking too much gets you nowhere?

A suicide note? Some days I think yes. Other days I'm not so sure.

A lost kid, disillusioned and alone. All the hours she must have spent in her apartment with the television on low. Sometimes I write out, in my own hand, the list of men she reveres. Kennedy? Depending on when she wrote the note, he was already dead or about to be. Actors: Peter O'Toole and Albert

The Gossip Columnist's Daughter

Finney. Russell, a philosopher. Sydney Harris, a columnist like her father. Theodor Reiks? Does she mean Reik? German psychoanalyst, a buddy of Freud's?

It's late. I'm in this still mostly empty living room of the apartment on West Pratt. Two guys are fighting in the alley. I listen to their happy grunts. It's me and Rudy, Friday night. When I moved out of our house on Jarvis, Hanna thought I should take Rudy so Snook would feel at home in my new place.
"It's continuity," she said.
"The cat is continuity?"
"Yes."
"I thought this was a trial separation."
"I'd like you to take Rudy with you."
"Cats don't like to be displaced. He'll freak out."
"You know I'm allergic."

When Snook's here she chases Rudy, and Rudy tolerates it, up to a point. Then he scratches for blood. That's continuity.
What happens to me — or my Andy?
I need furniture. I got to make some friends. I have friends. They're around.
The other night Rudy and I watched half of *Lawrence of Arabia*. Or I fell asleep halfway through. Rudy might have kept watching. Peter O'Toole plays Lawrence. It's in Technicolor. O'Toole's eyes so blue you could swim laps in them. His eerie golden hair glows radioactively. Often, in order to show that

his conscience burdens him, he appears constipated. In one scene, he blows up a train. In another, he shoots at point-blank range an old and trusted friend.

"I have no tribe," Lawrence says.

And therefore no loyalties.

ANDY PRINE TOLD detectives that Cookie called him around 6:30 on Wednesday night. He said they'd had a lovers' quarrel. Except at that point they were no longer lovers. Cookie also spoke to her father. Irv said that the call was brief and that she seemed happy. He's quoted in the *Los Angeles Times:*
"She had no problems."

The same night, Cookie had a dinner date at the home of a young couple, Marcia and Mark Goddard. In a couple of years, Mark would play Major Don West on *Lost in Space.* Marcia was the daughter of a big-time publicist, a friend of Irv's named Henry Rogers. Irv had asked Marcia to keep an eye on Cookie in Hollywood.

During dinner, Cookie was listless. The Goddards told investigators that she didn't eat and mostly pushed food around her plate. Her eyes were glazed over, and she held her head at a strange angle. The Goddards also said Cookie had told them that she and Andy were spending Thanksgiving at Glenn Ford's villa in Beverly Hills.

When they were questioned, Andy Prine and Glenn Ford both said they knew nothing about it, that they'd had other plans.

Before dessert, Cookie called a cab and left for home.

After 9 p.m., a friend, a freelance writer named Ed Rubin, knocked on Cookie's door. She invited Ed in and the two watched TV for a while. Cookie told Rubin that she needed some air. Walking around the neighborhood, she ran into Robert Hathaway, another actor friend. Cookie invited Hathaway to join her and Rubin back at the apartment. The three of them, Cookie, Rubin, and Hathaway, watched *The Danny Kaye Show*. I imagine the scene. It might have been a forgettable night, had it not been only five days since the president was killed. But by then they were all tired of talking about it. How much more could they possibly talk about it? Three friends watch TV to let their minds wander. Danny Kaye and friends camp around. Songs, skits, monologues. Kaye's so charming. At home in his own skin. The way he looks directly into the eye of the camera, as if he's talking directly to you. Danny Kaye's fast friends with her father, too. Rubin and Hathaway sit on the floor. Cookie's on the couch with her legs outstretched, painting her nails. The pills she'd taken before she went to the Goddards' have worn off. Still, she's enjoying herself, enjoying the company of two friends. Every once in a while the three of them laugh together. In one bit, Kaye prances around wearing a little Hitler mustache. In another he falls asleep while fishing.

Cookie asks Rubin and Hathaway if they want any cake.
Rubin says he's full.
Hathaway says yes, please, I'd like some cake.
Get it yourself, Bob. I don't want to mess up my nails.
And the three of them laugh, they laugh.
At around 11 p.m., Cookie announces that she's going to

sleep. Keep making yourselves at home, boys, she says, and toes dry, gets up off the couch, goes into the adjacent bedroom and shuts the door. Rubin and Hathaway leave sometime before midnight. Accounts in the record differ as to whether they locked the door. (In one interview Rubin said he did, in another he said he didn't. Hathaway said he couldn't remember either way.) Both consistently said that the television was still on when they left the apartment.

IN THE STACKS at the college the other day, I found a book by Theodor Reik, the psychoanalyst. In an essay called "Fragments of a Great Confession," Reik tells an anecdote about the death of his father when he was a boy. The attending doctor sent him to fetch a lifesaving medicine from the pharmacy. When Theodor returned home, his father was dead. And so he asked himself a single question for the rest of his life: *Could I have saved my father if I had run faster?*

Cookie stood in her own small kitchen and wrote a list of names on a memo pad.

Was she trying to save herself with names?

Maybe it's only the unanswerable questions themselves that allow us to commune with the dead.

THE GODDARDS TRIED to reach her by phone. She wasn't answering. On Saturday night, the couple drove down from their home in the hills to 1227½ North Sweetzer. Marcia stayed in the car. Mark went through the brick tunnel at the entrance. I've stood in this tunnel. It's like a brick grotto with mailboxes inside. A brief darkness you pass through between the street and the apartment complex. Goddard hustles through the tunnel and across a courtyard crowded with plants, in the center of which was a burbling fountain. A sharp right and up the flight of steps to the second floor. Cookie's door to the right at the top of the stairs. Newspapers stacked, three or four days of them. He knocks. No answer. Knocks again. There are silences that stretch for miles. He tries the door. It's open. The lights are out, the TV's on. That blue glow. Goddard doesn't make it past the threshold. The odor so potent his throat constricts. He flees. It's Marcia who holds her scarf to her nose, marches in, flips on the lights. Already knowing what she'll find, she doesn't scream.

BETWEEN SATURDAY, NOVEMBER 30, and Tuesday afternoon, December 3, the day she was buried in Chicago, the investigation made little progress, at least not in terms of solving any murder. What newspaper readers did learn was a series of facts about Karyn Kupcinet's personal life that the Sheriff's Department seemed to gleefully want to share with the public.

SHE HAD A criminal record. The morning after she was found, the papers reported that a year earlier on November 10, 1962, Cookie had been caught outside a department store in Pomona with an unpaid-for pair of capri pants, a sweater, and two books. The capri pants (green) cost ten dollars and forty cents. The sweater she'd lifted from a different store. Of the books, one was called *Genius* (author unknown) and was priced at four dollars and fifty cents. The other was the *Tao Te Ching* by Lao Tzu, which went for a dollar.

Six weeks later, Cookie pleaded guilty to shoplifting in Pomona District Court. She paid a one-hundred-and-eighty-dollar fine and was sentenced to three months' probation.

THEN THE WHOLE deal with the notes.

The more times Andy Prine was interviewed (the cops were closing in on him as a suspect), the more he told detectives. He must have felt that whatever he had to tell, he'd better go ahead and tell it. That's when Prine told sheriff's deputies about the bizarre notes he'd received two months earlier. He said he figured some crackpot fan must have sent them. Yet, he'd held on to them. The notes were created using different letters cut from magazines and taped to blank pieces of paper. When he told Cookie about them, she'd said, Weird, the same crackpot sent me similar notes...

FORGET FAME AND ROMANCE WITH
AGING GLENN FORD DEVIL MUST KILL YOU

YOUR LADY NEEDS SURGERY SUDDENLY
EXPECT TO GET BAD BREAKS WHEREVER
YOU GO. YOUR RICH BEAUTY HAS NO TIME

* * *

The Gossip Columnist's Daughter

YOU MAY DIE WITHOUT NOBODY
WINNER OF LONELINESS WANTS DEATH
UNTIL ONE SOMEONE SPECIAL CARES

The Sheriff's Department vowed to pursue this tantalizing new lead with vigor.

IT DIDN'T TAKE long. The *Los Angeles Times* broke the story on the following morning.

> Al Edsel of the Los Angeles County Sheriff's Department announced today that slain actress Karyn Kupcinet sent threatening notes to herself and her TV actor boyfriend Andrew Prine. A print found on the underside of a piece of tape on one of the notes matched a print of Miss Kupcinet's right middle finger on file from a previous shoplifting arrest...

WRECKAGE OF THANKSGIVING. Lucy has gone back to the city with Rachel. The Kenosha cousins snore in unison on the couch. I always forget they have names, Todd and Wendy. My mother and I are watching CNN. My mother watches CNN at a decibel level that must scare the neighbors but doesn't wake the cousins.

During a commercial, she complains that CNN is mostly commercials. I say, "Do you remember the notes that Cookie sent to Andy Prine?"

"What?"

I shout, "Do you remember that Cookie sent —"

"I can't hear you."

"Could we turn down the TV?"

"Where's the remote?"

"Cookie sent crazy notes to Andrew Prine. You don't remember?"

"What?"

I find the remote under Wendy's thigh and turn the sound all the way down.

"Like bizarre secret messages. She sent them to Prine. You don't remember? At first they thought it might lead them to the killer, but then they found her fingerprints."

My mother scoffs. "The killer was a figment of Essee's imagination. Otherwise, she might have had to look in the mirror."

"You don't remember the notes?"

"Hal, bring me a mouthful of vermouth, would you?"

"The papers were all over the notes. Just seems like something you might remember from the time."

"I guess I was preoccupied."

On the giant screen, muted Anderson Cooper moves his lips.

"Oh, Mom, I —"

"I could fit her in the palm of my hand, Lucy was so tiny, but they wouldn't let me touch her the first three days."

"Mom, I'm sorry, I wasn't thinking."

My mother looks me over, clucks her tongue.

"Are you dating anybody? There must be some —"

I shrug. "Need time."

"It's been, what, four years?"

I let it be. Three years. Four years. What are years?

"Cookie sent secret messages? About what?"

"Loneliness. Death. The devil. One was about Glenn Ford. Another about Tampax."

My stepfather comes in with the vermouth.

"What am I missing?" he says.

...the notes are believed to be one of the many peculiar things the twenty-two-year-old did to keep Prine from breaking off the romance. According to Prine, on the night of Wednesday, November 27, Kupcinet told him, "Someone left a baby on my doorstep." Prine told detectives that he suggested she notify police and inform them about the presence

[Continued on page 33, column 6]

MY MOTHER LOOKS up at the ceiling. Raises her glass, looks at it in the light.

"This vermouth isn't dry," she says. "Hal, this is Bianco — "
"She also said someone left a baby."
"What?"
"She said somebody left a baby."
"A baby?"
"On her doorstep."
"I don't remember that at all. On the doorstep?"
"Right."
"Oh, that poor kid. Jed, why can't you leave this alone?"

[Continued from page 1]

of the infant and Kupcinet agreed. There was no record of a baby being turned over to police. Captain Edsel said he believed the baby to be a "pure fantasy."

SHE TOOK PILLS. She shoplifted. She sent wacko notes. She conjured a baby.

One item wasn't reported at all. Mark Goddard told investigators that he and Marcia drove Cookie down to Tijuana in July of 1963.

In 1963, it wasn't just illegal in California and pretty much everywhere else in the U.S., it was too salacious to even print. The sheriff's office had leaked it anyway, and the story eventually found its way to Chicago. My mother tells me that, yes, this she remembers. At some point, she couldn't recall exactly when, she'd heard about Cookie's abortion.

"Who told you?"

"God knows. A story like that, it just got whispered and whispered."

...and in yet another aspect of this baffling case, police checked a report that Miss Kupcinet hid in the attic of Prine's house while he was out on a date with another girl. Detectives said that while police were being called, Prine reportedly flushed out Miss...

AT BEST, I'M a haphazard, distractible researcher with an indifferent cat for an assistant, but as far as I've been able to tell, after roughly the second week of December 1963, the Karyn Kupcinet murder case dropped out of the news. After days of intense coverage, especially in Chicago and Los Angeles, her story vanished from the papers, all the papers.

Completely.

At least two years would pass before her name would resurface, and these stories mostly have to do with things her parents were naming in her honor, including a gallery at Francis Parker, a theater at Shimer College in Mount Carroll, and a forest in Israel.

Yes, of course, plenty of other people in Los Angeles and Chicago were murdered after Cookie. And yes, of course, the country had a lot of other things on its mind in December of 1963. Even so, splashed over the front pages — and then gone?

IN THE 1980s, Irv and Essee Kupcinet hired a psychic to crack Cookie's case once and for all. Peter Hurkos, "telepathic detective," was well known in Hollywood for having worked on the Manson murders. His specialty: direct communication with the dead. First, Hurkos named Prine as the murderer. He said that Cookie told him she'd order her father to wreck his career if he left her. So, he'd strangled her. When Irv and Essee told Hurkos Andy Prine was old hat, Hurkos said, *Wait, I'm receiving new information from the other side.* He said that Cookie's spirit was now saying it was most definitely her downstairs neighbor, a guy named David Lange, and that Lange had murdered her in a fit of drunken rage because she refused to sleep with him.

When Cookie's parents stopped paying Hurkos, the psychic ran out of suspects.

Yet the Kupcinets eventually did settle on this neighbor as the killer. In *A Man, an Era, a City,* Kup fingers David Lange and faults the Sheriff's Department for screwing up the investigation. Lange was a failed screenwriter. He once dated Natalie Wood. His sister was the actress Hope Lange, at that time known for her role in *Peyton Place* (suitable only for adults!). David Lange was also a friend of Cookie's. In fact, it was Cookie who'd found him his apartment. Kup describes Lange as a "heavy drinker, a hanger-on, and a gofer." On the night the Goddards discovered the body, Lange was in bed with a girlfriend, not Natalie Wood. This never-named woman later told police that she and Lange heard all the commotion, people running up and down the stairs, but that Lange didn't react. She also said that someone did knock on the door and that Lange went to answer it, but he immediately came back to bed. Kup writes that police believed that the person who'd knocked on the door must have told Lange about Cookie's death but he chose not to go upstairs *because he already knew what had happened.*

He also writes about an allegation that Lange had confessed, to another friend, that he'd killed Cookie, but that Lange, then hiding behind his sister's attorneys, wouldn't answer any questions. Given that there was no other evidence, Lange's behavior alone was never enough to charge him.

This isn't a detective story or a police procedural. It's not a mystery. A mystery would leak through my hands like water. God knows I'd write one if I could. But the truth is I've never been drawn to stories with answers. I'm lured to the ones where people, for whatever reason, don't want an answer.

Cookie's case remains open.

Jayne Mansfield's Shoes

Let your wheels move only along ruts / This is known as mysterious sameness.
— *Lao Tzu*

BARBARA (BABS) ROSENTHAL née Tucker and Essee Kupcinet née Solomon grew up in different neighborhoods, five miles apart. Babs in West Humboldt Park on Augusta Boulevard, Essee on the Gold Coast, by the lake, at the corner of Astor and Goethe (pronounced "Go-thee" in Chicago and don't let any twit of a highbrow tell you otherwise*). In the late twenties, this was like being born into different nation-states. Borders were fortified. A daughter of a Humboldt Park tailor didn't mix with the daughter of a Jew who'd made it that close to the lake. To my grandmother's family, five miles and two different streetcar lines away, Lake Michigan might as well have been in Colorado.

Essee's father owned a drugstore. One-half of the store sold medicine, the other half, liquor. A bootlegger during Prohibition, Morris Solomon had gone respectable. Babs and Essee met on neutral ground, Merriel Abbott's dance studio in Rogers Park. They were both twelve. Soon enough, they were inseparable. Both girls had talent, but Essee had trouble learning the routines, and Babs would spend hours teaching her.

---

* I confess to using this same line in the two previous books, *Here Is Eisendrath* (Indianapolis: Bobs-Merrill, 2003) and *Montrose Harbor, Winter* (San Francisco: MacAdam/Cage, 2009).

The two rose through the ranks, and by high school they were dancing for Merriel Abbott professionally in regular shows at the Empire Room and in clubs and theaters across the city. Like an early Chicago version of the Rockettes. They'd perform numbers like "Jingle Bells" and do high kicks with bells on their ankles.

Babs once told me and Lucy that Merriel — *She pronounced it "Mary El," though God knows, to her face we never called Miss Abbott anything but Miss Abbott* — would charge the girls three dollars for every pound they were overweight.

Lucy said: Three bucks back then? Damn, adjust that for inflation.

By 1938 both Babs and Essee gave up dancing and dropped out of the troupe in order to go to college/get hitched.

Babs followed Lou down to Champaign.

Essee enrolled at Northwestern, where she met Kup.

While Babs was downstate, she and Essee kept in constant touch by mail. They joined the same sorority: Sigma Delta Tau. When Babs and Lou moved back to Chicago, Babs and Essee, Essee and Babs, were, once again, inseparable.

Then came children — both women had one boy and one girl.

During the war Lou volunteered, but his feet were flat as Illinois. The Coast Guard took him. A much-repeated family story is that Lou Rosenthal did such a fine job patrolling the Calumet River for U-boats that they eventually shipped him to the South Pacific, the navy being short on officers. Kup spent those years on the home front "columning," as he put it, and raising money for bonds. Chicago bought more war bonds than any other American city, thanks, in large part, to Irv Kupcinet beating the drum. At the end of the war, Harry Truman personally thanked Kup for a column he wrote in support of the atomic bomb.

Then: the fifties.

Kup later wrote, "Everything was booming in the 1950s, not just babies."

All those parties. People sometimes asked Babs and Essee to perform a few of their old moves, and the two friends would lock arms and high-step around the room to cheers.

The view on the Rosenthal side has always been that Babs was the purer artist. When Babs left for college, she mourned the loss of dancing. Essee only missed the possibility of fame. And it was this ambition she foisted upon her daughter. Her husband's fame, such as it was, was never enough. It had to be in her daughter's name. Fame at any cost — and while she may not have charged Cookie three dollars a pound, Essee, among other things, according to my mother, never forgave Cookie any extra weight.

CERTAIN NAMES, THROUGH the osmosis of repetition, become part of the permanent vocabulary of any city. LaSalle, DuSable, McCormick.
    Big Bill Thompson, Mayor Daley, Jesse Jackson.
    Bozo.
    Studs
    Oprah.
    Ye.

Jane Byrne, Ed Vrdolyak, Harold Washington. There are Chicagoans who might not know exactly who these three politicians even were, but no Chicagoan of any age has ever escaped hearing their names. The past tense isn't entirely correct. Last I checked (four seconds ago, as of the eighth of June 2023), Fast Eddie is still breaking the furniture, having been released from his second stint in the federal pen (tax evasion) this past March.
    All the names we lug around. Through an accident of geographic fate and birth year, we've all got our own horde of names. It's personal, these names we'll never shake no matter how long we live, no matter how many new and glitzier names crowd out the old ones.

The Gossip Columnist's Daughter

* * *

Ray Rayner.

Frazier Thomas.

Ernie Banks.

Dave Kingman, Ivan De Jesus, Manny Trillo, Steve Swisher, Rick Sutcliffe, Ryne Sandberg, Leon Durham.

Bill Veeck, Harry Caray, Greg Luzinski, Harold Baines, LaMarr Hoyt.

Artis Gilmore.

Sid Luckman.

Gale Sayers.

Butkus.

Bob Avellini, Vince Evans. Noah Jackson. Revie Sorey.

Payton.

Mike Singletary. Steve McMichael, Jim McMahon, Richard Dent.

Ditka. No, fuck Ditka.

The third quarter of the '86 Superbowl, up 37–3 on the Pats, first and goal, and he gives the ball to the Fridge instead of Sweetness?

Buddy Ryan.

Buddy Guy.

Curtis Mayfield.

Belushi.

Fahey Flynn, Walter Jacobson, Linda Yu, Bill Kurtis, John Drummond, Jim Tilmon, Tim Weigel.

Donahue.

Steve Dahl.

Oprah, Oprah, Oprah, Oprah, Oprah.

Algren, Wright, Bellow, Hansberry, Brooks, Terkel, Forrest, Howland, Mamet, Cisneros, Dybek, Steinberg, J. Wolf...

And though discriminating readers will be pained to see these two columnists joined even by the twip of a comma:

Kupcinet, Royko.

It's their names, we'll never shake their names.

Chicago didn't name Kup "Mr. Chicago." Kup crowned himself. But he repeated it so often, and for so many years, that the city had no choice but to accept it, if only to tune him out a little. Okay, okay, okay, have mercy, you're Mr. Chicago. Now leave us alone. We're reading Mike Royko on page 2.

And if he was "Our Kup," it was less out of pride than simply because, as my mother says, what's ours is ours whether we want it or not.

AT THE HEIGHT of his career, from the fifties through the early eighties, Kup thumped out six columns a week for the *Sun-Times* and was syndicated in over a hundred papers. And for at least a couple of those decades, if you wanted to make it in show business in America, you had to go through Chicago, and to go through Chicago, you had to go through Kup. Irving Kupcinet, son of a Lawndale bakery delivery driver. Now look at him.

The man's clout.

His face on the yellow *Sun-Times* trucks that delivered the paper in the morning.

Anybody quicker with a quip?

Ouch! This just in off wires too hot to touch. **Zsa Zsa Gabor**'s *house caught fire yesterday in Malibu. Maybe she's not as burned out as we'd thought...*

Or you might be in line at the Osco and you'd hear the woman ahead of you say to the cashier:

Did you read Kup?

Not yet. Too busy working. What's he got?

Liz always calls him first.

No! Again? Already?

She phoned Kup from Tijuana. Reversed the charges.

And if you couldn't sleep, there was Kup after Johnny Carson and Tom Synder's *Late Late Show* with his own late late

late show. First it was called *At Random* and later, *Kup's Show*. He was on television for twenty-seven years, first on our CBS affiliate, then on ABC and NBC, and later on PBS channel 11, and his show was a great favorite of Chicago insomniacs. Five or six guests would sit around and yak about whatever. Conversations would carom from gardening to race relations to life on Mars. In the early years, the show had no official end time and would wander deep into the night, sometimes till dawn, the cameras still rolling, until either Kup got tired of talking (not often), or one of the guests — Carl Sandburg or Liberace or Dick Gregory or Dorothy Lamour or Dinah Shore — slumped over from weariness, whichever came first.

At the Vatican, Kup had an audience with Pope Pius XII. I think of him kneeling to kiss the pope's big ring, like an oversize eyeball. Most Holy Father, I bring a big hiya from the Archdiocese of Chicago and Archbishop O'Connor, who, incidentally, Your Holiness, if you don't mind my saying, would make a hell of an excellent-looking cardinal in one of those tall red hats...

Or Sundays. In the radio broadcast booth at the Bears games, Kup did color for Jack Brickhouse. Neither of them paid enough attention to the game, and often Brickhouse would sail off topic and say something like You know Kup, the mustard on this kielbasa is a truly outstanding contribution to culinary excellence, and Kup would pluck his cigar out of his mouth and say, That's right, Jack! The mustard on your kielbasa is most certainly an outstanding contrib —

As said earlier, no ribbon in the Chicagoland area was safe from Kup wielding a pair of gigantic scissors...

Charity event? Unthinkable unless Kup emceed. Impresario

The Gossip Columnist's Daughter

of Philanthropy, Maestro of the Telethon. Easter Seals, United Way, the March of Dimes, St. Jude, Big Brothers Big Sisters of America, the American Heart Association, the Jewish United Fund, the Muscular Dystrophy Association, the Audubon Society, the League of Women Voters...

Kup's own annual Purple Heart Cruise on Lake Michigan racked up untold thousands for injured veterans.

And friends? Friends? Where to begin?

Kup lunched with Bogart and Bacall when they stopped off in Chicago the day after their wedding. He had Nat King Cole's private phone number. Nobody had Nat Cole's private number. Bob Hope? The two of them were like this. He and Old Ski Nose did USO shows together. Kup played a decent straight man to Hope's antic wisecracker.

Sinatra?

See the back jacket of Kup's first book, *Kup's Chicago.*[*] There's a photo of Kup staring at Sinatra as he eats a hamburger. That's true love, to watch someone munch a burger with that kind of attention.

For years, Kup shared booth number 1 at the Pump Room with Sidney Korshak, the Chicago-born Mob lawyer who conquered Hollywood and Vegas.

Other pictures in *Kup's Chicago:* Kup with Truman, Kup with Marlon Brando. Kup with Dinah Shore...

Very, very chummy with Jerry Lewis.

---

[*] (Cleveland: World Publishing Co., 1962; Melbourne: Hassell Street Press, 2011). The reprint listing: "This work in the public domain has been selected by scholars as being culturally important and is part of the knowledge base of civilization as we know it."

Sammy Davis, too.

When the rabbi heard that Sammy had converted, he said, "Fabulous, but can he sing?"

Of course he knew Bing. Inexplicably, he called him Der Bingle. Joan Crawford and Spencer Tracy and Sidney Poitier (who often joined Kup's annual fishing trip to Bimini which included my grandfather as ship commander) and Jack Paar (before a well-publicized feud) and Liza Minnelli, Mort Sahl, Jimmy Durante, Golda Meir, Groucho Marx, Jayne Mansfield, Otto Preminger, Nipsey Russell, Ronald Reagan, Dennis Hopper, Faye Dunaway, Danny Kaye, Betty Grable...

His friendships spanned epochs, from Perry Como to Mr. T...

The back cover of *A Man, an Era, a City* itself is a solid wall of names. It starts with Michael Jackson and Princess Di and then goes alphabetical, Muhammad Ali, Woody Allen, Ann-Margret, Richard Attenborough, Lauren Bacall, Burt Bachrach, Joan Baez, Warren Beatty, Simone de Beauvoir...

KUP IS THE model for Mike Schneiderman, the vapid, social-climbing gossip columnist in Saul Bellow's *Humboldt's Gift*. Schneiderman appears in a scene at the Playboy Mansion. Schneiderman is described as "large heavy strong tanned sullen fatigued." Bellow leaves out the commas as if he's trying to get the description over with as fast as possible. Schneiderman's entire existence consists of sitting around restaurants and with his greedy beak pecking up copy for use in his inane column.

At the time, Kup wasn't amused.

Word is your correspondent has been immortalized in the latest snorer by our muy famoso jet-setter and sometime Chicago resident **Saul Bellow.** *I fell asleep before I got to the part about me... Yucks and some clucks for* **Buddy Hackett** *last night at the Empire Room... On Wednesday,* **Warren Beatty** *sneezed,* blah, blah, blah... *My pal* **Henry Kissinger** blah, blah, blah...

IF KUP HAS remained a known quantity in the town where he was born, his friend Lou Rosenthal, also Chicago-born, was never known coming or going. It's the way he wanted it. He had no desire to be known or remembered. I'm descended from a man who chose to remain on the periphery, and I like to believe, despite my chosen line of work, that I've inherited some of his preference for going unnoticed.

One of my grandfather's heroes was another reticent Chicagoan, Robert Todd Lincoln. Not only did Robert live through the murder of his father (and the death of two of his young brothers) but he was forty feet away when President Garfield was gunned down — and within earshot when McKinley was plugged in the abdomen. At that point he stopped hanging around presidents, and for the rest of his life he tried to call as little attention to himself as possible. According to my grandfather, Robert never sought to cash in on the family name. This is debatable. He died an extremely wealthy man. Robert Lincoln served as ambassador to Britain and secretary of war and was the chief counsel to the president of the Pullman Company for many years.

My grandfather liked to tell the story of the time when, as a messenger boy, he delivered a sheaf of papers to a mansion at the corner of Lake Shore Drive and East Scott Street. Robert himself, not a butler, opened the door. A stocky, far less elongated version of his father. It was February and cold and Robert Todd Lincoln invited my grandfather inside to warm up. The eminent lawyer led him into a large study, where a fire was going. The two sat silently for a while before Lincoln began to quiz my grandfather about his life.

"And your father? His profession?"

My grandfather thought for a moment, ran his hand through his head of thick hair, hair I never saw in person, hair I've only ever seen in photographs.

"He's a barber."

My great-grandfather Max Rosenthal wasn't a barber, he was a small-time bookie who ran a handbook operation out of a pool hall on West Garfield Boulevard.

Robert Lincoln stared at him for a few moments. My grandfather's cheeks were like little purple plums and his eyes were beginning to water. The need to lie was humiliating.

"Jew?"

This time he was honest. My grandfather nodded, not once, but three times.

"Well, we all carry our crosses, don't we? Forgive the metaphor."

My grandfather, trying to find somewhere to direct his tear-filled eyes, noticed a sheet of paper on the table between them. It was scattered with numbers and symbols.

"Ah, that," Lincoln said. "I enjoy doing algebra in my spare time. Equations calm one's nerves. Conundrums with solutions. So many other conundrums in our lives have no solution. Don't you agree?"

The fire popped. My little grandfather sank deeper into his leather chair. Across the cavernous house, multiple clocks were chiming. All those years later, he'd tell my sister and me that there was an exquisite loneliness in Robert Lincoln's every move, the way he rubbed his beard, crossed his legs, even the quiet way he coughed. He walked my grandfather to the front door and, without a word, sent him back into the cold.

I STARE AT the phone with the intensity of a Jew who guards a corpse all night before burial. I expect as much life out of this inert piece of titanium. Hours I watch it and watch it and watch it and then it happens, the fucking thing lights up.

"Hey."

"Hi."

A pause as if in recognition of what's lost. The things we might have said. I can see her holding the phone away from her face. She's on speaker. She's not in bed. She's on the couch. When she hangs up, she'll read on the light blue couch with the coffee stains and the red wine stains until she falls asleep. Then she'll wake up, check on Snook, brush her teeth, and get into bed and read again until she falls asleep again and the book will fall out of her hand and thump onto the floor, but it won't wake her up. Later, hours later, something else will, and she'll wake to the light and flick it off and try and sleep again.

"Are you set to pick up Leah for swimming at two thirty?"

"I got it."

"You can't be late."

"I got it."

"The lesson's only twenty minutes so if you're late by the time she gets her suit on, the lesson will be half-over. It's the

Kosciuszko Pool on West Diversey. It's to hell and gone but I couldn't find any other lessons that weren't booked. In traffic it will take at least half an hour. Maybe forty minutes. Take Touhy. No, Western."

"I said I got it. I'll take Western."

"You say that and then you're late and then you drive like a lunatic and it scares Leah."

"The kid cheers when I run red lights."

"You think I'm being shrill," she says.

"I didn't say that."

Another pause.

"Don't forget the hand sanitizer."

"Never would I forget — "

"You think I'm a caricature."

"I didn't say that."

"It's in your breathing."

"You want me to come over?"

"No."

"You know who Kosciuszko was, right?"

"Good night, Jed."

"Fought in the Revolutionary War. Buddy of Washington's. Not only a pool, but he's got an expressway, three schools, and a brewery. Never set foot in this city. It didn't even exist. Pays to be a Polish war hero in Chicago."

"Night."

"Night."

ONE THING MY grandfather didn't do was read "Kup's Column." Lou didn't read the *Sun-Times* at all. He read the *Wall Street Journal*. He read the business section of the *Trib*. He said anybody who didn't read the business section every day was fated to be a perpetual child. And he read Fielding. He read Trollope. Dickens. Wilkie Collins. His favorite poem was Stephen Vincent Benét's "John Brown's Body," and he liked to recite parts of it:

> *John Brown did not try to sleep,*
> *The live coals of his eyes severed the darkness...*

There were other Chicagoans who didn't deign to read "Kup's Column." For instance, Hyde Park intellectuals, the sort of people who would use the word deign in a sentence. Hyde Park intellectuals might have read Royko, but they never stooped to read Kup—except for maybe Saul Bellow, who only read Kup to laugh at Kup. Also, Bellow read everything. Lou wasn't a Hyde Park intellectual. Like most Chicagoans, he never set foot on the campus of the University of Chicago. He went to DePaul and eked out a law degree in six years of nights. Still, though he wasn't born into it and never quite looked the part, despite his suits and erect carriage, he cultivated the character of a Midwestern patrician, a night school lawyer, yes, but one cut from old cloth. Probate. Wills and trusts. Estate planning. Whenever a fellow attorney greeted my grandfather on LaSalle Street, he'd shout happily, *Counselor!* and then tip the hat he never wore in his direction. Lou Rosenthal, a small, bald, hatless man in a city of hat-wearing men. A hat, any hat, would have given the impression that he was at least slightly taller, but Lou never went in for this sort of crutch. He went bald in his early thirties. When Babs suggested he experiment with a toupee, my grandfather dismissed it. God or biology sees fit to render me hairless, who am I to make a rebuttal?

Nor did he doctor his shoes to give himself an inch.

He didn't know who Dinah Shore was and he didn't care to find out.

I wonder if the fact that Lou didn't even read his column made Kup feel more at ease around him. He had so many friends, but how many who didn't want their name lit up?

My grandfather used to take me to lunch at the Cape Cod Room in the Drake. Once, I remember, he peered at me over his Bookbinder soup (red snapper with sherry) and said, "Listen, kiddo, I'm a dying breed."

"You're sick?"

"No, not that. Not yet, anyway. What I mean is that my way of seeing things has become, for lack of a better word, piquant."

"What?"
"Call it quaint."
"Like you're not cool?"
"Exactly."
I took a slurp of soup.
"Why don't you change?"
"Don't slurp," he said.

My grandfather smiled but only barely, a slight inward pull of his cheeks. Like a wince of pain. He called over the waiter, an ancient man with long sideburns and a gleaming white uniform embroidered in gold. At the Drake, all the waiters dressed like naval officers.

"Morris, would you get this child some cheesecake? It's rather an emergency."

"I'll alert the kitchen of the situation, Mr. Rosenthal."

"You're a good man, Morris. A gentleman and a scholar."

"Scholarship was never my strong suit."

"School of life, Morris, school of life..."

My grandfather rubbed both his small ears. He had allergies and he said rubbing his ears helped ease his throat.

He turned back to me.

"Your question deserves an answer."

"Which?"

"As to why I haven't changed with the times."

"Oh."

But he never did answer it, not that I remember, anyway. Morris arrived with the cheesecake. The old man's hand trembled and the fork bounced as he set it down in front of me.

My grandfather's great trick, now that I think about it and

see him again as he looked in the Cape Cod Room, was that half smile he deployed no matter the occasion. A smile with more ache in it than any sort of joy. During all those good years, it must have calmed his clients, who might have read in it: finally, a man who's not trying to sell me anything.

SWEATY CHLORINE-SOAKED AIR lines the nostrils. Heads bob in the water like seals. Their little legs thrashing. Is there a more useful life skill than learning to tread water? Welcome to life on earth, kid, now jog in place for the next eighty-plus years if you're lucky. I'm plumped on the bleachers with the other parents. This wet swelter. We all stare only at our own kid. We stare with zombie-like intensity. Not a single moment of this childhood will go unobserved. At least for the moment. In our hands, our phones. Tot swim at the Kosciuszko Pool. Long live the Patron Saint of West Point! The instructor lines them up on the pool deck. One by one, they jump back into the water. Snook is dutiful. Shivering, she concentrates on the shoulder blades of the boy in front of her, and when it's her turn to jump, she jumps.

I THINK OF the heaps of crushed ice in the urinals at the Drake Hotel and how sometimes there was fresh fruit, too. What a thrill it was to piss onto halved lemons and sliced apples and chunks of honeydew melon. I think of the way, after lunch, Lou would smoke his pipe and look me over without a word. He wanted me to know that I had a place, that here with him at the Cape Cod Room I had a place. I turned away from it. I didn't become a LaSalle Street lawyer. There's not a restaurant in the city of Chicago where a waiter knows my name. (There's a bar, the Sovereign, on North Broadway, Roz jerks her chin in my direction when I come in, but this is as close as I come to being acknowledged as a regular.) As an attorney I'd have been a bust. Even if I had become one, there are no more Lou Rosenthals. Nobody lingers after lunch at the Cape Cod Room. Once, I did have a place. I haven't had many other places since. Hanna used to say that I love nothing more than to wallow. I don't dispute this. I'm a champion wallower. But I do believe there's a difference between wallowing and trying to claw your way back in time.

KUP DIDN'T DROP names. He secreted them. Kup reveled in the vowels and the consonants that formed to create the physical ecstasy of fame on the tips of his fingers as he typed. He typed *Jack Paar* and for a few glorious, fleet milliseconds he was Jack Paar. (Also, he once filled in for Paar on the show that became *The Tonight Show*.) Typed *Ann-Margret,* same thing, he felt the heat of her breath in his finger pads. The entire column consisted almost entirely of names, bold-face names mingled with a few sentences and phrases, a name-studded prose, name after name after name. This isn't to say, as I've said (admittedly backhandedly), that it was all so easy. The grueling hours on the town, the hours on the phone, the hours he spent clacking out the names to meet the 1 p.m. deadline for tomorrow's paper. And it isn't as if he didn't have his moments.

When he interviewed Marilyn Monroe in '59, he asked her if she'd read Freud. She said she'd wait for the movie.

How about holding still for a radio interview?

"Certainly."

"Mind if it runs about thirty minutes?"

"I don't know you that well."

Bada bing.

There was the time the Queen's sister, Princess Margaret,

visited Chicago. This was in 1979. During a luncheon with the mayor, Jane Byrne, the visiting princess blurted, "All Irish are pigs." Jane Byrne was as Irish as Maureen O'Hara. Mr. Chicago was a witness. Kup jotted it down on a napkin and it was a scoop heard around the world.

What matters to me is not who he knew (everybody) or what he did, but that I've come to see Kup, or the idea of Kup, especially in his heyday, as a way of seeing a certain time, the sixties, in particular the early sixties, those first three years of the decade when the sixties were still the fifties. His columns are forgettable, mediocre, and yet at the same time they're a record of a moment that was about to vanish. Chicago partied nearly all the way through 1963, a kind of Midwestern Weimar. Maybe Kup and Essee, and by extension, always by extension, always at a remove, Babs and Lou, should have seen the end coming, that the party (even if my grandparents weren't at it) wasn't going to last. Chapter 7 of *Kup's Chicago* is called "Night Life, Anyone?" After spending seven pages on the Pump Room and Mister Kelly's, Kup recommends Hugh Hefner's Playboy Club, but there's a catch. The Playboy Club isn't open to just anybody. You have to pony up.

Or, as Kup puts it in a Kupism: *You're up a tree if you lack a key...*

The nights, the nights, the nights, the names, the names, the names, as if all that was needed to keep it all going was to pay a membership fee to Hugh Hefner.

Congressional record—U.S. Senate, November 11, 2003

MR. DURBIN. Mr. President, today the city of Chicago, IL, is marking the passing of a legend. Just yesterday, Chicago, and the rest of the Nation as well, lost a giant... As any reader of his columns can attest, right up until the end, Irv Kupcinet still wrote with passion and wit about the subjects on which he built his career—famous people and his native Chicago... Today we woke up to a world without Irv Kupcinet, and we are somewhat poorer by that loss. But a little part of Kup will always be with us... If an aspiring columnist were to ask my advice on reaching the highest levels of that profession, I would offer the following advice: study the life of Irv Kupcinet.... The real question we now face in Chicago is whether we can get up in the morning and face a day without "Kup's Column."...
    I yield the floor.

IN ITS TWO-COLUMN obituary, the *New York Times* wrote that Kup had "a wide-eyed love of celebrities, movie stars, tycoons, popes, presidents, beautiful people, kings and potentates of every description, even princes of the underworld..."

I looked up *potentate*. Now I can use it in a sentence.

I TELL MY students it's the kiss of death to include everything. I squeeze my chin and sigh, sage-like: "What if Michelangelo had just left the block of marble sitting there? Would we have David?" Now, I'm not even sure what I mean. Does the sculpture analogy even work? And who listens to their own advice?

Because I've scrawled Kup's former office phone number on an index card, I feel compulsed to record it here:

Randolph 6-2038.

Don't you wish you could pick up a phone and say, "Operator, connect me to Randolph 6-2038 immediately. I've got an item for Kupcinet. Otto, the gorilla, just escaped from the Lincoln Park Zoo..."

Lenny Bruce once accused Kup of being a moralist during a routine at the Gate of Horn theater in 1962. Then he wrote Kup to complain about the bad review. Bruce said he couldn't help it, even when he poured Lysol on his putz, he still talked filthy.

In 1980, Jane Byrne called Kup one of the two biggest freeloaders in Chicago, the other one being a columnist at the *Tribune*.

Kup retaliated by writing that Byrne had dozens and dozens of unpaid parking tickets. She didn't have to pay parking tickets like everybody else?

Not that Kup paid his own tickets. He *was* a first-class freeloader. At one point in the eighties even his bosses at the *Sun-Times* thought his quid pro quo was too obvious and ordered him not to accept any more Fleetwoods from Steve Foley Cadillac in exchange for positive mentions in the column.

These notes on Kup. Piles of them. I spend far too many hours documenting a distant civilization that never needed to be documented in the first place.

The medievalist across the hall calls me Jed Kaczynski.

In Kup's archive at the Chicago History Museum, I copy

The Gossip Columnist's Daughter

down forgettable jokes he compiled for the speeches he gave as a toastmaster at numberless forgotten functions.

So many mink coats here tonight, it looks like a PTA meeting in Texas.

When in doubt, there's always Zsa Zsa.

Don't listen to me. I'm the boob who predicted Zsa Zsa Gabor would join a convent.

Ba, dum, tss.

I won't be able to sleep tonight unless I impart (upon whom?) that on February 9, 1960, Marilyn Monroe sent the following telegram to the chairman of the Chicago branch of the Variety Club:

> CONGRESS HOTEL CHGO DEAR MR. CHAIRMAN: I'M HAPPY TO KNOW THAT THE CLUB HAS SELECTED KUP FOR THE HEART AWARD. HE IS ALWAYS DOING NICE THINGS FOR OTHERS.
> MARILYN

I've got a list of guests who appeared on his TV show between 1960 and 1974. Rex Harrison, Douglas MacArthur, Audrey Hepburn, Raquel Welch, Alfred Hitchcock (no doubt, to Kup he was "Hitch"), Richard Nixon (numerous appearances, another longtime friend), Richard Pryor (once, the two Richards were on together; what I'd give to have seen this episode), Charlton Heston, Joe Frazier, Judy Garland, Guy Lombardo, Cloris Leachman, Nelson Rockefeller, Bette Davis, Bill Cosby, Haile Selassie...

Haile Selassie!

One night, Betty Friedan and Gloria Steinem went for each other's hair and had to be broken up. Who's Betty Friedan again? Another time, Lorraine Hansberry told off Otto Preminger because she thought his *Porgy and Bess* was a cesspool of stereotypes. Then she told him where he could stick his good intentions.

In 1965, Malcolm X predicted on *At Random* that he'd be shot. Two weeks later he was assassinated.

Kup might have been a lightweight, but people opened up to him. One reason, I think, is because at least the thing wasn't canned. At the top of each show, Kup would say, "Welcome to the lively art of conversation. Unrehearsed, unscripted, broadcasting live in Chicago..." And it was true. You never knew what he was going to ask, or what direction the conversation would take, if it took any direction at all. The fact that the show had no set end time must have made it feel, for his guests, anyway, like a dull cocktail party that would never, ever, ever be over, so you might as well say something interesting or even something you actually believed.

In one episode, Sammy Davis Jr. appears on *Kup's Show* alongside an IBM robot named R2 More. Kup, ignoring the robot, takes a puff on his cigarette and asks Sammy, after plugging "the world's greatest entertainer's" upcoming show at the Holiday Star in Merrillville, Indiana, "What's this thing I hear about you and satanism?"

"Oh, that." Sammy sighs. "It turned out to be too much of a commitment."

R2 More beeps in approval.

Then Kup, still completely disregarding the presence of the robot, says, "You made a lot of mistakes in your life, huh, Sammy?"

Sammy gazes upward as if searching the rafters of the studio for some escape.

"I invented mistakes."

Beep. Beep.

"I hear you don't live such a wild life anymore, Sammy. Is it true what I hear?"

"You know, Kup, I find I really dig cooking and spending time with friends. As I get older, I value the quieter times. You know, you don't have to go out every night to lead a fulfilling life."

That's when an Irish actress named Geraldine Fitzgerald, who up to that point hasn't said a word, chimes in: "You don't?"

Beep. Beep. Beep. Beep. Beep.

What kind of interest could I possibly have had in all this as a kid? By the time I came along, Kup had been bumped from network TV to channel 11. And yet I'd watch the show by myself in the den downstairs, scrunched under a blanket on the big black leather chair, one or two in the morning, the sound down so I wouldn't wake anybody up. That I didn't have much of a clue what they were talking about made no difference. So boring it hypnotized. The talk went on and the talk went on.

Lucille Ball asks Kup when the commercial break is and Kup says, "Lucy, my dear, we don't have commercial breaks," and Lucy looks like she is going to fall out of her chair.

It wasn't just the guests who fell asleep. Once, the cameraman dozed off and the camera jolted upward, and because the producer had already gone home, the rest of the show consisted of a shot of the ceiling tiles accompanied by the drowsy, meandering voices down below.

Often, Essee would be just off set, waving at Kup to stop, please stop talking and let the guests go back to their hotels...

John and Yoko, Margaret Mead, Alger Hiss, Elijah Muhammad...

Elijah Muhammad, who as a matter of principle considered all white people blue-eyed devils, sent Kup and Essee Kupcinet a bouquet of flowers after Cookie's death.

Who didn't Kup talk to?

Among the condolence letters he received is one from J. Edgar Hoover.

Another is from Nathan Leopold of the Loeb and Leopold murderers. Richard Loeb was stabbed to death at Joliet, but Leopold was released on parole in 1958, thanks in large measure to Kup's help.

He always did keep it local. Give this to him. And no matter who he talked to, he never left Chicago behind. He never tried to reach beyond it, though as he often repeated, he had many offers to move to New York or Los Angeles.

When Queen Elizabeth departed Chicago in 1959, Mayor Daley said, "Next time bring the kids."

That sort of talk. Local talk. Neighborhood talk. Like the mayor, Kup was a master.

It's ridiculous, I know it, but I feel an obligation to set this all down again because (why the almost pathological need to repeat this?) we were connected by a thread to all the action. Somewhere on the periphery were Babs and Lou Rosenthal.

IN *KUP'S CHICAGO,* Kup writes that early in his career Essee wrote a column in his stead because he was traveling and couldn't file it. Turned out she had chops. The kid could write, Kup says, and so I never let that happen again...

In the archives, I came across a piece with Essee's byline, a front-page story she wrote for the *New York Journal-American* after the death of her friend Diana Barrymore, the daughter of the tragedian John Barrymore (and also Drew's aunt). Diana had success onstage and in film, but she'd become, by her own account in her memoir, *Too Much, Too Soon,* a wreck, "a thrice-divorced alcoholic has-been."

In the *Journal-American,* Essee described her attempts to save her friend from herself. To cheer her up, she'd recently given Diana an Arabic gold charm.

> I have one part of it. I gave Diana the other part....
> She held up the charm, and kissing it, said, "I'll never take it off. In fact, I'll be buried with it."

Maybe she was. A maid found her in bed in January 1960. Multiple sources say that she died of acute alcohol poisoning and a drug overdose, but an autopsy conducted at the time couldn't determine a direct cause of death. What is known is that ten days earlier, she'd been so blotto and noisy as an audience member during a Broadway show that it took four cops to get her out of the theater.

Essee's story was illustrated by two large pictures, one of Essee holding her half of the gold charm, the other of Essee attending Diana's funeral. She was wearing a fur coat and dark glasses with leopard-patterned frames. Next to her in the photo was Cookie. In the caption, Essee was named, but Cookie wasn't: *Girl at right is unidentified*.

On the clipping, someone had scratched out the word *unidentified* in pencil and drew a line to KARYN KUPCINET (all caps) handwritten in the margin.

Something eerie about the insistent way her name is written, as if whoever wrote it — I compared it to other samples in the archive and believe it to be Essee's handwriting — needed Cookie to be part of this story, no matter what. God forbid she go unnoticed.

Barrymore postscript:

Tennessee Williams was the great love of Diana Barrymore's life. Sounds like she missed a memo. For years, she waited for him to pop the question. In *Memoirs,* Williams writes that Diana Barrymore was "a girl with talent but not enough and it haunted and was destroying her." He also questions the official account of her death and suggests the possibility of a violent death. He writes that Diana's manager, not the maid, found her, and that the room was in complete shambles. Diana was lying naked, facedown, blood streaming out of her mouth. A heavy marble ashtray had been shattered against the wall. Williams writes that this mystery wasn't reported in the papers at the time. Her manager had whispered it in his ear during the funeral services in Manhattan.

THIS MORNING WASN'T my morning. It's still Tuesday. I didn't realize it wasn't Wednesday until I was nearly at the door of our house on Jarvis. When did yesterday remain today? That's either a profound question or a nonsensical one. But when I was nearly at the door, the door had a Tuesday look. Like it wasn't about to open. Shit, it's Tuesday. Instead of turning around and leaving, I went around back and stood on my toes and looked into the kitchen window and spied on Hanna making breakfast for Snook. Her back was to the window. She was wearing a faded maroon sweatshirt. Her brother's. On the front, if she'd turned around, it would have said Minnesota Golden Gophers with a bucktoothed mascot wearing a collegiate sweater. By making breakfast, I mean she was pouring milk into a cereal bowl. Sugar cereal, I noted, in direct contravention of decrees prohibiting such nonfood food. We are our contradictions. If I fed Snook Frosted Flakes, Hanna would call Cook County Social Services. On West Pratt, I give the kid dry wheat toast and avocado for breakfast. Snook noticed me almost immediately. She was sitting facing the window. Her little round head and big eyes she inherited from Babs. Lucy and I got her nose, Snook got her eyes. She stared at me, at this sudden appearance of her father's face in the window on the wrong day, and didn't say a word. Good, good kid, she already knows when to keep her mouth shut. The art of family confidentiality. Kids keep secrets like nobody. We learn it early. And she betrayed no wonder or even any curiosity about what I might be doing in the backyard, among the tangled skeletal March bushes, peering into the window at breakfast. Because she knew. She knew I was looking into the window at what should be my life.

I ducked down and slipped away. As I walked east on Jarvis, Saul Bellow tapped me on the shoulder and reminded me he wrote the same scene in *Herzog*. It's all trodden ground, Rosenthal. Everything you say, I've already said it better. Irv Kupcinet? I finished off that schmuck in two paragraphs. And now you're doing the divorced-daddy-in-the-window bit?

Hanna and I never married.

That matters? Marriage is in the mind. No, the spleen. Anyway, I covered the mournful papa routine like snow on L tracks.

God knows he's right. When Moses Herzog peers into the window of the house he once lived in, he sees his ex–best friend bathing his daughter. And the traitor has wild carrot-colored hair and one arm. No, I can't beat that. His is a scene of domestic horror laced with comedy, mine's only something that just happened, just a kid staring at her father as if she'd been expecting his head to pop up on a Tuesday.

FAMOUS CAMEO! KUP gets off a train in *Anatomy of a Murder*. Jimmy Stewart plays a lawyer who is defending a soldier accused of murder. The soldier claims the dead man raped his wife. Ben Gazzara plays the accused. He broods on-screen for two and a half hours. Lee Remick, who plays the wife, rarely takes off her sunglasses. The trial scenes go on for days. Everybody and his brother is called to testify. It's like sitting in traffic. At one point Jimmy Stewart requests that the accused be examined by a psychiatrist, and so court is adjourned while one is sent for. What follows is a brief scene where Stewart's sidekick, an old drunk named Parnell (most excellent shaggy mustache), goes to the train station to fetch a certain Dr. Smith, an army shrink...

And that's when Irv Kupcinet steps off the train wearing a long coat and a fedora.

Parnell seizes Kup's arm and shouts, "Dr. Smith!"

Kup glares at him and shouts back, "You must be mistaken!"

Then he charges directly toward the camera before veering out of the frame.

I rewind.
"You must be mistaken!"
"You must be mistaken!"
"You must be mistaken!"
Kup's sense of indignation at being misidentified borders on rage. It's over-the-top and weirdly personal. You don't know who I am? How dare you? Me? A nondescript Dr. Smith? Some schlemiel off the street? Some doctor nobody?

But the man himself was a fiction. The creation of a lower-middle-class son of a bakery delivery driver from Lawndale. Nothing complex or even tricky about the creation — all bootstraps and hard work and look at me now. But there were times when he detached from the character, times when Irv wasn't "Kup."
Saul Bellow picked up on the distance. Of the otherwise-insipid Mike Schneiderman, Bellow writes that there were times he looked blank, as if the emptiness of his life made him physically sick.
It runs counter to Kup's hail-fellow-well-met and man-about-town persona, but there is an absence about him in some of the pictures. Even in the photographs that predate Cookie's death, you can almost see the void behind his eyes. Here he is in 1952 with Tony Bennett, pale, ghostly, the right side of his mouth wrenched into a tight smile.

True, he might simply have been zonked. He and Essee out on the town every night, and with the TV show going sometimes to four or five in the morning and back in the office at the paper by nine...

A DINOSAUR WHO never became extinct, he just kept at it. He remained a man about town long after that wasn't a thing anymore. Year after year he showed up to his fifth-floor office at the *Sun-Times*. Because of names. Because there are always names, old names, new names, names, and more names. Six columns a week, forty-plus years. Like Lake Michigan itself, always to the east of us, glooming, lurking, shining, Kup was there, whether we bothered to look his way or not. And let's be honest it took work, a colossal amount of work, to be that trivial for that long, day in, day out.

WHO'S CALLING WHO trivial?
So he wasn't Mike Royko. He wasn't even Bob Greene. At least Saul Bellow had the imagination to give him a different name. And aren't I biting the hand that also fed me? Because over the years, my name, too, appeared from time to time in the column. As did the names of everybody else in my family: my father, my mother, my sister, and, before the rift, Babs and Lou.

In the bibs and diapers department, the stork has delivered a boy, **Jedidiah,** *to* **Mr. and Mrs. Aubrey Rosenthal.** *Papa is an up-and-coming solo practitioner who's just hung his shingle (cases and controversies, anybody?), Mama is the enchanting* **Clarice**... *Among the guests at* **Joan Crawford**'s *Mental Health Ball at the Conrad Hilton Friday was crooner* **Vic Damone** *and Blackhawk* **Bobby Orr**...

In Kup's world, young husbands are always up-and-coming and young wives are always enchanting. And when my father acted in the Chicago Bar's yearly variety show, when my mother won a substitute-teacher-of-the-year award, when my sister kicked General Assembly ass in Model UN — all were name-checked in the column.

Author! Author! Little **Jed Rosenthal** *is in a sailor suit* no more. *The twenty-nine-year-old scribe has penned a short story for the venerated* Atlantic Monthly *(founded in Boston in 1857!)... A little birdie spotted a* **Dan Quayle.** *The ex-veep was in town yesterday keynoting the Illinois Bankers annual shindig at the Palmer House...* **Kermit the Frog,** *blah, blah, and* **Miss Piggy,** *blah, blah...* **Kenny Rogers,** *blah, blah...* **Kim Basinger,** *blah, blah, blah.*

We might have made fun of it all our lives, we might have shunned it as shallow and stupid, even anachronistic, but didn't my grandfather save the clippings? Babs might have snipped the items out of the *Sun-Times,* but it was Lou who filed them away for posterity. He may not have read the column, but he hung on to our mentions.

"DADDA?"
  "Yeah, bud?"
  "What are we eating for dinner?"
  "Eggy rice and hamburger."
  "Eggy rice again?"
  "You love eggy rice."
  "Pizza."
  "Leona's is closed, honey, next time — "
  She stomps a plump foot on the linoleum.
  "Giordano's."
  "We're doing rice and hamburger."
  "Zimi's."
  "No."
  "Lou Malnati's."
  "You hear what I said?"
  She's got Babs's huge eyes and she knows how to use them. Just like she knows every pizza place from here to North Avenue. I had a professor in graduate school, a father of five, who said that all children are ostensibly interchangeable until they turn eighteen. I remember jotting this pearl of idiocy down in my notebook.
  "Pizza or nada," Snook says.

SO WE APPEARED in "Kup's Column" a few times? So did tens of thousands of other names. Who gives a damn that some Rosenthals nobody ever heard of had a little proximity to fame sixty years ago? An uncle on my mother's side who'd always say: *Shake the hand that shook the hand that shook the hand that shook the hand of John L. Sullivan.* That's how it was. But my grandparents were only once removed. Talk to Babs and Lou and you were talking to a couple who'd spoken to a couple who'd spoken to everybody who was anybody. But the fact of it is, to them, none of it mattered. Babs and Lou, at the end of the day, didn't give two shits who the Kupcinets knew or didn't know — they simply loved Irv and Essee, Essee and Irv, period, whoever they were. But see, Babs and Lou Rosenthal themselves weren't anybody. Why else would they have been so expendable?

AS A FORM of self-flagellation I watched *Kramer vs. Kramer* with the cat. Rudy enjoyed it. For a cat it's a comedy.

There's a scene early on, just after Meryl Streep leaves, when Dustin Hoffman tries to make French toast for his kid. Hoffman hams up his incompetence. There's a close-up of his bewildered fingers fumbling around trying to figure out what to do with the slice of bread. Finally he dips the slice into a coffee cup full of egg and milk, but the bread doesn't fit, and so he folds it and stuffs it into the cup and the kid protests because it's not the way Meryl Streep does it. Meryl Streep doesn't fold the French toast. And Hoffman, panicking, says something like, No, no, no. You do fold it. Folding is the way it's done. The finest chefs, in the best restaurants, they all serve French toast folded.

THE ROSENTHALS WERE an off night, a break, a pause in the action, a respite from being seen to be seen. Babs and Lou would come over to the apartment on East Lake Shore and the four of them would sit in Essee's big white living room. You stepped down into it, as if into a swimming pool, and there was a crowd of white couches and giant white pillows, and beyond the big picture windows, beyond their own reflections in the well-lit room, was the vast black lake. Irv might put on a little music — local Waukegan boy, Benny Goodman — but more often than not they'd sit and drink and smoke in near silence and gab about nothing. That was the beauty. They didn't need to say anything at all.

Essee and Babs huddled in the corner of a couch, Irv and Lou sank side by side into those twin puffy white chairs, holding their pipes.

Half-completed thoughts, murmurs of agreement.

Or maybe they'd get a table at Gene and Georgetti's, upstairs in the quiet part, or a booth at the Singapore and they'd order prime rib all around, old friends and old friends' kind of talk. Essee would ask Babs about Judith and my father and nod as she gazed languidly at my grandmother's familiar, full lips, hardly listening. Irv and Lou might talk a little politics. They'd been Truman Democrats and now were Kennedy Democrats and considered themselves liberals on race and economics, though both, out of a sense of duty, voted twice for Ike in the fifties. Times were changing. So long as they didn't change too much, it was all fine. Fine. No, nothing was ever expected, and that's why these nights became so precious in my grandmother's memory. How many times in our lives are we truly at ease? When there's nothing in the offing that could possibly throw anything off.

A NEIGHBOR DIED yesterday. He lived across the hall. Three-plus years here and we never spoke. A well-dressed old man, shiny-shoed, furtive. I have no image of his face. Quick with his keys when he opened his door and even quicker with the locks after he shut it behind him. One lock and then another and another. Often late at night, he played piano, not well, hesitantly, but I'd lie here and wait for him and nights he didn't play I was disappointed. There was some hullaballoo. Shouting in the corridor as they pulled the stretcher out of the apartment. They'd zipped him up in a bag. Before he was all in, the elevator kept banging closed on the stretcher until a cop held the door open with his foot. Then the elevator closed like a fist. Silence in the basement again.

SOME NIGHTS THOUGH Babs did get her own taste of glamour. Lou would stay home and read. Sometimes, not very often, Babs would accompany Irv and Essee out on their rounds. Those were sparkling nights. When Babs was one of the gang, careening drunkenly from the Buttery to Chez Paree to Al Siegel's Living Room to the Bistro to the London House for jazz. A plebeian, seeing the entourage, would know it was Kup and Essee and Tony Curtis and Janet Leigh. But who's that other one? Couldn't possibly be a star, with that nose. And once, once, Jayne Mansfield stopped in the middle of the sidewalk and told Babs she liked her shoes, and Babs, in a moment of abandon and bravado, took her shoes off right then and there and she and Jayne Mansfield traded. They fit! We're twins! Right there in the slush on Wacker Drive. Traded shoes. Even after the rift, Babs would tell this story, though she'd never say how it was that she happened to be walking down Wacker Drive with Jayne Mansfield.

No, it's not that Babs craved a return to any of that. It wasn't the secondhand connection to movie stars, to the anointed ones. It wasn't her sense of having missed out on her own possibilities in show business. She'd reconciled that long ago.

It was the quiet nights. Babs mourned the loss of those nights when they'd just sit, with or without music, talk and a little laughter, nothing forced, nothing bombastic, and the lake out there in the dark that they couldn't see because of the light and their reflections on the glass.

II.

A Hateful Errand

A LONG BLACK Lincoln eases up to the curb. The driver immediately pops out. He's as small as a jockey. He's dressed in livery. A double-breasted suit, a couple of sizes too big, white shirt, black tie. Atop his head is a miniature hat like a child policeman's. With exaggerated haste he struts around the hood of the limousine and plants himself before the columnist. He waits a moment before calling out, carefully enunciating all the consonants, "Mister Kup-cin-et!"

The columnist stands motionless and stares right through the little man's little hat.

The driver waits another long moment, allows time for the nonanswer to become an answer. He opens the back door. Irv gets in stiffly, without folding his body. It's reminiscent of the way a man who's been arrested is shoved, with the helping hand of a cop pushing his head, into the back seat of a squad car, except in this case nobody has laid their hands on him. It's like his body itself won't bend in order to accommodate having to sit down.

The driver closes the door as if it's fragile. Everything about this driver — the ill-fitting livery getup, the deliberate movements, the obsequiousness — suggests to Lou not only that the outfit is a costume but that the man wants them to know it's a costume.

I'll be driving you, but you think I'm anybody's chauffeur?
"And, sir? You are?"
"Rosenthal, Lou Rosenthal."
The name means nothing to him. The driver eyes him.
Should it mean anything?
No.
"Please, sir."
The driver leads Lou around to the other side of the car and opens the door. Lou gets in and slams the door himself.
Irv's flopped lifeless, chin sagging to his chest.
Once out of sight of the two men in the car, the driver jerks his chin at Solly.
"Trunk's open."
Uncle Solly doesn't nod, or rather he nods without nodding.
"And ride up front."
Solly carries the suitcases over to the Lincoln and sets them down. He opens the trunk and loads the cases inside. For a moment, he stands alone behind the car. Solly squeezes his eyes shut, then blinks a few times to revive himself.

IT'S CAVE-LIKE, THE Lincoln. A den of leather. There's a satisfyingly luxurious crinkle every time you move, even slightly. There's a jar of cashews. There's a decanter of bourbon. A small bowl of ice with a pair of tongs. The bourbon sways as the limousine jolts away from the airport. Nobody speaks. Uncle Solly sits beside the driver in the passenger seat, silent as a mountain. The driver keeps his eyes on the road, only a few times does he flick them upward to check on the two men in the rearview.

The Lincoln gains speed on the freeway. Irv has left his hat on. The top of it grazes the velvety roof. Lou shuts his eyes. The silence of four men in a car, even one as roomy as this one, is thick. The proximities, the weight. Hot flesh and perspiration. Noisy breathing. What a relief it would be, Lou thinks, to talk, to simply talk, to talk and exchange nothing at all, if only to hear a voice other than the one in my own head. Irv Kupcinet hasn't spoken a word since they left Chicago.

LOU GAZES AT block after block of flaming glass. A netherworld that's too bright and at the same time blurry. Maybe I need new glasses? The boxy, sand-colored buildings seem to bob in the morning glare and even the streets themselves seem on the verge of evaporation. But you could dry up and float away here, couldn't you? A place this bright before 10 a.m.? This is December? At one intersection, waiting for a light to change, stands a girl with a short torch of red hair and, Lou can't help but take note, the skimpiest skirt imaginable. No, not imaginable. Looking at it, he can't even imagine it. That skirt would be small on a doll. My god, she looks like a rooster without pants. The girl swivels her head to look at the limousine (yes, like a rooster, like a chicken!). She's unimpressed by any shiny car. Looks away, nose up at the sky in search of something, anything more interesting.

No wonder the kid had such a hard time here.

How do you act when everybody, all the time, is acting?

The Lincoln swings into a turn and Irv and Lou bump shoulders. Neither man keeps his shoulders rigid as you would if you were sharing a car with a stranger. There's comfort in this, isn't there?

Two old friends, their shoulders bumping.

IF I COULD bring her back, Irv, I would.

My grandfather thinks of that story of the lover, the kid with the flute. What's his name? Oedipus?

Has anybody gone down to the lowest depths on behalf of a friend? Draw me a map, you murderous god, and I'll go down.

I'll learn the flute.

I'd bring her home, Irv, I would. On my back.

THE COUNTY MORGUE on West Temple in downtown Los Angeles. It lurks behind the courthouse. A low-slung brick building, looks like it's hiding. A tall man stands alone in the otherwise-empty parking lot. He's wearing mirrored sunglasses and an impeccable cream-colored suit. He's like an apparition and yet at the same time he's not out of place. It's like he belongs right where he's been standing, and he may well have been rooted to the spot for days. Sidney Korshak doesn't need a car to occupy a parking space. He's not even smoking. Korshak doesn't smoke. His hands are clasped together in front of him like a patient priest. As the Lincoln glides to a stop beside him, my grandfather studies the man from the car window. Korshak is taller than he remembers. I'm surrounded by tall Jews. Didn't we all used to be so much closer to the ground?

Is it the water in America?

Lou and Sidney Korshak went to law school together. Night school at DePaul. Korshak was a year ahead. They never spoke. Even then, Korshak was a well-coiffed hooligan. His face, what my grandfather can see of it behind the glasses, is heavier now. A soft-looking bulb of a nose and jowls that sag off his cheeks like a basset hound's. Above his broad forehead rides a wave of badly dyed black hair. Not handsome, never was. Even so, Korshak is famous for his women. Power trumps ugly every time.

He's the Fixer. The Myth. The Sphinx. Mr. Silk Stockings. The syndicate's kike brains.

Specialty: labor negotiation.

Korshak sent the limo. Though always a Chicagoan, Korshak, years earlier, had moved the base of his many operations west, to Los Angeles and Vegas. Now he lives in Beverly Hills.

How to make it in Chicago? Truly make it?

Get too big to live there anymore.

The driver scurries around the front of the car and opens the columnist's door. Slowly, Irv Kupcinet emerges into the daylight. Korshak looks him over, assesses the extent of the damage. Lou also steps out of the car and plants himself beside Irv.

"Oh, buddy," Korshak says, "buddy."

Sidney and Irv had been boys together in Lawndale. The Korshaks lived on the east end of Douglas Park, the Kupcinets on the west. The Korshaks were better off. Sidney's father was in the construction business. Also hustled real estate. Mostly aboveboard. But Sidney had an arsonist uncle for a role model. When you wanted an insurance payout, you called the firebug David Korshak to burn your place down. At twelve, Irv and Sidney broke windows together on Roosevelt Road. They rolled dice at Putty's until Putty chased them away for being too young. They'd join the fray when Davey Miller's gang beat up Polacks who'd been beating up Jews. Irv and Sid would land a few punches before taking off across the park, laughing.

Elbowing aside my grandfather, Korshak pulls Irv to his chest.

"Oh, buddy, buddy, buddy."

The clamor of traffic and jackhammering across the street, and yet there's this silent embrace, one man holding up another. Irv convulses and his hat falls off. My grandfather stoops to pick it up. Korshak thrusts Irv away and, still gripping him, looks his boyhood friend in the eyes. Irv stares back without blinking. Only his bloody pupils are hard. The rest of his body is slack. Korshak again pulls him close, this time nearly lifting Irv off his feet. All the while, Lou is standing so close he can smell Korshak's cologne, vinegar mixed with vanilla. Another half minute or so, and only then does Korshak release him.

Irv speaks for the first time since O'Hare.

"Sid, you know Lou."

"Not sure I do."

But of course Sidney Korshak knows my grandfather. Maybe not by name, and definitely not from their law school days (Korshak never noticed him then). But he knows Lou Rosenthal the way all Chicago Jews know each other — through somebody or through somebody else or through somebody else's somebody.

Korshak yanks Lou's hand. It's a vigorous, full-bodied handshake, as if to pull Lou out of a hole. Looks him straight in the eye. Here we are, commiserating. Korshak is known for not condescending to a small-fry. It's a way he has of not immediately dismissing men who have nothing to offer him. Even if they're straight. Because you never know. Depending on the jam he finds himself in, any man might come up with something worth taking. He's got a brother in politics back home in Chicago, and by most accounts Marshall Korshak is clean, if not squeaky. Sidney Korshak knows from Boy Scouts. But there comes a time when even an Eagle Scout needs a favor. That's when you make him beholden.

"Lou Rosenthal," my grandfather says.

"Ah," Korshak says. "Rosenthal."

Irv begins to stagger toward the morgue, as if dragged by an invisible rope. Korshak makes a little underhanded paddle motion with his fingers, indicating that Lou should go on ahead of him, the way a kindergarten teacher might motion her pupils to fall into line one behind the other. My grandfather, still holding Irv's hat, does follow Irv, but not because Sidney Korshak just told him to. He catches up and tries to hand Irv his hat.

"Keep the fucking hat, Lou!"

Solly? He's still in the passenger seat of the Lincoln, the little driver having told him with his eyes not to get out of the car, not even to move.

ONCE INSIDE, IRV and his two friends are met by a woman in a white lab coat. Another tall drink of water, Lou thinks.

Put a white coat on a woman and I'll fall at your feet, you angel of mercy.

My grandfather always had eyes for the ladies. Babs never much noticed. How could anybody who works in a house of death, he thinks, keep their coat so clean? Lou conjures an infinite closet, a sea of milky coats, one for each body she collects. Though the woman (doctor?) can probably feel my grandfather's eyeballs crawling all over her (in spite of himself and the circumstances), she's got eyes only for the columnist. They're fixed on Irv like buttons. She must be able to tell a father right away. Not that she needs much intuition in this case, as Irv stands slumped and dazed before her as if he's already carrying the weight of the body he's come to see. What a job, day after day, to greet the shell-shocked.

Sidney Korshak has already, for legal purposes, as the representative of the family, identified Cookie's body. His signature appears on a certificate that is, to this day, held in a filing cabinet at the Los Angeles County medical examiner's office.

But Irv needs confirmation of his own. What father wouldn't?

The Gossip Columnist's Daughter

He falters, sinks in the knees. Lou reaches. Sid reaches. Irv steps backward, away from both of them.

"Where?" he says. "Where?"

The good doctor extends her arm toward a hallway that my nearsighted grandfather can't see the end of.

FADING CLAP OF distant footsteps. The waiting room isn't much bigger than a coat closet. Maybe it was a coat closet. There's a rack. No coats. Three chairs are jammed together in a row. They're attached, as if they might be stolen. Who's going to run off with a chair from here? Korshak squats into the middle chair, his stance wide. He'll take all three chairs, thank you. He smooths his be-ringed hands on his perfect pants. A few moments of silence before he releases a prolonged sigh.

"Grim business," he says.

Lou, standing a few feet away, is examining a pile of dead flies in the bowl of the light fixture above their heads. They come for the light. All the corpses of their brethren who've come before are nothing to the call of the light.

Korshak, not a man to raise his voice to be heard, says it again, more or less in my grandfather's direction.

"Grim business."

Lou lowers his eyes and meets his own unassuming mug in Korshak's glasses. He smiles a very faint yet distinct smile. Though it's no more than a hint, a suggestion, really—his mouth is closed, his cheeks barely rise—it's enough, if only for an instant, to unsettle Sidney Korshak. Sorrow's smile:

inscrutable, bottomless, superior. Because this is about friendship, which after all is a form of love, maybe the purest form, all the more potent for never having to be attested to in any formal ceremonies or even with empty phrases like "Oh, buddy, buddy." So Irv and Sid broke a few windows together? After high school and college they went separate ways. Irv into the newspaper racket. Sid into the racket racket. What's not, at the end of the day, a racket? Over the years, sure, they saw each other. And, yes, through much of the fifties, before Korshak decamped to California, they famously "shared" booth number one at the Pump Room. And yes, yes, they'd cross paths when they made the rounds at night, and of course, Irv would sometimes put in a word for Sidney in the column. Bad boy with a heart of gold sort of stuff. *A birdie tells me the anonymous Samaritan who pledged ten grand at last Thursday's March of Dimes Telethon at the Aragon Ballroom was none other than* **S.** *Korshak, Esq....*

But Kup and Lou? Lou and Kup? Theirs was a bond untethered to power or notoriety or money or glitz. And isn't this my grandfather's loss also? Wasn't he by Kup's side, pocketful of Arturo Fuente cigars, pacing the halls of Michael Reese the night this child was born? Lou holds his ground. His loyalty, his love, will not be degraded by mucking around in the filth with a Jewish savage in a five-hundred-dollar suit. The gentiles don't have enough reasons to think we've got horns?

Grief emboldens. Not only does Lou Rosenthal know who Korshak is, he knows what the man is capable of demanding that other men do. He's heard the stories. At least some of them have to be true to keep the myth alive. Never seen in any court. Doesn't carry a briefcase. Doesn't even have a license to practice law in California. Doesn't need one. No office, either. Works out of a restaurant. And yet they say he's the highest-paid lawyer in the country? His client list goes on for miles. Gulf and Western. MGM. United Artists. Hilton Hotels. The Los Angeles Dodgers. Korshak's not a lawyer. I'm the lawyer, Lou thinks. I'm the frickin' lawyer. Korshak's a phone call. Trouble with a union? Strike? What strike? Call Korshak. He'll handle it. He'll make a call. And if that doesn't do it — nine times out of ten that does it — then yeah, he'll call Tony Accardo from a pay phone and Accardo will call some goons who'll call some other goons and they'll break a few arms, or bludgeon a head. Korshak always keeps his distance. He's the Mob's link to legitimate business. He's not — the Mob likes to keep it this way — the Mob itself. You have to understand the difference. He's refined, elegant, above all the fray. Sidney Korshak's got class.

But grief, it also intoxicates, and it's gone way to my grandfather's head. In family lore this has become known as the standoff in the coat closet. Rosenthal's Alamo. Sidney Korshak takes his glasses off and peers more closely at this small, bald bosom companion of Irv Kupcinet's. Who's what? Proprietary? Territorial? At a time like this? You think I didn't bounce that kid horsey on my knees, too? Korshak's eyes are small and peppery. Few people aside from his latest mistress — in December of 1963, it was Jill St. John — have the nerve to look straight into them. Korshak presses his hands into his thighs and unfurls. When he's standing up, his head nearly grazes the ceiling. Not that he needs height or anything else to accentuate his advantage. He's only curious. Lou steps his right foot forward and squares his shoulders, and Korshak recognizes something a lot more familiar. The war in the Pacific aside (which he entered too late to see any fighting), Lou hasn't thrown a punch since middle school and even that was half-hearted. A kid named Evan Salke and Lou had missed. And yet his stance now is of a man ready to let one loose in the name of unsullied friendship. Legs wide, right fist squeezed into a fat little fruit. Korshak grins. More with his teeth than his mouth. He grins at this little egghead of a probate attorney, my now long dead grandfather, and almost lazily swings a preemptive counterpunch laced with truth.

"Didn't your old man run a handbook on Garfield Boulevard for Jimmy Doughnuts?"

Because he's the Fixer, the Myth, Mr. Silk Stockings.

"Maxie Rosenthal? Am I right?"

Lou had his own myths. He liked to project the notion that he'd emerged from the womb upright wearing a sensible off-the-rack suit and sensible brogans, ready to walk hatless down LaSalle Street. But you've got to come from somewhere.

"A bookie's kid?" Korshak says. "And now, what, you've got your own three-man firm, an office on East Monroe? Handle the wills of a few biddies and chuckleheads?"

Lou can't stop himself. "I've got two partners, seven juniors, and half a floor of the Monadnock Building. The Bar Association recognized our firm with the Golden Plate two consecutive—"

"Hallelujah," Korshak says. "And the Korshaks, we were horse thieves in Galicia."

My grandfather again gazes at the heap of flies in the bowl of light.

"And the lug outside in the Lincoln? Don't I know him, too?"

"My brother."

"Ah, yes."

Lou looks at his brogans, as if to plead with his shoes that Korshak keep his brother out of this.

"Didn't he muscle for Jake Guzik?"

"Solly drove for Guzik."

"Right," Korshak says under his breath. And the more quietly he talks, the more he talks. "And I only draft contracts. But you? You're the Righteous Jew. I've been searching, and here you are. With your half a floor in the Monadnock Building. I'm scum and you're Louie Brandeis. I got Louie Brandeis here in cheap shoes."

The Fixer sits back down and fondles his glasses. He talks to himself. His voice nearly not a voice at all anymore, like it's something Lou is overhearing from a great distance, as if something heard on the wind, though they both remain in this tiny stagnant room.

"Because we're all square now," Korshak says. "America loves the Jews. You did your time in the Pacific and came home and rolled up your exemplary sleeves? Got your nice little firm and your nice little house and nice little wife and nice little couple three kids? Maybe a grandkid? You think Maxie Rosenthal's that far out of Egypt? America loves the Jews? Kennedy? That dead cocksucker loved the Jews? He loved the Jews as much as his father. And LBJ? LBJ loves the Jews?

The Gossip Columnist's Daughter

And guys like me? I make us look bad? Yeah? Yeah? Listen, you hairless cunt, if you think I didn't bounce that kid on my knees, too — "

In the hall, Irv can be heard, faintly, moaning.

My grandfather holds up an open palm to shush Sidney Korshak, and Korshak's so surprised he actually stops talking. The old legend, the time Lou Rosenthal shushed the man who offed Jimmy Hoffa. Maybe he didn't, but he knew who did. Korshak shoves his glasses back on and stands up. With his hands behind his back he begins to pace, priest-like, the confines of the little room. Lou pulls his belly in, holds his breath.

HE SHUSHED HIM. Lou did.

But aren't all victories, even our grandest, ultimately illusions?

Irv appears in the doorway of the waiting room, wobbly, and so pale it's as if he's been bleached. My grandfather opens his arms. But it's Sidney Korshak who receives him. And it is Sidney Korshak who, with hardly a twitch of his left eyelid (enough for Kup to read it), jettisons my grandfather from the scene.

"Lou," Irv says. "I need a few minutes with Sid, okay?"

"DID YOU KNOW this girl?"

Solly doesn't turn to look at the driver, who's really just a kid himself in his ludicrous bellhop hat. A street-level thug of Korshak's, the outfit never being short on delinquents and punks. It's always been a buyer's market.

"Well, did you?"

Solly rubs his left earlobe and considers the question.

"Did I know her?" he says.

"Isn't that what I asked?"

Solly looks out the windshield at the parking lot, at the county building adjacent to the morgue. She's inside there somewhere.

The veins in Solly's neck begin to visibly pulse.

She was Kup's kid. Of course I knew her. Like everybody knew her. Standing in the kitchen of the house on Fargo Avenue. Some occasion or another. Her laugh from another room. She was maybe fourteen, fifteen. No, I didn't know her. Her face on TV. The fact of her now.

"What's your name?" Solly says.

"No name," the kid says. "I don't have a name unless Mr. Korshak says I have a name."

"I'm Solomon," Solly says.

The two sit in silence, the windows up, the hot car.

"Edrick."

"What?"

"Edrick," the kid says. "Some Brit name. My mother liked it."

"Pleasure to meet you, Edrick."

"Know your way around LA?" the kid says.

"No."

"But you know your way around?"

Solly shrugs. Sure. I know my way around.

"And the girl?"

"We're bringing her home," Solly says.

IN THE CORRIDOR, my grandfather leans against the wall. He should walk out of earshot, but he doesn't. Lou Rosenthal matters so little that Korshak doesn't even bother to close the door, or maybe there is no door. Maybe that little coatroom never had a door in the first place.

Either way, Lou, holding Irv's hat, listens. Where to put his eyes? He reads the inside lining of the hat. Adam Hat Co., New York. And under that: *Deus Major Columna*.

His high school Latin. God's greatest something.

At first, Irv murmurs something Lou can't make out.

"I know," Korshak says. "I know."

Irv, louder now. "I saw her, Sid."

"I know, I know. I did, too."

Lou resists the urge to reenter.

"Just lying there."

"Yes," Sid says.

"Like a piece of meat."

"No, no, Irv—"

"I saw her."

"Yes."

"Why didn't I go down on my knees?"

"Buddy," Korshak says. "Listen. Can you listen to me?"

"Yeah?"

"I need your attention."

"Yeah."

"It doesn't have to look like it looks."

"Yeah?"

"We've got a guy in the Medical Examiner's. The coroner's a little kinky. And we've got a doll to pin it on, this two-bit actor Prine—"

"I'll kill the motherfucker myself."

In the corridor, Lou grips his friend's hat like it's flesh.

"Not that." Korshak coughs to clear his throat. Gets down to business. "And the charges, they won't stick. There's nothing. Not a print. No witnesses. No history of knocking any girls around. Nothing. And he's got an alibi. He was with some other actress most of the night. But for the moment, anyway, they'll kill him in the press, and that's a death worse—"

"I will," Irv says. "With my bare hands I'll—"

"Think about Essee," Korshak says.

"Essee," Irv whispers. Pauses. Whispers it again: "Essee. You know what she says?" My grandfather leans his ear closer to the door, if there even is a door.

"She says Cookie did it to spite her."

"No," Korshak says. "Don't say that."

"Pin it," Irv says. "Pin it on the doll."

WOOZY, LOU WANDERS off. He finds a different exit. He thinks of what his mother used to say. Always leave by a different door from the one you'd come in.
    Why?
    Otherwise, you'll never get back inside.
    But, Ma, what if a place only has one door?
    You don't go in.
    Lou opens the door and steps into an enclosed courtyard. A sprinkler leisurely scatters water over the grass. Even the morgues have perfect lawns in California. Wait, he thinks, wait!
    Why would anybody want to go back into a death house?
    I should have gone out the same door we came in and run like hell. Isn't he a man with his own daughter? Lou Rosenthal has a vision so vivid it's as if it's already happened. His own Judith on a gurney. And he does fall to his knees in the wet grass. A spray of water belts him in the face. He remains like that, and waits for the rotating arm to swing around again, for the water to whack him again. Soaked, he obeys an inexplicable impulse. He tosses Irv's hat on top of the sprinkler, and for a couple of moments the hat rises, twirls, spins, a little flying saucer, before being flung and landing on the grass. And my grandfather, through tears, laughs into the face of a merciless sun.

IRV AND LOU jammed side by side into a booth at the Culver Hotel, a few miles from downtown. They've taken off their jackets and sit with rolled shirtsleeves. The booth has tall leather walls like a padded cell. They've been drinking for six straight hours. Lou's not a drinker.

Korshak booked Irv a suite at the Beverly Hills Hotel, but Irv didn't want to attract any more attention. Reporters pounced when he left the morgue. Solly and that kid Edrick had to fend them off. Irv's in the attention business, built a name feeding off the attention of others. In a private moment, he was the first to admit it. Irv once told Lou, Without a host, I'd shrivel and die.

Now he's on the run from the press. Holed up in this third-rate hotel in Culver City that, if it's famous for anything, which it isn't, it's because some drunk munchkins once trashed the place after a long day on the set of the Yellow Brick Road. The sort of tidbit that Kup relished. *And in other Hollywood news, turns out pint-sized drunks are still drunks. Police in Culver City say diminutive cast members from the MGM production of* The Wizard of... Even so, they've traced him here, a few men from the *Tribune* and the *Daily News* (a classy paper, but you've got to pay the bills) and the *Los Angeles*

Times are scattered around the bar, plus a few tabloid hacks. A juicy story. A gossip columnist's daughter, aspiring starlet, et cetera, et cetera. So far they're giving Irv space, but they're going to need copy soon. They've got editors clamoring. Solly is parked in the booth next door. He's reading a book. Aside from the clothes he's wearing, it's the one thing he brought with him from Chicago. A paperback copy of Howard Fast's *The Edge of Tomorrow* he'd carried in his jacket pocket. In the dim light, Solly holds it close. Every once in a while, without moving the book from in front of his face, he eats a french fry.

It's nearly one in the morning and Irv refuses to go upstairs. Lou's head droops. Two untouched T-bones, ordered hours ago, congeal in their own juices. Lou pushes Irv's plate toward him.

"At least eat some potato."

"Not hungry."

"It doesn't matter if you're not hungry."

"I should be drunk by now. Are you drunk, Lou?"

"Just eat a little potato."

Irv calls over the leather wall. "Sol, am I drunk, true or false?"

"Drunk," Solly says.

The waitress stands before them. She's got gray-blue eyes and ruby lips. Lou can't see her eyes in this light. Earlier, he'd asked her. Irv had fallen asleep for a few moments, and while she was setting down the steaks, he'd come out and asked.

"What color are your eyes?"

Sorrow and this much booze and my grandfather's many inhibitions are back in Chicago.

"Gray-blue. Blue-gray."

And oil-black hair. It's pulled back tight.

"Would you be so kind as to bring us two more of whatever we've been drinking?"

"You've been drinking Glenlivet."

"Right. Two more. Please. Please and thank you."

She rounds her lips as though she's about to sing and she floats floats floats away.

Across the room, one of the reporters coughs, a loud hammed-up cough.

"When I get back," Irv says, "I'm going to break Don Maxwell's neck in eighteen places. Fucking *Trib*. I'd send a scrum if his kid — "

"You're news, Irv."

Irv rams the back of his head against the leather.

"I'm news."

"You got to eat a little something and then sleep, or if not eat, sleep."

Irv turns his head slowly to look at who just spoke. Like he's been talking to himself all these hours and just noticed that Lou Rosenthal's right here next to him.

"So she took pills. Everybody takes pills. I take pills. You take pills?"

"Sure, I take pills."

(Antacid tablets.)

"If she was sad, wouldn't I have known? All the kid did was laugh."

"Of course you would have."

"No makeup. That kid didn't leave the house without it.

I used to tell her, 'What's with all the paint? You don't need any paint on your face.' She was right there on the table, Lou. Right there. Right there. I wanted to shake her awake. I knew they'd stop me but I thought, If only I could shake her, you know? And I didn't, Lou, I didn't."

Irv lays his hands flat on the tablecloth and rubs. Heat. If only he could burn his hands off.

Solly lowers his book and gazes around the room without looking at any face in particular, a skill he perfected long ago. Not unlike an actor scanning the audience to gauge the mood. Animals getting restless.

Irv covers Lou's bare forearm with his hot, wet palm. Something about the transfer of heat from one friend to the other, Lou thinks. What? What about it? That will save us? Irv's talking—

"...a week in September. Said she wanted to see her parents. I took her to see Johnny Mathis at the Amphitheater. Essee stayed home. Believe that? Passed up Mathis. She loves Mathis. She thought Cookie and I needed a little time together. I took her backstage and she ate it up like she'd never been backstage before. A pro now, just finished a movie with Jerry Lewis, and she's jittery to meet Johnny Mathis? And Mathis, that fake dago, says, 'Sweetheart, where have you been all my life?,' and Cookie without missing a beat drops the shy routine and says, 'Seek and you shall find.' Kup's kid? I opened all the doors? Bullshit. She was good, Lou, she could act—"

"I know it."

"Out of nowhere. 'Seek and you shall find.' Who said that?"

"I don't know. Moses? Mathis isn't Italian?"

"Black as the night is long," Irv says. "It's the makeup. I should have locked her up in the basement."

Irv's grip on Lou's arm tightens.

"I don't even have a basement. A garage, no basement. You got a basement, Lou? On Fargo Avenue? A basement?"

"You know we do. We did a remodel just last — "

"I should have locked her up in yours."

"You have to sleep."

"Sad? About what? That two-bit Prine? NBC canceled *Wide Country* six months ago. Prine's a sinking stone."

Lou takes a breath and says what's been bobbing around in his mind for hours.

"We can't know them," he says. "Even our own. Maybe especially our own. I think of Judith, Irv. I mean, how well do I know Judith? They live their own lives. You know? Irv? Irv?"

Irv releases Lou's forearm and stands up. He wraps his hand around a glass and raises it and for a moment squints at his old pal Lou Rosenthal.

Solly lowers his book again and stands up also. Certain kinds of silences. He knows them well. The breath before a man snaps. When things could still go one way, or they could go another way. In this case, Irv's either going to give a strange toast or he's going to ram that glass into the tabletop. In the dark, reporters reach inside their jackets for notepads. Neither happens. Irv just stands there until his legs give out and he finally crumples.

SOLLY LIFTS IRV and tosses him over his shoulder like a sack of laundry. All the more remarkable, as Irv himself is six feet one. Did that just happen? Did I see that? Lou watches his brother head for the elevators, knowing he'll remember this. Maybe one day he'll even tell it. Irv draped like a child over Solly's shoulder. The ease, the familiarity. Is loyalty more reflexive when it's only a matter of physical strength?

"ARE YOU ALL right?" the waitress asks.

Lou reaches to his face to take his glasses off but they're already off. Fingers dangling idly, he squishes his nose.

He's not sure.

"Hold on."

Scattered across the table, empty glasses, those steaks. A small crime scene.

The place has mostly cleared out. The debris of other tables. Not as much of a mess as this one. A hotel bar, late.

When the waitress returns, she sits in Irv's place. For a few moments they don't speak. They're both, for different reasons, well past tired. Her eyes, her lips. Her hair pulled like that. Lou wonders if it hurts, the constant yanking.

"You alone tonight? I mean out here, all these tables — "

"A new girl quit. Just me and Chuckie tonight. It happens."

"I'm harmless," Lou says.

"Sure. Though I've been wrong before. What's going on with your friend?"

"They found his daughter."

"Found her where?"

"On a couch."

"The actress?" she says. "I read about her."

"Yes."

"Hadn't heard of her."

"Watched her grow up," Lou says.

"And the big one?"

"He's my brother."

"He doesn't eat with you? Not that you ate."

"My friend's a big deal and so my brother watches —"

"Your brother can't eat with you?"

Lou sinks deeper into the cushions.

"What's your name?" he says.

"Gwen."

"Gwendolyn?"

"Just Gwen."

She reaches for Lou's cheek and grazes it with the backs of her fingers.

And he thinks there's nothing so rare on this earth as a stranger's sudden touch. What drives him to say this out loud? The sorrow? The booze?

"There's nothing," my grandfather declares, "so rare on this earth as a stranger's —"

"Go to sleep, honey."

"I'm Lou Rosenthal."

She stands and begins to stack her tray.

"Gwen," he says.

Her hair pulled so tight it must hurt a little, but constant pain is no longer pain but something else. If only he could name it. The hurt that's part and parcel of every moment.

    This hateful errand.

    What am I thinking? I'm sharing a room with Solly.

ON THE ELEVENTH floor, Irv's flung across a bed like a wrung rag. Solly had gently tugged off his shoes and done his best to tuck him in, but Irv keeps thrashing around.

In the adjacent room, Solly, now on his own bed, goes on reading his book. In the story, a man, a writer, has also settled down to read a book. The writer is alone in his fishing shack in the mountains. He's lying on a cot reading and munching a chocolate bar. Languidly, he reaches for a cigarette and it is only then that the writer notices the giant ant lurking at the foot of his bed. He grabs a golf club. He happens to have one handy. Wait, isn't he fishing? Anyway, the writer brains the ant's skull with his five iron.

Solly reads. He likes a story where one thing happens after another thing.

Nobody reads Howard Fast anymore. Lots of people used to.

There's something pretty strange about this ant. Its size, for one thing. Biggest ant the writer ever saw. He puts it into a basket and drives back to Manhattan. In the morning he phones "the Museum" and makes an appointment to see the chief insect curator.

Solly laughs when the writer's wife says he never seems to tire of hanging around places like museums, police courts, and third-rate nightclubs. Amen, Solly thinks. Amen.

The next day the writer is met by the curator as well as an unidentified man and, hmm, a US senator with an interest in entomology. The curator makes his examination, and it turns out the giant ant is not an ant at all but a highly intelligent extraterrestrial life-form. The curator asks the writer if the ant attacked him. No, he says. Did it make any move toward you at all? No, the writer says. It was just there at the foot of the cot. The curator asks the writer, So then why did you brain it with a golf club? Because I was scared to death, he says. Then the US senator (or maybe it's the other person in the room who may or not be with the CIA, Solly can't keep track) says, No, the answer is simple. *You killed it because you're a human being.*

Hold it right there! If this thing was so damn smart, why didn't it use a weapon to defend —

"You asleep?" Lou says.

"No," Solly says.

TWO TWIN BEDS. Two heaps. Two brothers in a hotel room not sleeping. They've pulled off their shoes and socks but are still in their suits. You reach a point when you're too tired to unbutton, unzip. Even tearing off is beyond you. There's a vague swampish smell. Solly's dozing, his book tented on his chest. In the narrow alley between the beds, two pairs of sweat-stained leather shoes—Lou's size 8 brogans and Solly's size 14½ loafers (galoshes still appended)—are tumbled together like overturned boats. The curtains are still open. Scattered lights of an unfamiliar city. It lacks a lake, but there's the ocean somewhere. Solly's never been much of a sleeper. Since he was a kid, whisper to him at any hour of the night and he'll answer back like he's waiting for you to say something. It's a way of being together, this waiting for sleep in an alien room.

Me and Solly?

When was the last time we shared a room?

In the flat on Fifty-Fourth Street, before the family moved north to Rogers Park, Solly would crawl into Lou's bed and curl his bulk against him. It was like being nuzzled by a small bear.

That only lasted a few years, because soon enough Lou was

down in Champaign and only a few years after that he was married. At Babs and Lou's wedding at the Drake, Solly was, what, eight or nine? Now he's how old? Common blood. You can drop your guard. You don't have to be Lou Rosenthal with half a floor in the Monadnock Building. You don't even have to know what you're going to say after you've said your only brother's name in the dark.

"Solly?"

"Yeah, Lou?"

"I can't sleep."

"No kidding."

"You want to take a walk?"

"Your legs talking?"

"No, but they'll do what I say."

"I'll take a walk, sure."

And they rise from the dead. Solly pulls the chain of the bedside lamp and there they are, Lou and Solly, in the sudden blatant light, a couple of rumpled pasties, one big, one small and plumpish.

"Cut the light," Lou says.

THEY WALK A few blocks away from the hotel, along Culver Boulevard. Darkened stores. No traffic. Lou turns off onto a side street. They're walking single file down the sidewalk, Solly following. Small houses set back from the street behind low fences. Night throbs with the hum of the electrical wires over their heads. Trees and plants of dizzying variety in the half-light of the streetlights. On Fargo Avenue, Lou only knows the maples, lindens, rhododendrons. Here, every corner, fertility. He walks faster, and even Solly, with his long legs, has to work to keep up. Even when he's not going anywhere, my grandfather's in a hurry. Block after block they walk. In the quiet houses all the sleepers in their beds. Strangers and their breathing. And then what happens? Poof, one bed or half a bed is empty. And then, poof, another. And another. Is there a more perfect word for here now, gone the next?

"Poof," Lou says out loud.

"That's right," Solly says. "Poof."

The dark houses. Lou's footsteps like staccato gunshots. The squeak of Solly's rubber soles.

"It's like he got hit by a bus," Lou says. "Am I right? Who sees this kind of clobber coming? Oof. Nobody. You don't even know it's a bus. Because you don't even know your own name anymore. Which for Irv—Christ, what difference does it make to you whether it was a bus or not? You see what I'm saying?"

"Sure, Lou."

Maybe Solly sees, maybe he doesn't. Though he's seen a few people get hit by buses. CTA buses. Solly's seen all kinds of out-of-nowhere wallops.

"You know where he was when he heard?" Lou says.

"No, where?"

"Sara Lee. You hear they opened a new factory in Deerfield?"

"Who doesn't love cake?" Solly says.

"Irv's there as master of ceremonies. Essee, too. Someone calls him to the phone. You think he knows it's a bus?"

"It can always be a bus."

"You know that. Maybe I even know that. But Irv?"

"No," Solly says. "Not Irv."

"Right, and tomorrow he's going to wake up and it's going to hit him again."

"That's right."

"They're going to dice the cowboy actor like a tomato."

"Yeah?" Solly says.

"Damn it," Lou says.

"What?"

"Dog shit."

Solly had seen it coming. He'd seen it ahead of them on the sidewalk, waiting there ahead of Lou, a little hill of crap. But that's the rub, isn't it? You can't warn everybody about everything. Always a bus, always a little hill of dog crap. The brothers walk in silence. The night drifts to ash with some pink in the distance, over the roofs of the houses.

LOU MADE THE arrangements and accompanied the body as far as he could, which was the tarmac. He stood by the casket and waited for the men to load her into the plane.

The casket was made of steel, of the kind used to transport soldiers.

The airline wouldn't have let him into the cargo hold even if it had known about our tradition of never leaving a corpse alone.

III.

Winner of Loneliness

SHE WAS BORN Roberta Lynn.

When she was three she handed her father a cookie and said, "Here's a cookie for your cookie."

In high school she called herself Bobbe. It was only after she got serious about acting a few years later that she named herself Karyn. She thought it went better with Kupcinet, that the repetition of the hard *K* made it easier to remember. Essee must have approved, because I don't think she'd have gotten away with it otherwise. Cookie was never (outwardly) rebellious against her mother, even after she moved to Hollywood. When she graduated from Francis Parker, she enrolled at Pine Manor Junior College. She might have intended to transfer to Wellesley College down the road, a common thing to do then, but instead she dropped out and moved to New York to take classes with Lee Strasberg at the Actors Studio. That lasted about six months. She moved back to Chicago and briefly changed her full name to "Lynn Roberts" before changing it back to Karyn Kupcinet.

In 1960, she moved to Los Angeles with her grandmother, Essee's mother. Something went wrong. Maybe they didn't get along. Whatever happened, the grandmother returned to Chicago after a few months. That's when Cookie began renting a one-bedroom apartment on North Sweetzer.

THE PUBLICITY PHOTOS are probably typical of the time, the early sixties, but I've noticed something, or I've willed myself to notice something. Some hint in her eyes of the wildness that was to come later in the decade? Maybe Cookie was a little ahead of her time. Her look is always different. In one, her hair's in a short bouffant, in another it's longer and flowing past her ears in waves. But it's her expressions, as if she's constantly testing out a new way to look at the camera. In one she's sulky. In another, demure. In the next one, she's reckless, fierce, Don't get too close to me. Her facial structure seems to change, too. My mother says Cookie was the first person she ever knew who had "work done." Always, whatever the look, her eyes are wide. She's got dreams of making it big. Or maybe they're really only her mother's dreams and she's just playing the part. Who's to say how much she wanted it? She expected it, this I believe. It went without saying that she'd be a success. Did she crave it? The take on Essee has always been that she pushed and she pushed and she pushed. If I'm not going to be famous, my kid sure as hell better be. Essee got her hooked on the diet pills? I don't doubt it, but at the same time it feels too easy to blame Essee for everything. She's too obvious an ogre. Stage mother from the gates of hell. And what about Kup? Didn't he push, too? By pulling so many strings, it's clear he had the same expectation. The kid gets famous. Period.

HER FIRST SUMMER in California she played Annie Sullivan in a summer stock production of William Gibson's *The Miracle Worker* at a theater in Laguna Beach. A review in the *Los Angeles Times* said that she did an admirable job, got the faint Irish accent right, and that the dark glasses she wore throughout the play couldn't hide the shine in her eyes.

> Annie: She won't starve, she'll learn. All's fair in love and war.
>
> Captain Keller: This is hardly a war!
>
> Annie: Well, it's not love. A siege is a siege.

I'm on the floor of the kitchen on West Pratt holding a Loyola library copy of *The Miracle Worker* over my head, reading out loud words Cookie once spoke, as if my lips forming the words could bring me a little closer...

> Rudy: You're not much of an actor, either. Can't you put a little spirit into it?

Annie and Helen spend much of the play whacking each other around. The stage directions go on for pages describing in detail how they chase and hit each other. But in due time the Miracle Worker triumphs, and Helen comes to a hard-won understanding that there's a universe beyond herself and this universe is made up of words that represent not only the physical world where she can punch and bite, but also abstract concepts such as fear — and love. Helen is no longer entombed in eternal darkness. But Annie's gift isn't merely a gift to a single mute deaf blind girl in the Deep South but a bequest to us all, because Helen becomes Helen Keller, a very, very great American.

> Annie: I wanted to teach you — oh, everything the earth is full of, Helen, everything on it that's ours for a wink and it's gone.

On the floor, cat drama critic asleep under the bed, I read this pure schmaltz, this unadulterated sugar, and buy every fucking word of it. I think of my own wink.

The distance between West Pratt and Jarvis, nine blocks west, two and a half blocks north. The other day my phone said it took me two thousand one hundred and three steps.

Also, where was Annie Sullivan when Cookie needed her?

IN THE ARCHIVES there's a press release from Paramount Pictures announcing:

> FOR IMMEDIATE RELEASE
> DECEMBER 21, 1960
> IRV KUPCINET'S DAUGHTER JOINS
> CAST OF JERRY LEWIS' "THE LADIES MAN"
>
> Karyn Kupcinet, daughter of Chicago newspaper columnist Irv Kupcinet, has been signed for <u>a top role</u> in Jerry Lewis' "The Ladies Man," a Technicolor comedy currently filming in Hollywood.

"A top role" is underlined in pen.

Paper-clipped to the press release was an ad that appeared in the traitorous *Tribune* in July of 1961 promoting the Midwestern premiere of *The Ladies Man* at the Oriental Theatre.

> It's Jerry's Biggest, Funniest Yet!!!!!!!!!!
> Everybody's talking about Jerry Lewis as The Ladies Man?????????
> Costarring Helen Traubel, Pat Stanley, Gloria

Jean, Sylvia Lewis, Dee Arlen, Francesca Bellini, and Hope Holiday as Miss Anxious!

In the credits, Karyn Kupcinet is listed as a working girl. Her character isn't named.

I've never been able to get through the whole thing. Lewis's squawking is just too impossible to endure that long. Cookie nearly steals her scene, accompanying her announcement of Herbert Heebert's breakfast with a well-executed eye roll, but by my count she doesn't have more than four lines.

A top role? What happened? I ask a half-empty garden apartment, a sleeping cat, Was the original Paramount Pictures press release wrong about Cookie from the beginning, or did it become wrong in the course of shooting the movie? Was there a moment when Jerry thought, No, the kid doesn't have it?

Or what?

THINGS GOT BETTER. In November of '61, Cookie appeared on two different network shows simultaneously, as a beauty contestant on *Hawaiian Eye* and a college co-ed on *Mrs. G. Goes to College.*

An ad ran that week in the *Hollywood Reporter*:

Kup, too, put in a plug. Pardon a point of parental pride, but we'll be glued to two TV sets Wednesday night, watching daughter **Karyn**...

... Three months later and twenty pounds lighter, she returned to the Warner Bros. TV lot for *Hawaiian Eye* and the lead role in an episode called "The Queen from Kern County." The now-svelte daughter of Chicago columnist Irv Kupcinet moved to the West Coast a year and a half ago. The young cutie has considerable stage experience, but while she was widening her stage talent, she was also developing a width problem...

— "Stay Slim For Fatter Roles," *St. Louis Post-Dispatch,* April 29, 1962

What do I know about any of this? My own theatrical experience began and ended when I bombed as Chief Brown Bear in a seventh-grade Elm Place School production of *Little Mary Sunshine*. I forgot a line. Something about forbidding my daughter to go off with that Colorado Ranger Jim, I don't care how stalwart a scout he is. I tore off my duct-taped headdress and stalked offstage. But it does seem that for a twenty-one-year-old actress at the start of her career, she received an inordinate amount of press in newspapers across the country. The *St. Louis Post-Dispatch*'s story appeared in a slightly different form in the *Buffalo News* as "Plump Girls Get Thin Parts" and the *Hartford Courant* as "Plump Girls Don't Get Fat Parts." In each of them she extols the virtues of a high-protein diet, with special emphasis on raw vegetables. There are also stories about her in the *Atlanta Journal, Kansas City Star,* Norfolk *Ledger-Star,* Cleveland *Plain Dealer, Oakland Tribune*... In these articles, she's variously described as curvaceous, big boobed, not willowy, a delight to the eye. She's also called self-doubting, giddy, shy, ambitious, witty, highly intelligent, and unassuming.

In one episode of *Hawaiian Eye,* Cookie runs around in a bikini with a surprised look on her face.

Something else I've noticed about her acting, or at least in the footage I've managed to watch. On *The Gertrude Berg Show* or *The Red Skeleton Hour,* there's an ambivalence in her affect as if there's part of her who isn't sure she even wants to be in the scene. Though I'm not sure this makes for great acting, I find it arresting when it seems like any moment she—Cookie or Karyn or Bobbe or Lynn or Roberta—might meander right off the set.

THERE'S ALSO A murky quality to some of the photographs. A vagueness in her eyes that allows whoever looks at her to make up their own story about who she is or might become. Pictures where her gaze is almost too welcoming, too inviting. At the same time, she's hiding?

All her life, in and out of the apartment on East Lake Shore, she'd been surrounded by people who were so loved, revered, fawned over, and worshipped for their capacity to become other people. How hard could this be? She'd been doing it forever already. When had she ever felt much like herself?

I'm going in circles.

AS FAR AS I can tell, she never tried to distance herself from her last name. She recognized that it was a boon, an unsecret weapon. Her huge brown eyes, her developing talent, and her last name. But this doesn't mean it wasn't another kind of weight. She told the *Philadelphia Inquirer* (or she was edited to say because nobody on earth talks like this):

> "I have never completed an opening night, an audition or a TV show but that someone hasn't said to me, 'I was surprised at your good performance. Confidentially, I had thought to myself: I know how she got that job; through her father. Actually, I was pleased to see that you really do have talent.' The first time I heard that, I ran to my room and sobbed," Karyn confides. "It shocked me that others had the same feeling I was secretly afraid of."

IN *WIDE COUNTRY,* Andrew Prine plays a rodeo rider named Andy Guthrie. Mostly he stands around looking tall. He's got an older brother, Mitch, who does the talking. When Mitch says something tough, Andy juts his chin out and grunts, "That goes for me, too."

I'm not being entirely fair to Prine, who'd come out to Hollywood fresh from Broadway, where he'd been celebrated for a role in *Look Homeward, Angel.* But *Wide Country* made him a minor celebrity. He wasn't a dope. He told an interviewer that he used to make a lot less money doing a lot more work.

In her guest spot, Cookie plays a damsel in distress, a schoolteacher with another passable Irish accent, who's kidnapped by a band of Apaches. On horseback, Andy Prine/Andy Guthrie rescues her wearing only a towel, his face half-covered with shaving cream.

IN JANUARY OF 1963, a magazine called *TV Star Parade* ran a photo spread featuring Prine and the new love of his life under the headline: WHAT A DIVORCED MAN WANTS ON A DATE. The opening sentence: "Andy Prine doesn't want a wife again—he wants to date a gal who will set him free. Karyn Kupcinet is the answer..."

In the photographs, Andy and Cookie frolic around what appears to be an abandoned farm. Cookie's attempts to look like she's having fun are painful to look at even sixty-plus

years after the fact. In one picture she's smiling in such an exaggerated way, she looks borderline hysterical.

She probably is hysterical. I'd be hysterical if I had to endure that photo shoot.

The unsigned story yabbers on for six pages of text and photographs.

Andy's ideal date is "a sweet simple girl who knows that the man is the boss."

For a guy who finds Hollywood a "boring town" what this divorced man wants is companionship that doesn't impinge.

He and Karyn like to commune with nature, and they prefer the simple things, such as climbing rocks or walking in the country.

> When the "tide of seriousness flows too heavily"
> Andy will always back away.
> But currently and perhaps permanently he's found
> a gal who doesn't demand answers to the future.

Call me a curator of nonsense. But knowing that Cookie will be dead in less than a year haunts that last phrase.

a gal who doesn't demand answers to the future.

There's no byline. Did this unknown (and I'm sure underpaid) magazine writer see something in Cookie without even knowing it?

A KID FROM a tiny town in rural Florida, Andy was living it up while the living was good. He must not have known what to make of this Jewish princess from Chicago, who, once she started, never stopped talking. Cookie talked about everything. Art, literature, philosophy...

"You know what Bertrand Russell says?"

"Who?"

"He says there's nothing more stimulating than totally useless knowledge. For Russell, it's the human interest in the arcane, the esoteric, the obstruse that separates us from barnyard animals. He's got a point, don't you think?"

"Huh? Barnyard animals what?"

And Andy would lie back with his hands behind his head, his feet extending past the mattress, and just listen to her chatter until she ran out of words, or he fell asleep.

AND BECAUSE I spend so much time scrounging around in this rabbit hole, I feel compelled to report (again to whom?) that there was one person Cookie Kupcinet was not:

She wasn't Tammy Windsor.

There's more useless information out there about television shows and movies than I ever imagined, or wanted to imagine, but for some reason, somewhere along the line, Cookie Kupcinet got mixed up with another actress who apparently went by the pseudonym Tammy Windsor. It's for this reason that Karyn Kupcinet is credited on various websites with TV and movie roles she never had, including guest spots on *The Andy Griffith Show* and the original *Little Shop of Horrors* with Jack Nicholson. I've watched the episode of *The Andy Griffith Show*. It's a riff on the Hatfields and McCoys feud, and the actress who called herself Tammy Windsor, whoever she was, is good, funny, and quick with her delivery. She doesn't overdo the hillbilly accent. But she's not Cookie. I've also watched the interminable *Little Shop of Horrors* (a Rudy favorite; he thought the man-eating plant was a positive Darwinian adaptation) and Tammy Windsor plays one of the excitable high school girls. Here, I can see why someone might have mistaken her for Cookie. There's a slight resemblance, though more in manner than appearance.

"LUCE?"

"Uh-huh."

"How are you?"

"What?"

"I asked you how you were."

"It's 2:10 in the morning."

"If I said I've fallen in love with Cookie Kupcinet, would it be any more ridiculous than any other ridiculous things —"

"Like falling in love with your wife?"

"We're not married."

"Cookie's dead."

"Why limit ourselves to the living? It's a cramped view. It's also discrimination. Don't the dead deserve as much romance as —"

"What was the original question again?"

"Would it be ridiculous —"

"If the dead are an option, then why not someone with, I don't know, more substance? Like Janis Joplin or Harriet Tubman or Eleanor Roosevelt or —"

"She's my loneliness, Luce."

"She's what?"

"Cookie's my loneliness."

"I gotta go back to — "

"Did I tell you about the whole Tammy Windsor controversy?"

"Who?"

LOYOLA GRANTED ME a little pot of research money. I had to sign a waiver certifying that I wasn't conducting any experiments whatsoever on animals. Is reading out loud to a cat torture? Some felines would say so. Hanna did agree to come over and feed him, but she said Rudy couldn't come back to live at Jarvis while I was gone because that would only confuse him. Also, that she was still allergic. Good luck, cat, I said. I'm off to California in the morning. Spirit to LAX with one stop in Denver. No checked bag. Twenty-five bucks to stick my backpack under the seat. Four and a half hours of turbulence.

For the first few hours on the ground, I was ecstatic. Field research was everywhere I looked. The rental car counter was field research. The NPR station (KCRW) was field research. Parking. Starbucks. I booked a room at the Culver Hotel. On the walls of the bar downstairs were framed pictures of solemn-looking munchkins. Must have been taken before they trashed the place. After a nap, I went to where the morgue used to be before they tore it down. I got out of the car and paced along the sidewalk, pensively, hands behind my back and performed contemplative research.

I drove over to 1227½ North Sweetzer. The ½ had always seemed fantastical, as if it had never been a real address at all. The fraction was right there on the sign. Monterey Village Apartments. And nothing seemed very different from the photographs I'd studied. Swap out the cars like they do in the movies and (insert that French word that starts with a *v*) it's 1963. Tall palms out front. Trees that must have been here when she was here. Trees she might have smelled or seen without looking at them, the way I didn't look at them as I hustled through the tunnel with the mailboxes, the dark little cave. I ran my finger across the dust of the mailbox for 7B. There was that narrow frame where you slip in a piece of paper with your name, but it was empty. On the other side of the tunnel, a fountain softly gurgled as it had gurgled when Mark Goddard rushed past it sixty years ago. A living museum of a place that had existed in my mind for so long. A bike was chained to a post. Lots of plants, well cared for, but also slightly unruly. I climbed the stairs. Her door. The first one on the right. The only one on the right.

I stood at the top of the stairs and waited, as if at some point she was going to burst out of 7B late for an audition with wet hair.

Cookie paid $150 a month, utilities included.

On my wall, a photograph of two deputies carrying a stretcher down the same set of stairs.

I don't know how long I'd been standing there when a young woman began climbing the stairs carrying groceries, a tall bag in each arm. Out of one of the bags poked a bunch of bananas. She was in her late twenties, early thirties. Sunglasses shoved up on her forehead. A flood of curly black hair. Long earrings in the shape of grasping hands, like they were holding on to her lobes for dear life. When she reached the top, she was frazzled, annoyed. Monday and already a lurker?

"Cary Grant? Across the courtyard. 3A."

"No," I said.

"Randolph Scott? He was really only here a month. He never signed a lease, but he was in — "

"Karyn Kupcinet."

"Who?"

"She lived in 7B for two years and ten months."

"What was she in?"

"Some shows and a Jerry Lewis movie."

"Offed herself?"

"Why do you ask?"

"Jerry Lewis."

I love you.

"Free for a coffee?"

Kind of her to shake her head with slight regret.

"The way you added the ten months. Did she?"

"My mother thinks so."

"What do other people think?"

"That she was strangled."

She put her bags down outside her door. When Mark Goddard took the stairs two at a time that Saturday night, the first thing he noticed in front of the door was the pile of newspapers.

"What does your mother say to that?"

"She doesn't get that far into it."

"But you do?"
"I'm on a grant."
"Strangled is a better story."
"Is it?"
"Why are you wearing hiking boots?"
"Field research."
We stood there outside her door.
"You can't come in the apartment."
"I totally get it."
She shifted her key ring from one hand to the other and back again.
"If she did, why do you think she did?"
"The list goes on. Trouble with a boyfriend. Not a lot of work. She got caught stealing. Also, an abortion. And she wrote these notes or threats, but they didn't make a ton of — Anyway, there was an autopsy. A broken bone in her neck. Same bone as Jeffrey Epstein. But if she did, she didn't do it like Epstein. It's confusing."
"Who'd she threaten?"
"The boyfriend. But also herself."
"I don't get it."
"The case is still open."
She bit her lip and raised her sunglasses higher on her head. A signal. She'd had enough. This was a little interesting, but that was enough. There were people in her life who knew what it meant when she pulled her sunglasses up higher on her head.
"Can I just take a quick peek, just to see where —"

The Gossip Columnist's Daughter

* * *

As I was passing by the fountain, she called down to me: "Things go missing. I'm not kidding. I'll drop something. Lipstick. My favorite pen. A twenty-dollar bill. I could look for days, it's gone. Not in the cushions of the couch, not under the rug. I mean *gone* gone."

THERE MUST HAVE been good mornings. Out there on the steps. In spite of everything that had already begun to pull her down. Slippers and an old cashmere topcoat of her father's. She'd make a cup of instant coffee and sit on the steps and read. If she was out of cream, she didn't mind it black. The library wasn't far and she'd stagger out of it with a stack of books. Why finish one when there's always another to start? And maybe those days when she was home, when she had no auditions or rehearsals, she'd take a break from reading and wander down the streets and listen to people taking showers. Some of her neighbors worked nine to five, but many didn't. She'd come to love the sound of people taking showers in the middle of the day. Something hopeful about that rush of water.

Up in the Attic

LATE MORNING. CURLED up against Andy, who's turned away. Morning after a long night of drinking and arguing the same argument. Andy wants more freedom. Cookie shouts, "Define *freedom!*" Andy says if he has to define it, he doesn't have it. Cookie: "See, there it is, you can't!" She was twenty-two and he was, what, twenty-six, twenty-seven? Back and forth like that until they were both so drunk and zonked they flopped back into each other's arms.

Now the light through the windows. She wakes but doesn't open her eyes. For a couple of moments she has no idea where she is. She's hot, there's skin. Not hers. A pleasant disorientation. Like remembering you're alive. Mostly we forget. Andy's bedroom. 2211 Stanley Hills Drive. She opens her eyes to all that light in the trees. It could be noon already. Sunday? Tuesday? Cookie reaches across his body, boggy with sleep, and kisses his gaping oaf of a mouth. He murmurs and edges away.

She wonders if love is always independent of everything else, including the object being loved. That mutuality not only isn't a requirement, it's got nothing to do with it. Love is freedom? There's your freedom, Andy. What did Sartre say? We absorb the other but the other cannot absorb us? Do I have that right? What do you think of Mr. Sartre, Mr. Prine? Care to comment?

If only she could shut her mouth sometimes. Of work, she talked a blue streak. About handsy producers: "They're like crabs constantly nipping at you." About the catty bitches on the set of *The Ladies Man,* especially that one who, in the movie, plays the trombone in bed, Lillian Briggs. Cookie couldn't stand Lillian Briggs. She carried that stupid trombone everywhere even though she couldn't actually play a note. In the movie, she told Andy, they overdubbed her.

And Jerry? One minute he'd smack you on the lips with his sloppy, wet mouth, the next he wouldn't know who you were or what you were doing on his set. Two years ago now and she's still talking about it.

She tried so hard not to be a chatterbox, because she knew that too many paragraphs in a row confused him. It never worked, because even when she was silent and only staring at Andy, words, words, words would fall out of her eyes.

Cookie uncurls and gets out of bed. The sheets so tangled. Yanks one off the bed and wraps herself up. The light through the trees. Andy snores loud, watery snores. Needs a longer mattress. Her father once took her down to Springfield. She remembers a picture of Lincoln on his little deathbed, his feet dangling.

Maybe you'll play him sometime, Andy.

Hold this moment of peace, she thinks. Grip it.

She reaches and grabs a fistful of Andy's thigh and twists it. He groans but doesn't wake up.

"I'm pregnant, you dumb galoot."

SHE NEVER DID tell him. Not while he was awake, anyway.

BEFORE SHE PASSES out in the back seat of Mark Goddard's Buick, Cookie tells Mark and Marcia that she wants to get the hell out of Mexico, that she doesn't want to strut around Tijuana like some postdivorce Elizabeth Taylor. Nightfall, and they're in a traffic jam on the Avenida Revolución.

"Your daddy's friend Liz," Marcia says.

"Just ask him," Cookie says.

"Nobody's strutting anywhere," Mark says. "We'll be in San Diego in an hour and a half, if I can find the border."

A few minutes later, Cookie's out cold. Painkillers and exhaustion. They'd started driving south from Los Angeles at the crack of dawn that same day.

"There should be a sign," Mark says.

"There's lots of signs. They just don't want us to leave."

Marcia rolls her window down. The street's already crowded. Marcia isn't impressed by Liz Taylor, or any other star. Her daddy knows everybody and anybody, too.

Inside the clubs, the bands are warming up. A man in a tuxedo stands outside one club and beckons directly to Marcia. "Tonight!" he shouts. "Tonight!"

She reads one of the signs on a marquee.

"Wonder what skin dancing is."

"No clue."

She reaches across the front seat and pokes Mark in the stomach.

"Don't be such a tight-ass. Let's get a drink."

"And what? Leave her in the car? Scooch closer."

She nudges against him, rubs his ear. They'll divorce in a few years, but right now Mark and Marcia can't keep their hands off each other.

"Saint Mark. Won't leave the kid in the car. And he wouldn't say no to this mission of mercy, either."

"What choice did I have?"

"You could have refused."

"And then what?"

"Then what? She has to run home to Mommy and Daddy, that's then what."

"I hear the mother's a piranha."

"Would that be so terrible?"

"What?"

"For the mother to knock some sense into this kid. Or she finds another chauffeur. What about Andy? Or Bob Conrad or Skip Ward or Troy Donahue or Dwayne Hickman. It's not like she's got any shortage of men."

Just a few cars on the Mexican side. They wait. Marcia slides back across the seat, leans her head against the window, closes her eyes.

"Marsh," Mark says. "We'll come back. You and me. We'll make a weekend of it."

"I'm tired. I'm tired and no Mexican quack even did anything to me."

The border guards wave them past. On the American side, an officer wielding a flashlight points it into the back seat.

"What's with her?"

Mark starts to speak but the officer directs the light at Marcia.

"I'm asking her."

Tongue working in his cheek. Gray buzz cut. Wrinkled skin. A little old to be standing on the border at night?

"She started with whiskey in the morning."

He points the light back at Cookie, who's balled up tight as possible. He's seen worse. Once, they had to pull a girl who'd begun to hemorrhage out of the car and fetch a doctor from National City.

A CLEAN LITTLE room reeking of bleach. A table with a plate of silver instruments and a stack of towels. In the corner, a padded chair like a barber's. Attached to the bottom of the chair, metal rods. At the end of the rods, buckles for your feet. The doctor, a squat man with a compassionate, almost jovial face. He reminded Cookie of a fat priest she'd seen in a movie. What movie? He spoke flawless English, though he didn't say very much. He went about his business with slow, deliberate movements. He breathed loudly through his nose. Before he used any of the instruments, he'd light a match and sterilize it. Then he'd hold it up to his face as if ordering it to do his bidding.

A young girl, his daughter, acted as his nurse. She couldn't have been more than fourteen. She had her father's eyes. She did most of the talking, in Spanish. Cookie didn't know a single word, but she understood everything the girl said. When she said, He's going to give you a shot, Cookie rolled up her sleeves. When the girl told her, Get undressed, Cookie took off her clothes. And as she became sleepier, the nurse-daughter caressed her shoulders until she could no longer feel those gentle fingers.

Cookie woke up in a bed in a different room, also

rigorously clean. The sheets had been washed so many times they were nearly translucent.

So they ripped it out of you and you didn't feel a thing.

Mark had done his homework. He'd found a reputable place. It hadn't been difficult. Goddard himself was a Boy Scout, but it seemed like every actor he talked to had an address in his wallet. Still, it was as illegal in Tijuana as it was in California. When he handed the doctor the payment, the man shoved the wad into the pocket of his white coat without a word.

NORTH OF SAN DIEGO on a two-lane highway. The Buick's headlights only pierce the darkness so far before they fade into nothing. On either side of the car, orange groves, vast shadows. Mark nods off for a moment. The car strays into the oncoming traffic. He catches himself and swerves back into his lane. Marcia, whose head rests on Mark's thigh, sleeps through it. But the jolt wakes Cookie. Her sweat-drenched face is stuck to the seat. She peels it off the leather.

"Whoa there, partner."

Barely a whisper. Sudden, disembodied. Like her voice comes to me some nights. A little hoarse, parched. One thing all our dead must have in common is thirst.

"How do you feel?" Mark says.

"Hazy."

"Hurts?"

"I don't know."

"Go back to sleep."

And for a few moments, she tries, but it's no use. She sits up. Same thing happens at home, once she wakes up there's no turning back.

"Now I'll keep you awake."

"I'm fine."

"You know what Bernard Baruch says?"

"Who?"

"Friend of my father's."

"Another one."

"There are battalions. He and Malcolm X are like this."

"And this guy Baruch?"

"A zillionaire, lots of opinions."

"Okay, what's he say?"

"'Those who mind don't matter, and those who matter don't mind.'"

"Don't mind what?"

"Well, he was talking about the seating at a dinner party. When you mind who gets seated next to you, you mind. But when you don't, you don't. That's you. You don't mind."

"Sure, I don't mind."

"You know Sisyphus?"

"Him I know. Pushes a rock up a hill."

"Right," Cookie says. "It's a mountain. But you're — "

"Two years of college right there," Mark says.

"You know what makes him happy?"

"Happy? Doesn't the rock roll down again when he reaches — "

"It's the walk back down."

"What about it?"

"Sisyphus thinks, he contemplates."

"What? The rock?"

"Yes, but the rock isn't just a rock. It's everything. Love, death, fate."

"I don't get it."

"It's because he's conscious. Sentient."

"But if he's got to push the rock — isn't the whole thing a punishment? Over and over?"

Cookie hoots, she hoots in a dark car on an empty road outside San Diego in July of 1963.

"The gods thought it was a punishment! But he knows that when the boulder rolls down the mountain again, he'll have it all back again. Sisyphus pushes it back up so he's able to live after. Every time. It's like he's immortal, he's dead or he's in hell or wherever but at the same time he's eternal, see?"

Marcia raises her head off Mark's lap.

"Where are we?"

"Lord knows," he says.

SHE STOLE BECAUSE she was good at it. She'd been ripping off stores since middle school at Francis Parker. She and Judy Rosenthal. Didn't they make a little business out of it? Resold Hershey bars to fifth graders? She moved on to clothes that year at college in Massachusetts. She'd take the bus into Boston and return with new outfits. Amazed her roommates. She'd buy pants and take a skirt. But she came to see this bait and switch as cheating. The real trick was to walk into a store without any money. That way she wasn't tempted to spend it. It helped that after she moved to California she was mostly hard up. She earned peanuts for the guest spots. Her father sent checks but she'd forget to cash them. She practiced. She rehearsed. She could slip on a blouse sleeve first, hardly tilting her head. She smiled. Throws people off, as if thieves don't smile. Thieves smile plenty. A private thing. Andy didn't know. The Goddards had no idea either. She only got nabbed that time at Buffums in Pomona because she'd had a greedy moment. On her way out she spotted those cute pants she couldn't live without. A better thief than an actress. She knew it. They should give out awards.

SHE ONLY KNOWS it's possible to get up there because she once noticed a little door in the ceiling of Andy's closet. She wanted to know him. You want to know anybody, inspect their closet.

"Where does it go?"

"Heaven," Andy said and kissed her again. They were in the closet together. This was in the early days. He'd followed her in there.

"It's a cute door."

"Must be an attic."

Turns out it's more like a crawl space. She still has a key to his door, not that Andy ever locks his house. Easy enough to climb up here. She carried a chair up from the kitchen. Tiny and snug. A private darkness. She's brought a lighter. There are a couple of exposed beams and some pink fiberglass insulation. Also, between the floorboards, what almost looks like feathers. The only thing she's afraid of is being nibbled on by a mouse. The insulation makes her think of the cotton candy her father used to buy her and Jerry at Wrigley Field.

But for the occasional bark of a dog, it's quiet. Cookie waits. Hot, she takes off most of her clothes. She'd like to smoke a cigarette, but she doesn't want to burn down Andy's house, she only wants him back. It's so simple. Sometimes people need to be reminded not to kick other people to the curb. To take the long view. Short-term urges? He loves her, he's said so. How many times has he said so. And when he comes home and gets into bed, she'll step down onto the chair and back into his closet and back into his bed, think about it, imagine it.

All he has to do is come home alone.

During my swashbuckling field research in Los Angeles, I stood outside the house Andy Prine once rented at 2211 Stanley Hills Drive. A modest house for the neighborhood. A bachelor's house. It had recently been repainted. Three packages from Amazon were piled on the stoop. Nobody was around.

He doesn't come home alone. And still she waits. For what? When she hears them giggling in the bedroom, she can't hold still anymore. Andy says, in his Andy Guthrie voice, "Either a coon or a man up there." He calls the police, but before they arrive he opens his closet door and sees the kitchen chair.

The *Los Angeles Times* said Andy Prine flushed her out from up there. But the truth is she climbed down on her own.

"Let me get dressed first," Cookie says.
   "You're naked?"
   "I'm broiling."

HIS DATE IS an actress named Ahna Capri and now she's waiting in the kitchen for this tedious scene to be over. She's also trying to make her way. Couple of guest spots on *Leave It to Beaver*. Who needs this drama on her off-time?

Andy, six feet four in his socks, stands in the living room and looks down at Cookie, who's huddled on the love seat. For a change, the big lug does the right thing. He listens. Without telling her she's nuts. She is nuts. She's been hiding in his crawl space, naked, for how many hours? But for now he listens to her as she quivers and sobs and forgives him, she forgives him for being such a dunce and for all the other girls, including that Wendy in the kitchen. Andy doesn't correct her. What Cookie calls his date is the least of his worries right now, but it annoys Ahna Capri, who can hear every word from the kitchen.

How's he going to get rid of her? Not just tonight but generally?

Andy kneels on the rug before her like he really means to accept all the forgiveness she's been bestowing. He's acting better than he does on TV. Using the Method technique, he conjures the funeral of a beloved grandmother, and tears begin to collect in his eyes.

The doorbell rings. Andy asks Ahna to get it.

"What am I, the maid?"

But she does it anyway, and comes into the living room to report that two officers from the Los Angeles Police Department would like a word with the man of the house.

"Wendy!" Cookie points.

"What do you want me to tell them?"

"It's okay. It's not a prowler."

"You think I'm a prowler?"

"You were hiding in the attic."

"It's a crawl space."

"Shit, I'll talk to them."

Andy gets up off his knees, leaving Ahna Capri alone with Cookie.

"I'm not sure he's worth the trouble," Ahna says and joins Cookie on the love seat.

Cookie, a little less exhilarated now that the cops are on the premises, turns to Ahna and says, "What is your name?"

"Ah-na. Anna but with an *h*."

"Oh."

Two women on a love seat. It's late. All the lights are on in the room. The scene makes me think of Daisy Buchanan and her friend the tennis player in *The Great Gatsby*, when their dresses begin to rise and billow in the wind. Two women in their twenties, their entire lives ahead —

I'm weak. I can't just leave them be where they are right now. Impossible to resist looking up what happened to Ahna Capri. It's a kind of hell. The idea that we can know a life in milliseconds. Some fame in the seventies. A Bruce Lee movie. Died after a collision with a truck in 2010.

Andy's still talking to the cops.

A cop guffaws. "One in the bed, one in the attic. I should audition for something."

"It's a pretty name," Cookie says.

"Hungarian," Ahna says.

After the cops leave, Andy offers to drive both women home. Cookie refuses, says she'll walk, and she does. She walks, four-plus miles in the dark, from Laurel Canyon to her apartment on Sweetzer, barefoot, swinging her shoes.

THE PHONE'S STOPPED ringing as much as it used to, even a few months back. I wonder if word hasn't gotten around about her, that producers and directors have become wary.

But there are times now, even when it does ring, that she doesn't pick up. She stops paying the bills, too. Pacific Bell sends threatening letters. She doesn't read them.

FOR DECADES A critic named Claudia Cassidy wrote a column for the *Chicago Tribune* called "On the Aisle." They called her Acidy Cassidy. Also the Viper, the Executioner, Medusa of the Midwest, the Hatchet from Shawneetown, and most damning of all, That Woman from the *Tribune*.

Of a fellow Chicagoan, a pianist named Rosalyn Tureck, she wrote:

> ...in the face of the inexhaustible vitality, the splendor, the scope, the joy of the great Bach, hers is pedantic, even bigoted.

Acidy Cassidy must have forced more than one artist to take a good look in the mirror. As my high school cross-country coach, Jordy Hanson, used to say when I, again, failed to reach the top of the hill at Ravine Drive, "Are we going to be honest with ourself now?"

In July of 1962, Cookie returned to Chicago to take a lead in a play called *Sunday in New York*. They put it on at the Edgewater Beach Playhouse, a temporary theater on the beach.

They put the tent up in June, took it down in August. Often gusts threatened to send the entire tent and everybody inside into the lake.

Her parents, of course, were in the audience. As were my dutiful grandparents.

There was a moment during Act 2 when Essee winced at how wide Cookie — not her character — opened her mouth.

When the curtain fell, Babs Rosenthal applauded the longest. Everybody else had stopped, she continued to slap her hands together. Not only out of loyalty to Essee and Irv, there was always that, my grandmother was ever the good soldier, but also because she knew what it meant to perform before a hometown crowd, in front of people who know you. Amid all the applause, jealousy, even rage, born of familiarity. And so Babs, whatever she thought of the play and Cookie's performance, kept clapping...

I've always been a little transfixed by the curtain call, that brief minute or two when the actors haven't entirely shed their characters, but the stresses of their lives have already begun to fill their eyes again. A divorce, a father in the hospital. They hid it all so well for a couple of hours. I think of Cookie basking in the applause, and at the same time wanting to get the hell out of Chicago.

Under a kinder star, she says, Cookie might have made it all the way.

After Cookie's death, Claudia Cassidy remembered that the direction of *Sunday in New York* had been shoddy, that the play was as inconsequential as it was poorly written, that she was bored stiff, and yet... "this slender girl with the huge dark eyes held on, and it seemed to me that in the right hands she might become something special."

Kinder star? All the way? I just want her to make it past 1963.

IN THE GUEST spot on *Perry Mason* that aired in January of 1964, Cookie plays the sister of a woman accused of murdering an ex-lover. Under penetrating yet manfully gentle questioning by Raymond Burr, she does a convincing job of loyally declaring her sister's innocence. My sister? No, she's not capable of such treachery. How can you even suggest it? And yet there's this glint in her big eyes, which are open just a hair wider than they should be, that says, Hell yeah, she shot the bastard.

Afterlife of Karyn

DECEMBER 1991. Oliver Stone's *JFK* is released in theaters. Conspiracy theorists across the country enjoy multiple orgasms.

In February 1992, the *Today* show airs an interview with Stone and cohost Bryant Gumbel. In the segment that immediately follows, Gumbel presents a list of people who died violently in the weeks and months following Kennedy's death and who might have had a connection to the assassination.

First on this list: Karyn Kupcinet. Found murdered in Hollywood on November 30, 1963. Case remains unsolved.

In a column published days later, Kup blasts the *Today* show for what he calls an "outrage." He concedes that Cookie died violently: "but there is no link whatsoever between her and the assassination."

It isn't the first time Kup has heard of the possible connection between Cookie and JFK. He refers, without mentioning the title, to a book published more than two decades earlier. Here's where the rabbit hole gets deeper, the weeds denser, the quagmire more sinkholeish —

* * *

Rudy, on the office radiator, yawns. Please, please, not the conspiracy stuff. You've become enough of a nutbag as it is and now you're going to start in on all this —

Go back to sleep.

You're no better than Ellroy. You think you are, Mr. Iowa MFA. Get over yourself, Mr. Literary, the fewer books you sell, the better you think you are. Dead white actresses are catnip and you're just as happy to roll around in the muck as Ellroy —

Is it catnip, is that what you want?

The good stuff. Not the cheap stuff from Pet Smart. Go to Bentley's on Devon.

The book that Kup referenced without naming is called *Forgive My Grief,* self-published in 1966 by a Texan named Penn Jones Jr., considered by many to be the godfather of first-generation JFK conspiracy theorists. The title comes from a Tennyson poem: "Forgive my grief for one removed / Thy creature, whom I found so fair."

> This book gives names and details of
> THE STRANGE DEATHS OF 24 PEOPLE
> who knew something, learned something or saw something that was supposed to have remained secret.

Then comes a contents page so inspiringly bonkers it rises to the level of conceptual art, a kind of history of the world in eight words:

The Gossip Columnist's Daughter

1. Deaths
2. Deaths
3. Deaths
4. More Deaths
5. And More Deaths

Karyn Kupcinet's name doesn't appear in *Forgive My Grief* until chapter 4. Jones briefly sketches out the unusual circumstances of her death and why it made it into the book. In Jones's telling, it started with Jack Ruby. Back in Chicago when Ruby worked as a low-level union operative, he was friendly with Irv Kupcinet. Years later, after he became involved in a Mob plot to kill Kennedy, Ruby got back in touch with his old buddy Irv, now a famous columnist, and told him about it. Irv, in turn, constitutionally unable to keep any news to himself, told his twenty-two-year-old daughter, an actress out in Hollywood.

Are you following this?

No, the cat says. This part I've never understood. Let's say Ruby did tell Kup. Why would Kup tell Cookie? Why not the cops, or the FBI?

I'm just telling you what Jones says in his book. I'm not saying it makes any sense. Anyway, I thought you weren't interested in any of—

Just go on.

And Cookie, in turn, couldn't keep the information to herself, and on the morning of November 22 she attempted to notify somebody—anybody—by calling an operator in

California and shrieking into the phone that the president was about to be shot. Twenty minutes later —

Skip that, I know that.

And a week later, in order to send a message to her father never to open his trap again, the Mob ordered a hit on Cookie Kupcinet.

IS ANY OF this shit true?
That's the problem.

> 1. Kup did know Jack Ruby in Chicago the way all Chicago Jews know each other, either directly or through somebody or through... et cetera, et cetera. Were they pals? Kup had pals under every rock. Jack Ruby wasn't one of them. He just knew the guy. Were they in touch after Ruby moved to Dallas? Possible, but unlikely. Kup wasn't a snob, but there's no evidence in the Warren Report that Ruby —

This is in the Warren Report?
I forget. Ruby is, of course, maybe not Kup.*

> 2. A woman did call an operator at 10:10 a.m. California time, twenty minutes before the

---

* Kup *is* in the Warren Report. Back in Chicago, Ruby once approached Kup about helping a friend of his who was trying to break into showbiz. The act was "Jerry the Talking Dog," and Kup secured him a booking. (Warren Commission, Volume XXII: CE 1257).

assassination. This woman didn't shriek into the phone that the president was about to be shot, she whispered it. It's known as the "Oxnard call" because operators traced the call to the Oxnard-Camarillo area, fifty miles from Los Angeles. The woman also whispered that the chief justice of the Supreme Court was going to be killed, and the entire government was about to collapse. The *Washington Post* ran a story about the call a week later, around the time of Cookie's death, quoting one of the operators as saying that the woman had sounded rehearsed, as if she were reading from a script.

So how do we know Cookie was the one who made that call?
For a cat who wasn't interested, you've got a lot —
Just tell it.
Because some guy named Penn Jones Jr. said so.
That's it?
That's it.
He made it up?
Whole cloth.

CUT TO 1991 and Oliver Stone.

Karyn Kupcinet (or the Oxnard caller) doesn't appear in *JFK*, though there was, apparently, a character based on her in the original script. Yet the movie does include a scene where a woman strapped to a hospital bed says something like what the Oxnard caller is said to have said, i.e., that somebody's going to whack Kennedy in Dallas... (This character is based, as I understand it, not on Karyn but on another woman who also, the story goes, warned of the assassination before it happened. I forget her name, she's in my notes somewhere.) Where was I? Right, so Oliver Stone allegedly cut the Karyn Kupcinet character from the script, but Kup, given his connections in Hollywood, might have gotten wind of it anyway. Because Kup's hatred for Stone's movie goes far beyond the fact that Stone simply kicked the door wide open to whackadoodle theories about the assassination in general. It's personal.

In column after column after column, over the course of a year, Kup trashes Stone and the movie.

> **Oliver Stone**...*Another theory for his collection of astounding assumptions on the assassination of JFK, the butler did it...*

And that's mild. When Stone didn't win an Academy Award, Kup mocked him, wondering if he was going to claim a conspiracy against him. In 1992, a Chicago writer named Jim Kielty did a detailed examination of Kup's obsession with Stone in a *Chicago Reader* piece called "Kup vs. JFK." Kielty writes that Kup pummeled Stone at least two dozen times over the course of the previous year. The figure is inexact because Kielty stopped counting. Kielty agrees that Kup's animus toward Stone was driven by the suggestion that he and Cookie were somehow mixed up in the assassination.

At the same time, I'm convinced that Kup, like plenty of other people, believed firmly in the lone-gunman theory and the conclusions of the Warren Commission Report. In one column, he quotes a line of Kevin Costner, who plays the New Orleans district attorney Jim Garrison in *JFK,* from another movie — I'm told I can't quote it even though Kup did in the *Sun-Times* and it's everywhere on the fucking internet — but you know the line?

About Susan Sontag being overrated? And good scotch and Oswald acting alone?

Good kitty.

WAIT.

Yes?

You believe that the Warren Report is sacrosanct? Case closed?

Fuck if I know. My only point here is that Penn Jones opened the door to the theory that Cookie was somehow wrapped up in the assassination. Then years later Oliver Stone, in his way, kicked it open in the sense that now anything went, any crackpot association, and then the internet and Reddit or whatever and then every true-crime fanatic, that just exploded her entire presence —

And Ellroy?

ON MY FIELD trip to California, I also stopped by the Los Angeles County Sheriff's Department to see if I could get a look at Cookie's case file. The cop behind the thick wall of smudged bulletproof glass was a blur. Her hair looked like it was blowing around in the wind. Maybe there was a fan back there. I pressed the button for the intercom.

"Good morning, I mean good afternoon, I'm a professor of creative writing at Loyola University in Chicago. I'm conducting research into the unsolved murder of Karyn Kupcinet, who was found strangled in West Hollywood in November 1963."

"What can I do for you, honey?"

I hit the button again.

"I'd like to examine the case file. It's my understanding that the file is still open, that it's, you know, a cold case. Unsolved."

"A cold case?"

"That's right."

"Like on TV?"

"Right."

"Are you related to the victim?"

"No, I'm not. But my grandparents were close to the victim's parents. Very close, for years they —"

The Gossip Columnist's Daughter

"Do you have a notarized release from an authorized third party?"

"No, I don't, how do I —"

"Instructions on our website."

"You gave the file to Ellroy."

"Who?"

"James Ellroy, you handed him Cookie's entire case file."

"Who's Cookie?"

"Karyn Kupcinet."

"Is Ellroy the guy who wrote *The Black Dahlia*?"

"That's him."

"That book kept me up at night. Him and Elmore Leonard. I get them mixed up. Names kind of similar, you know? But those two, they really get it. They're out there. On the streets. And I mean the dialogue in *Get Shorty*! Book's even better than the movie. It pops off the page! You teach writing? You know who I really love, James Cain. *Double Indemnity*. If you can make an insurance scam interesting —"

"Would you like to get a coffee?"

"Excuse me."

I pressed the button again and held it. This thick smudged glass. Like staring into a murky aquarium. A blurry, windblown phantom. As if she was encased in ice.

"Drink later?"

"Check the website, okay, honey?"

ASIDE FROM Penn Jones Jr. and all those who followed — taking his fable about Kup and Cookie knowing something about the assassination ahead of time and running with it (*Crossfire: The Plot That Killed Kennedy* by Jim Marrs, *High Treason: The Assassination of JFK and the Case for Conspiracy* by Harrison Livingstone and Robert Groden, and the list goes on and on) — nobody's done more to keep Karyn Kupcinet's name out there than James Ellroy. To his credit, he's never expressed any interest in the JFK bullshit. What turns Ellroy on is the aspiring-actress-found-naked-and-dead-in-Hollywood angle. In 1998, he published a piece in *GQ*. It's provided fodder that's now been recycled by true crime ad infinitum. It seems that Ellroy, given his status as celebrity bad-boy crime writer, was given full access to Cookie's case file. My guess is that either he secured a release from an authorized third party, whatever that means, or the Sheriff's Department figured he couldn't do any worse of a job solving this case than anyone else over the decades so what the hell, give the file to Ellroy.

 Sheriff's Homicide File #2-961-651
 Date: 11/30/63

The Gossip Columnist's Daughter

> Location: 1227½ North Sweetzer Avenue, West Hollywood
> Victim: Kupcinet, Karyn (NMI), W/22/DOB 3/6/41

NMI. No middle initial. All of Cookie's names and she didn't have a middle one. Then come the details. How she was found. Already signs of decomposition. Ellroy calls it decomp. He's got all the lingo. Cookie's a hophead. A drug-addled, eating-disordered actress-dilettante.

He quotes chunks of the police report. They found a teddy bear on the floor —

You had a teddy bear?

Why wouldn't I have? Any law against dead, nude aspiring actresses having a teddy bear? Too sentimental? It's in the report, isn't it?

I'm losing it.

You say that as if it hasn't happened already.

The cops zeroed in on a red bathrobe on a chair in the living room. This robe looked as if it had been taken off and dropped on the chair "in a disorderly fashion."

Among the many books in the apartment, officers found one in the living room open to a page. A weird book, Ellroy says, open to a very weird page. About something called ecstatic dancing, how if you danced in the nude you could lose all your inhibitions.

Ellroy lists the pills that the cops found in Cookie's bathroom. Among many others were Miltown (a tranquilizer, "trank" in Ellroyese) and Desoxyn (a diet pill, an upper). No question he knows his way around a medicine cabinet. According to the police report, Cookie had filled two fifty-pill prescriptions of Desoxyn on the Monday before she died. Forty-eight pills were missing from one bottle, thirty-three from the other.

Ellroy's piece is called, inexplicably, "Glamour Jungle."

Where's the glamour? She died in a one-bedroom apartment. Diet pills and overdue library books.

But don't get me wrong, Officer, I never did catch your name, I'm a fan of Ellroy's. The rat-a-tat-tat prose, the way he never met a sentence he didn't want to behead.

After a while, though, it's fucking irritating.

Andy Prine, he says, wanted to keep things "cooool."

Also, he liked to ball Cookie on his own terms.

I know you had a mother, Mr. Ellroy. I read your book about her. I still feel what I felt when I read it.

Did you ever have a daughter?

Oh, but he comes around. Badass as hard-boiled softie. Cookie might be a hophead, an addict, a dilettante, a hot mess of a Jewish princess, but in the end the whole deal is a freak show and a heartache. She got lost, he says, in the uproar.

What uproar?

Also in File #2-961-651: Cookie's datebook. I quote here out of the conviction that James Ellroy doesn't own Cookie's words any more than you or me or anybody else who types them into a post on Reddit.

In October of 1962, she wrote that she cried herself to sleep. Then Andy. Much of spring and summer of 1963, it's all Andy, Andy, lovely Andy...

In July of 1963, there's an apparent reference to the trip to Mexico:

7/12/63: Traumatic. Glad it's over.

November of 1963:

11/20/63: —I'm losing reality.

11/22/63: President assassinated.

11/25/63: Ate to oblivion.

CREDIT FOR NOVELTY. Ellroy's theory is that Cookie, while dancing naked and ecstatically (per the instructions in the weird book) (and also loaded and junked-up), fell, and somehow broke her hyoid bone.

She then crawled up onto the couch, where she died.

PODCASTS, CRIME BLOGS, YouTube mini documentaries. Commentary, speculations, judgments. And nearly every bit of it recycled. Anyone who gets sucked into Cookie's story ends up repeating the same details, as if Cookie herself might be found in the repetition.

But to keep a story going, it's got to be fed, and to feed it, you need posts, comments, guesses, fantasy.

> *Karyn Kupcinet didn't make the Oxnard call. It was a Rosicrucian performing a ritual called radionics, using the phone. It's a form of preemptive healing.*
> *Debbie H., Super Member, edited October 12, 2010*

Or:

> *Lyndon Johnson didn't order Jack Ruby to kill Karyn. Red Dorfman arranged the hit to divert federal heat over the Chicago mob's hostile takeover of the Teamsters because Irv Kupcinet knew a wheelbarrow of secrets...*
> *Branmuffin891, March 20, 2014, 10:22 p.m.*

The stuff is searchable for eternity. Or at least until our machines melt.

But isn't the thing about conspiracy theories that at least sometimes they've got one little toe in some truth? Red Dorfman was a high-level Chicago thug (longtime associate of Sidney Korshak) who knew Jack Ruby from back in the day when Ruby was an organizer for the waste handlers union and Red was his boss, and, yes, Red was also a longtime friend of Irv Kupcinet's…

Why do I feel again compulsed (my brilliant, long-suffering copyeditor says this isn't a verb anymore but I'd like to bring an archaic form back) to include the fact that Allen Dorfman, Red's son, who was later gunned down in the parking lot of the Purple Hyatt in Lincolnwood, went to summer camp in Wisconsin with my father? My father said that Allen blackmailed the counselors for special favors and stole tennis balls and sold them back to the camp at a profit.

Off track again. There is no track. The only rails around here are the Red Line and I'm off, off—

What else? Andy Prine's first wife accused him of strangling her cat. Gives me some ideas.

Also, Prine was so hard up for cash in the years after being fingered as a suspect in Cookie's murder that he posed naked with a horse in a cheap knockoff of *Playgirl*. I've seen the photograph. Easy to find. It's now included in the permanent record of humankind. Along with the Magna Carta and the *Mona Lisa*.

> *At least she hitched a ride on Prine's massive member for a while.*
> Anonymous reply, September 9, 2014, 5:11 a.m.

And because there's everything. There's kindness out there, too.

> *Wowzers, she looks like Natalie Wood and Elizabeth Taylor fused together, with a little Jackie thrown in. The more I read, the more I feel for her. She had a flair and spunk. Looks like untreated addictions and psychological problems.*
> *DM eight years ago*

Four in the morning and I'm where? In a defunct chat room reading an old message board like it's vintage graffiti? Unless all stories are connected, somehow, someway, in the way all Chicago Jews know each other, as has been said already more than once, directly or...or...or...

What if I just went *home* home? From Loyola to Jarvis — two miles and change — and put my key in the door, quietly, so as not to wake you two?

RUDOLPH?

    Jesus, what now?

    Check out the spider.

    Can't you see I'm enjoying my leisure?

    A big one. It's crawling up the wall where the tenant before me must have had a flat-screen TV. You can tell by the placement of screwless screw holes. One big empty rectangle.

    Huh?

    The spider. See it?

    What about it?

    I just thought you'd be interested. You know, animal to animal. A fellow creature.

    An arthropod? You want me to be friends with an arthropod?

    I was making conversation. Maybe you could eat it.

    I'm not hungry. Would you let me sleep?

    Going for a walk.

    Go. Go.

Fargo Beach. No beach left. The lake's eaten it away. Wind lashing. Rising sand pelting my face. It's like being shot with BBs. That thing about Chicago not being all that windy, like we're only the eleventh windiest city or something, that the moniker is all about us, how we talk too much, that it's our words that amount to such a squall, that may be true but stand by the lake on a night like this and you shut your mouth and just try to stay on your feet.

Branmuffin891,

I read with interest your comment that Red Dorfman ordered the hit on Karyn Kupcinet in order to keep her father quiet about the outfit's infiltration of the Teamsters. While I believe this is batshit (the Feds knew about the Mob and the Teamsters since at least the early fifties, not that it has an ounce of a connection to Cookie's death), it did trigger a memory I thought I'd share. You see, my late father went to Camp Ojibwa up in Eagle River with Red's son Allen...

Dear Snook,

Every kid deserves a better father. This is a given. Take Nelson Mandela. Great guy. Lotta prizes. Big ones. No Father of the Year awards. Tomorrow night, at this time, you'll be at my place, I call it my place, but it isn't any place, you know that, and you'll be asleep on the cot in the living room, the room that when you come over we call your room, and it is, it is your room, my place isn't any place, but it's your room, and I'll be in mine doing whatever I do in here, but I want to say, even though you can't read yet (your mother would like you to read early, but I say why rush it, why crowd the brain when you've got your whole life —). What I'm trying to say is that I know I'm preoccupied and that even when you're here I'm only partly here, partly not here, and by partly not here I mean partly not here with you even though we're together because I'm staring at what you call my craaaaazy papers.

Dear Mr. Bellow,

I hope you understand that my shamelessly ripping off the letters Moses Herzog writes to anybody and everybody is part homage, part hero worship, and more than half recognition of my own inadequacy as an artist, but it's also time for me, pale as I know myself to be in any comparison under any possible sun, to come out from under your natty Burberry overcoat where I've been burrowed since I first read you on my own in, I can't remember what year, but it wasn't in school, because even when I was in school nobody was teaching you and now there isn't anybody teaching a creative writing class from Chicago to Mogadishu who'd teach your work (or a literature class, the real professors don't want you, either), which is too bad, but understandable. The idea being that we've all heard enough from you and your ilk already. Old white guys have been talking nonstop since time immemorial, please go away

The Gossip Columnist's Daughter

now. And don't think I don't know I'm heading for old white guy status, if I'm not there already. Allow me to add something on a somewhat related subject, i.e., that the remark you made in 1988 about there being no Tolstoy of the Zulus? Not only was it racist, which goes without saying, it was tone-deaf, and there's no greater violation of Bellowian principles than tone-deafness. In a way it even reminds me a little of your brilliant send-up of Irv Kupcinet in Humboldt's Gift, *a man who fed off others for his own ego and livelihood... Mr. Bellow? Mr. Bellow? Wait, Saul, please —*

The detectives assigned to the "Unsolved Unit" are the personification of the Bureau's "Bulldog" image... Long after the original case investigators may have retired or otherwise left the bureau, every clue or lead is investigated by this unit. It is not uncommon for cases that may have occurred more than 15 years ago to be brought to trial and conviction by the detectives of this unit. Recently, intrepid "Unsolved" detectives prosecuted a murder that was committed in 1974! It is never too late to provide information that will assist detectives in solving a case. If someone knows something about a crime, please contact...

ONE PODCASTER SAID that if only she had hung on a few years more, she'd have become an absolutely insanely decadent hippie chick.

COOKIE'S RED BATHROBE. Kup brings it up in the "Who Killed Karyn?" chapter of *A Man, an Era, a City*. He writes that when Cookie was found, the investigators observed that "her robe was folded neatly on the chair." Kup deduces from this that whoever murdered Cookie must have folded the robe. Why? Because he says that Cookie had always left clothes wherever they happened to fall.

I should leave it there. Let that robe be.

But because I'm a freak, I have to point out that if Ellroy's detail from Cookie's homicide file is correct (no reason to believe it isn't), it directly contradicts Kup's line about the robe. The cops noted the opposite.
    The robe wasn't folded. It was found in a disorderly fashion.
    It's possible that nearly thirty years later, Kup simply misremembered the detail. But maybe it's something else. How likely is it that Cookie's killer folded her robe before he strangled her? It's so illogical that Kup might have imagined this fastidious murderer because the truth—that she'd done that night what she'd always done, which was let her robe fall where it fell, in this case on the chair—had been impossible to take.

A KNOCK. TWO knocks.
    Holy shit. Morning?
    Answer it, Rudy whispers. It's two-thirty in the afternoon.
    No.
    The student knocks again.
    Do your job, Rudy whispers.
    No.
    The student slips a note under the door.

> *Professor? Are you here? It's office hours.* —Grace Contreras

Oh, Grace. He thinks the killer folded her robe because she always left clothes where they fell.

SHE SETS THE book down on the coffee table. It's a library book, but it's not overdue, because one day Cookie just walked out with it under her arm.

    She thinks, Wittgenstein's right. Birth is abandonment.

    September 1963. Outside, everything is so green. All the flowers she doesn't know the names of and never will. September in Los Angeles, a stealthy month, a pause after the winds of summer. The winds, someone once told her, go and hide up in caves in the hills. Now the crickets in the trees and in the tall grass (a gardener was out front yesterday with a machete) have begun to throb and seethe. A chica-chica-chica sound that gets more and more feverish as the night darkens. Mating calls. Who was it that told her that the chica-chica-chica is a mating call? Some man. Skip Ward? He knew a lot about nature.

    What makes one cricket want another cricket?

    We hear one flood of sound, they hear individual invitations.

    You. No, not you. You. Yes. You.

IV.

Solly's Diploma

WHEN I WAS a kid, whenever we had a day off from school, my father would take me with him to his office. I had to dress accordingly. At that time this meant wearing a sailor suit. Lucy, being older and a girl, was exempt from this humiliation. Little blue blouse, little white tie, little blue shorts, little saucer of a little white hat. I wore this getup when I went downtown to my father's office in the American National Bank building on LaSalle Street until I was seven and old enough to suffer mortification and refuse.

"Over my dead body," I announced, "will I ever wear that John-John outfit again."

"What if you become a sailor?" my father said.

"I'll drown first."

We'd take the train. Normally, my father drove to work. He preferred to sit in bumper-to-bumper traffic on the Kennedy than chitchat with fellow fathers. He only schmoozed with people he considered bigger wigs. But for some reason, on sailor suit days he felt the need to show me off, and so we'd board the 8:08 at the Ravinia station. I'd stride into the car and salute. I'd stand at attention. I'd scan the horizon for the enemy. It all seems fantastical now. I can't even conjure this without wanting to crawl into a hole.

My father had a naval fetish. He and my grandfather were never close, but the fetish had to be connected to Lou's service in the South Pacific. There must have been some grudging respect or even love in there somewhere. Still, my father and grandfather avoided each other at family gatherings like two planets that must, due to the laws of physics or gravity or whatever, maintain a certain distance from each other. If Lou took a step toward my father, my father would take a step backward, and vice versa.

Though physically they looked very much alike (they were short and top-heavy, Lucy used to complain that only the men in our family are big-breasted), to Lou my father represented a human embodiment of the crass takeover of a noble profession.

Nobody called my father counselor as he charged coatless down LaSalle Street. He was no better than a shirtsleeved commodities trader in the pit at the south end of the block.

A comparison that suited my dad just fine.

Noble profession my ass. Justice is blind? Yeah, it is. Blind as a bat. A cesspool's a cesspool. Why pretend we aren't swimming in it?

To my father, Lou's posturing as a barrister out of *Bleak House* was a farcical throwback to an era that had never existed in the first place. *Learned Hand! Oliver Wendell Holmes! Brandeis! The old man thinks he's Felix Frankfurter. But Frankfurter knew who's boss. The law? Nah. Power. Power's the boss. Remember that.*

Even so, there I was in my sailor suit.

A tribute to a father he didn't otherwise respect.

On the Chicago and North Western, I'd mince and preen before baffled men with briefcases between their legs.

Once we were downtown at the office, I'd sit in one of the tall wingback chairs in front of my father's desk and watch him work. He'd lounge in his big black leather swivel chair with one leg draped over a padded arm and shout.

"Banis! Zadowsky! Beck! Beck! Where's Beck?"

It was the same at home, those years when we still lived with him. If you were out of his sight for a half a minute, he'd start to holler your name.

My father's firm defended insurance companies against suits brought by their customers. He said if he didn't do it, somebody else would. He also said the average person has no idea how much fraud the average person is capable of committing.

"And large corporations?" Lucy once asked. "Allstate? State Farm? How much fraud are they—"

My father beamed.

"The kid gets it!"

The Standard Club for lunch. That plum dining room. Plum carpet, plum walls. There were tall cabinets that reached the ceiling, dishes facing out. There was the Croatian maître d' who'd fooled generations of Chicagoans into believing he was French. At a round table in the far right corner sat the plum-faced judges. They were always there, judicial potted plants. My father would pay his respects. He'd bow and present me.

"Your Honors, my offspring."

And I'd do my saluting-and-checking-the-horizon bit.

Judge Lincoln Marovitz would call out, "Land ho!"

The ancient district court judge, the wild brambles of his eyebrows. Head like a goose egg. The mayor's favorite judge. It was at Mayor Daley's request that President Kennedy appointed him to the federal bench in '63.

"Would you look at this kid? Would you? He's a little Rickover, this kid. The future. Steer the ship, little man, steer the ship."

Abraham Lincoln Marovitz. No kidding. His Lithuanian shtetl parents named him after the American Abe, a very great man. They'd heard he got shot in the temple.

Marovitz told that joke for decades until he wore it out.

In his younger days, Marovitz cut his teeth keeping syndicate bosses like Frank Nitti out of jail, and even then, years later, when we'd stop by his table, there remained a whiff of danger about the old goose egg, which only enhanced his reputation. He wasn't somebody you messed with. There was no more beloved figure in Jewish Chicago. He'd reached the highest heights. And maybe there's a point when you no longer need to be corrupt, when you're so dirty you're clean.

Once, on a Cub Scout trip to Starved Rock State Park, our den leader showed us how to wash dishes with mud.

Judge Marovitz, Judge Hoffman, Judge Edelstein, Judge Klein, Judge Holzer (later convicted in Operation Greylord, bribes, extortion) — all five paragons of the profession cheered for me. And then, with an abrupt chortle, Marovitz was done with us.

"That's enough now."

Lunch at the Standard Club. Roast beef, thick as a radial; big-ass french fries; and orange sherbet. Not necessarily in that order.

And after that, my father and I would walk ten blocks over to the *Sun-Times* building on Wabash. I liked to look at the giant printing presses through the plate-glass windows on the ground floor. They were idle in the afternoon, but there were always pages of today's paper visible on the conveyor belts, and I liked to imagine that somebody had only just shouted, Stop the presses!

Then the elevator to the fifth floor. In deference to Babs, my father (mostly) honored the ban on mentioning the Kupcinets in my grandparents' presence. Yet he'd always remained on cordial terms with Kup. When he was growing up, Kup had always been like an uncle to him. The association never hurt my father professionally. Kup steered business his way, and on occasion, yes, he dropped my father into the column. *Kudos!* **Aubrey Rosenthal** *has been named cochair of the Character and Fitness Committee of the Chicago Bar Association, whatever this means… Queen comedienne* **Phyllis Diller** *is stirring the pot tomorrow at…* My father would knock gently on the door of Kup's office, which was adjacent to the newsroom, and almost immediately it would open. My father must always have called ahead. And there he'd be. These were the only times I ever saw him in person. And like Judge Marovitz, he'd make the same Admiral Rickover joke. The old coot, the old blowhard. Buffoonish worshipper of Bing and Bob and Frank. He'd kneel and kiss me on the head, nuzzling my ear with that big honker of a nose. I wish I could say I'm repulsed by the memory of that fusty cigar breath.

IN THE SUMMER of 1965, Babs and Lou left Chicago. They sold the house at 1114 Fargo Avenue in Rogers Park, a house that had been in the family for three generations. What I'd give to own it again, a house I've never set foot inside. I think of the modest brick two-story with small dormer windows as ours, still. Sometimes I walk by in the middle of the day, open the gate, and plant myself in the patch of grass in the front yard.

They sold the old place on Fargo Avenue and decamped north to Highland Park. Because there were other Jews there. Highland Park had always at least tolerated Jews. There were no restricted covenants like they had in Kenilworth and Winnetka. 1414 Waverly Road! East of Sheridan. Built as a vacation home for a railroad baron, back when they used to make daylong treks in a carriage to get away from the fetid city, it was a ramble of a place with five bedrooms. Vines grew up the sides like the House of Usher. Countless hiding spots. Heavy drapes in the living room you could twist yourself up in like a mummy. A basement with broken storm windows we used to smash. Heavy reek of rot and decay. Lucy said there were bodies buried under the concrete. And an attic that ran the length of the house. An old-fashioned perambulator that had once been my father and Aunt Judith's when they were babies, black hood, big whitewall tires. A little hearse. Lucy would thrust me around in it and bash into the walls.

My grandparents were house-proud. They'd grown up in crowded flats. The moment they married, they'd vowed never again to live in an apartment. 1414 Waverly Road was a lot of house. Maybe too much. For a discreet man who never wanted to attract attention, it was extravagant, a near mansion, even if it was obscured by vines.

Throughout the seventies and into the early eighties, the family gathered on Waverly Road. Babs, I know, especially missed the city, but both my grandparents dearly loved that house. Lou gardened. He grew juicy tomatoes in the side yard. Babs entertained her new suburban friends in the family room with the enormous picture windows.

In the mornings, Lou took the 7:38 train into the city.

Babs taught dance and exercise classes at the rec center. She was a pioneer of aerobics. The first time I ever saw leggings, they were on Babs, not on Jane Fonda.

In the year I was born, 1970, my parents followed Babs and Lou out to Highland Park. No crime! Trees! Clean! Lucy kicked and screamed. At six and a half, she said, *The suburbs? You're dragging me out to a vast cultural wasteland for some trees? There's trees in Lincoln Park.*

After we left, the only Rosenthal remaining within the city limits of Chicago was Uncle Solly.

By the end of 1983, my grandparents had lost the house on Waverly Road and Solly was dead.

LIKE JEWS EVERYWHERE, Chicago Jews like to indulge in our connections to the Mob. Call it a point of ironical pride. We didn't all used to be orthodontists in Northbrook. You should have seen us back in the day when we were real tough. Warsaw ghetto tough. Don't-fuck-with-us tough. In *Kup's Chicago*, Kup writes, "As a columnist on the nightclub beat, I'm often in a peculiar position of figuratively rubbing elbows with the underworld."

Peculiar position? Figuratively?

Kup, you shared a table with Sidney Korshak at the Pump Room for over a decade.

Horseshit aside, he captures the gist. We get a kick out of rubbing certain elbows. Case in point, the delight my father used to take in retelling the Allen Dorfman tennis ball story. Have I told that?

But to be related, directly, to one of these dirtbags?

Solly lacked the necessary distance, which is why this was told only in whispers, if it was told at all. For Lou, in particular, it was deeply shameful. Not so much because of what Solly might have done or not done, but because Lou believed he'd failed in his responsibilities as a brother. He'd hardly known Solly as a kid. And then came college and Babs and the children, my father and Judith, and after them the war...

His big kid brother had had to fend for himself.

WHEN LOU DIED, I went over to the little house on Burton Avenue, the little place by the municipal tennis courts, where Babs and Lou moved after the quick sale of the house on Waverly Road, and, with Babs's permission, stuffed all of Lou's files into grocery bags. Babs said the last thing she wanted to see was whatever was in those files. I must have filled twenty or thirty bags. I've since lugged these files around with me from apartment to apartment, to a house, and back to an apartment. Most of them contain the financial records of long-deceased clients. There's something oddly comforting about columns of numbers representing dollars that don't exist anymore. Isn't money a metaphor, anyway? Your Honor, since cash is only a symbol of value and not actually the value itself, my taking it shouldn't be considered…

Mingled with these client files are manila folders marked "Personal." Lucy's is thick. All her award certificates from Model UN and state and national debate competitions. Articles about her in the school newspaper. Her acceptance letters to Yale, Columbia, Princeton, and the University of Chicago. (She shunned them for Middlebury.) And, of course, clippings from various mentions of my sister over the years in "Kup's Column." *Representing El Salvador at the United*

Nations Invitational in Washington, D.C., wunderkind delegate **Lucy Rosenthal,** *14, argued, successfully, for total world nuclear disarmament and the colonization of Jupiter...*

My file wasn't as thick. Some poems I'd published in the underground literary magazine at the U of I (*The Yawp*). A few mildly positive reviews of *Here Is Eisendrath*. My own two clippings from "Kup's Column." There was a file on my parents' divorce, containing information I didn't need to know. One with Aunt Judith's watercolor paintings, as well as her first application for a driver's license. Another with my father's dismal report cards. There was a file containing a sheaf of Babs's publicity photos from her dancing days. My grandmother and her remarkable contortions. And in one unmarked folder containing a single item, I found Uncle Solly's diploma from Roosevelt College. He'd graduated in 1970 with an associate's degree in commerce. The diploma is printed on very smooth, almost rubbery paper. You can't rip it. Vellum?

There are days like today when I take it out of my desk drawer and rub it.

> *The Board of Directors of Roosevelt College, upon the recommendation of the faculty and by the authority vested by the State of Illinois, hereby confers upon Solomon Rosenthal...*

I couldn't wrap my arms around one of his legs. Like hugging a redwood. He always let me try and then he'd glomp around with me monkeyed to his knee.

He never made good on his degree in commerce. When I

knew him, roughly the first thirteen years of my life and the last thirteen of his, Solly was a custodian at Lane Tech High School on West Addison. Jews didn't come so big, and they also weren't, even in our family's diminished view of itself, janitors. But the very fact that Solly had a steady, ordinary job was in and of itself a relief, especially to Lou.

HE WAS EIGHTEEN. He was having lunch by himself at Fritzel's. Jake Guzik happened to waddle by. A financial virtuoso. They called him Greasy Thumb. A man needs a well-lubricated digit to count all that money. Another story is that when he worked as a waiter, Guzik was so clumsy he'd stick his thumb in the soup. He was a better pimp than waiter. After moving from prostitution to bootlegging to gambling, Guzik rose to become Capone's number two, the highest-ranking Jew in the syndicate. When Dr. Al Brown left town — Capone had lots of aliases; the one he preferred was Al Brown, a podiatrist — Guzik was in charge of the city.

He walked like a penguin wrapped in an inner tube. Guzik hadn't seen his feet in person since the start of the Great War. Never carried a gun. He carried numbers, which were infinitely more powerful. As if some edict had been passed down by the pope. Italians must have at least one whiz-kid Jewboy to handle the income. Don't futz with the money yourselves. The newspapers also called him Little Fella, Top Noodle, Panderer in Chief, the Ogre of Ogden Avenue, Old Bossy Eyes. Guzik called himself Jack Arnold, and he told the Kefauver Crime Committee he was retired.

"Retired from what, sir?"

"I decline to answer on the grounds of my Fifth Amendment right not to criminate myself."

When he paused at Solly's table, the master accountant was in the twilight of his career, having served three years at Leavenworth for tax evasion. Something about my uncle caught his attention. It had nothing to do with Solly's bulk.

"Aren't you a melancholical bastard?"

Solly took a bite out of his corned beef sandwich. He didn't read the papers. He didn't know who Guzik was and he didn't care.

But Guzik knew melancholy. He trusted it. A melancholy man was a man with enough on his mind not to feel the need to stab another man in the back. Because such a man knew that stabbing anybody, even a boss, wouldn't remove the weight, that the weight was existential. Such had been Guzik's experience. Men with what he thought of as an "inner life" tended to be the most loyal. Not that he himself had any use for an inner life, but Guzik considered himself, like any decent pimp, a scholar of human nature.

This one had a droopy hangdog face, but intelligent, sorrowful eyes. What he thought about, which was a lot, he'd never say.

It was 1946. The war was over, but my grandfather was still in the South Pacific. Solly had only recently dropped out of school. He liked to read, but not what anybody told him to read.

He lived with his mother. His father was dead.

Jake Guzik stood there and studied Solly as Solly chewed his sandwich.

"Need anything?"

Here at Fritzel's, beside his table, was a big man, one of the biggest, offering himself up, no strings attached. Strings can wait. Beholden comes with time. Solly Rosenthal examined his sandwich before taking another bite. Guzik stood motionless, hands cradling his pregnant hill of a belly, feet pointing in different directions. The din and clatter quieted. People were starting to notice, and Guzik thought for a moment that this overgrown young ox might be razzing him. At Fritzel's, among his populace, Guzik was accustomed to fealty, if not outright cowering. Some of his goons, scattered across the restaurant, kept their eyes on the boss. *This kid trouble?* No, he's for real, melancholical. Guzik reached into his front pocket for the wallet that protruded like a growth. He always carried a few thousand in cash in case he got kidnapped. With a grunt he tugged out the wallet and peeled off a twenty. He released it so the bill floated gently toward Solly's table and came to rest beside his coffee. Then Jake Guzik waddled onward toward his regular table as diners shifted their eyes to their plates.

FOUR DAYS LATER, two goons, one clean-shaven, the other less so, knocked on the door of my great-grandmother's house on Fargo Avenue. My great-grandmother Willa knew better than to be hoodwinked by their manners. When I knew her she was a savvy old bird with a helmet of white hair that could ram a hole in a wall. At her ninety-seventh birthday party she told me, *Don't slouch. You look like a bum in a train station.* But in 1946 Willa was newly widowed. Solly had no prospects: a gargantuan man-child who mostly moped around the house. Lou was still thousands of miles away, fighting a war that was supposed to be finished. Who was going to take care of Solly when she was gone? She'd live to be ninety-eight, but how could she have known that then? Here were two men who accepted her offer of Frango mints with profuse thanks. They were goons, but they were Jewish goons. How terrible could they be? At his mother's insistence, Solly accepted the job at forty-five dollars a week. After they left, the clean-shaven goon came back and knocked on the door again. He handed Willa an envelope.

"The kid needs a couple of suits. Try Bradford's on South State. Myles makes them big."

ONLY THE TO-AND-FRO of a hoodlum accountant. All he did was drive Jake Guzik as he made his morning rounds of handbook joints across the West Side, from Milwaukee Avenue east to Cicero, to pick up yesterday's take. Guzik was still hands-on. It gave him something to do. Everyone knew that if you paid up and paid up right, Solly Rosenthal wouldn't twist your arm. A lot of guys would twist your arm as soon as look at you. But not Solly. And if you were short, Solly would shoot you a mournful look. That was usually enough for whoever it was to figure out a way to get themselves un-short in short order. Otherwise, yeah, Guzik would pucker his lips and Solly would twist your arm so fast and hard he'd rip a few tendons if not break it clean off. Or at least that happened once. There's a prison record. *Solomon Rosenthal DOB 2/16/28. Assault and Battery (Class B).* He served seven and a half months at Stateville in 1952.

Other days, he'd help Guzik out with the books. Guzik told him he had a good head for numbers and that one day he should split the racket and go back to school, get a degree.

PINK PADDED PAW rises.

Objection.

Please state the nature of your objection.

Your Honor, the idea that big old Uncle Solly was just a big hunk of peaceful vibes is all conjecture. Not a shred of evidence is being offered, aside from a criminal record that would suggest that the sort of behavior in the known conviction was the norm, as opposed to the suggestion above that it was an aberration.

All I know is what I know. Solly drove for Greasy Thumb Guzik.

Isn't your whole point — if you had a point, which you don't — that families lie to themselves, and that these lies get handed down as love —

Listen, mind your own Meow Mix. Either I know what I'm doing, or I don't.

That hasn't engendered confidence thus far and it's been —

I didn't ask you.

You didn't?

Stalks back to his radiator, tail rigid as an antenna, clean little butthole jeering at me.

GUZIK DIED IN 1956. The first reports were that he had a heart attack at an address on Stony Island Avenue. He'd been in bed with his mistress. His wife was in Arizona. The following day, out of deference to the wife, the initial reports were corrected. Jake Guzik, officially, died in his own bed on Fifty-Ninth Street. In his will, he left his favorite chauffeur three thousand dollars and a car, a Mercury Montclair convertible. After the funeral — which was so enormous and chock-full of underworld bigwigs they had to hold it across the city line in Berwyn, lest the Chicago cops be obliged to round up half the mourners — Solly retired.

For years, he ran errands for Lou.

Eventually, he took Guzik's advice and earned his GED. In the fall of 1967, he enrolled at Roosevelt College.

IN 1970 (THE story we tell goes), Solly shocked the family by arriving at Babs and Lou's for Thanksgiving with a woman. Her name was Pauline Haynes. It wasn't so shocking that she was Black, though it wasn't so un-shocking, either. Chicago is Chicago, and, let's be honest, many of its people, then as now, lived in entirely separate universes. But it was the late sixties, early seventies, and all kinds of crazy things were starting to happen, even in segregated Chicago, and Roosevelt, which was founded after the war, was known to be a hotbed of socialism where races mingled — and who knew what else — till all hours.

No, what rocked the family was the fact that Solly had found a woman at all, let alone a pretty one who wore high heels and spoke French like a Parisian.

He'd always kept to himself. He still lived with his mother. Solly? A woman?

The following spring, the two drove to Reno and got married. One last trip in Jake Guzik's convertible. There's nothing harder to imagine than other people's happiness, in this case the decades-old laughs of two people I barely knew.

Still, I like to imagine Solly and Pauline out west. Coasting down a two-lane road with the top down, Pauline's bare feet on the dashboard, and Solly, a man who rarely even smiled, he's outright laughing now. He can't even remember what she said. It was miles back. He's just laughing. Solly Rosenthal is laughing.

AT THE TIME they ran off to Nevada, Solly would have been in his early forties. Pauline was more than ten years younger. My grandparents and my parents encouraged Lucy and, later, me to call Pauline "Auntie Pauline." That's what she was. She was our aunt. But we called Aunt Judith "Aunt Judith." I remember that when we were all together everybody would repeat her name multiple times, in the most ham-handed way. Can I get you another drink, Auntie Pauline? Oh, Auntie Pauline doesn't want to hear that old story again, do you Auntie Pauline? I also recognized the novelty of Pauline being an official member of the family. Showing her my drawings, I'd shriek, "Auntie Pauline, Auntie Pauline, look, my dinosaur had babies!"

We must have been exhausting.

But those times we saw Solly and Pauline together, Thanksgivings, mostly, Pauline was always friendly and laughed a lot. And, we noticed, she touched Solly often. He'd be sitting on the couch in the family room of the old place on Waverly Road, sitting there in his silent way, not smiling but not unsmiling either, and she'd be casually rubbing his forearm or toying with his fingers.

My parents were always at each other's throats.

And Babs and Lou?

Those stoic single beds.

Thinking back, I realize that Solly's marriage was the only one in our family that seemed even vaguely passionate. But what did we know of them? Beyond the holidays? Some relations don't exist beyond the periphery of family, or maybe they don't exist at all until they materialize on Thanksgiving, only to vanish again after a few hours.

Pauline got a job teaching high school French at Lane Tech. Solly got a job at the same school, first as an assistant custodian, and later as the chief custodian.

An interracial couple on the North Side of Chicago in the seventies. They weren't common, but they weren't unicorns, either. It couldn't have been easy. But what I remember most about them is their ease with each other.

As far as I know, nobody in my family, not even Lou or Babs, ever set foot in the apartment that Solly and Pauline shared on North Spaulding, just off West Irving Park Road. They both liked jazz, so maybe at night they'd put on WSDM. Pauline grading papers at the kitchen table while Solly read a book or a magazine borrowed from the school library. Lester Young's on the radio. Or maybe Solly just stares into space, as we sometimes do when we're content and there isn't anything, now, that we want, given what we already have. They never had kids. Who knows where or when it went wrong, or even if it did? If we can't pinpoint such a moment in our own lives, why should we be able to pinpoint it in anybody else's?

MOST LIVES DON'T need close to a thousand words. Obituary writers know this. If you get one at all, at most you get a column, maybe two. If you're luckier you get what? Three hundred and fifty words? Five hundred? Seven hundred and fifty? Also, obituary writers write on deadline. Multitudes get left out, even for the very famous, but a good obituary writer can capture the contours of a life in a few broad strokes. This principle extends to the art of conversation, in which, sometimes, we also practice this sort of concision. Meet an old friend and catch up. How long does it take to get to the crux of it? The basics are exchanged before anybody opens their mouths. The way an old friend sits. Heavily in the chair or with a lighter touch? And then come the highlights. Success versus failure. Love versus its lack. Who died, who didn't.

And all that we can't shape into words, we say with our eyes.

Jed Rosenthal. Born at Michael Reese, Chicago, Illinois. 2/21/70. Mother, Clarice; father, Aubrey; sister, Lucy. Childhood in Highland Park. Lake Michigan. Paternal grandparents, Babs and Lou, a quarter of a mile away. At two and a half, swallowed bottle of paregoric. Stomach pumped. Indian Trail School. Mrs. Gerstad: "Gentlemen and gentle ladies only tie their shoes..." Sailor suit, rather not discuss. Elm Place Junior High. For four straight years remained shortest boy by a number of inches. Highland Park High School. Ran cross-country slowly. Met Rob Preskill ("best friend"). Junior year Lisa Bonetti shared her gum and saliva, not much else. AP English. Mrs. Engerman: "Your handwriting and grammar are atrocious, but you have some not unoriginal ideas." Bless you, Mrs. Engerman. University of Illinois. Virginity eliminated. Blur. Name omitted. C+ on Prufrock essay. Still loathe Eliot. "Let us go then, you and I." Fuck that. Creative writing major. Went to few other classes. Mark Costello, author of *The Murphy Stories,* generous, gruff, gave attention when probably wasn't warranted. Remain grateful. Hanna Abrams. Met in library late sophomore year. Glasses, no-nonsense. Long hair then. Practical ponytail. Theater major with concentration in performance art. Not quick with a smile, which is why when she did... Hanna, Hanna. 403 South Coler Avenue, Apt. 2, Urbana, IL 61801. Two years of nights and mornings. Broke up senior year. *Not saying you're clingy, I mean you are, but that's not*— Graduated. Waited tables in Wicker Park, Buono Fortuna on North Milwaukee (fired for being late for shift multiple times). Eurail pass. Spain. Grew beard. Graduate school, Iowa City. Barely made it out alive. Chicago again. Story in *Atlantic Monthly*. "Kup's Column" mention. First book, 2003 (short stories). Couple nice (short) reviews. Teaching job. Assistant prof. Thanks, Jesuits! Grandfather dies. Second novel tanks but helps tenure case. Close call. By a squeak. Thanks again, Jesuits! Years. Relationships came and went, mostly went. One not quite engagement. At Sovereign on N. Broadway, November of 2016, to drown election sorrows in a PBR. Or three or four or five. Curveball. Hanna Abrams happened to walk into that beloved dive with her friends. All this time, same city. Amazing. What's it been, fifteen years? *More like eighteen.* Jesus. What have you been doing? Still making art? *I'm a psychologist.* No kidding, wow. Married? *No. How about you?* Nope. Almost but nope. (Pause.) You want to meet up? *Sure.* Couple dates. Maybe three, four. Could have been five. *I'm pregnant.* No. Seriously? Really? No way. Honestly? *It happened. I mean something obviously must have—* Wow, that's terrific. I think. No kidding. Amazing, actually. I never thought I'd. I mean, why not? Those nine months. A country of us. Moved to the house on Jarvis. Hanna's father loaned down payment. July 2017, Leah (Snook) born at Northwestern Memorial. Kiddo so cute. Snug in that carrier thing named after a tennis player. But stress? Creeping dissatisfaction? Malaise? Third novel splutters, deadline passes. Publisher doesn't notice. Irritable, morose, sullen. Cat acquired. (Hanna allergies.) April 2019. Hanna: *A parting. A trial…Meanwhile, we co-parent.* What even is that? September 2019. Babs dies. Vague new idea for third book. Oh and yeah, and then an earth-wide pandemic. Hey, listen, now that we're cooped up anyway, why don't we— *Not ready.* Why? *Hard to pinpoint. But what are the tribulations of two relatively privileged people compared with the world as we know it collapsing?* Snook sticks a Lego up her nose at day care. Hour later sneezes it out and into the side of another kid's head. Obsession with Cookie Kupcinet takes further hold. Pretty directionless most days, but an obsession. Somewhere in there, father dies. Begins talking with (not to) the cat. We're about caught up. Died on / / in Chicago.

Who do you think you are? Worst obit ever. You'd flunk out of Medill. Need to cut at least five hundred words but that's not the half of what sucks about it. It reads like you're talking in your sleep.

Also, this cat's got a name.

THANKSGIVING, 1975, AND Solly arrived alone. Midway through the meal (after Lou had delivered his usual speech about the pilgrims), he stood up at the table and tinked his glass with a fork. He'd never done anything remotely like it before.

"Oh, Solly," Babs said. "You'd like to make a toast?"

"An announcement."

"All right, we're listening."

"Pauline has accepted a position at the Interlochen Center for the Arts in Michigan."

"Oh my, that's very prestigious."

"It certainly is," Solly said.

"And you'll be joining her in Michigan?"

At first he smiled at the thought of it. Then he shook his head.

"No."

He clamped his eyes shut and sat down.

The family had always considered Solly a little slow compared with the rest of the Rosenthals. Now I wonder if what we considered slow was simply his way of dodging us.

On those Thanksgivings in the years after Pauline left, he always let on that he was happy to see everybody, but it was clear he was going through the motions. I see him now, his paunch, his sweater vest, how his bulk would dominate the table and still he made so little eye contact. Present and not present. He wasn't a pathetic figure. If that's the portrait I've created, I've failed. He just had a lonely dignity we didn't bother to notice much. My father and sister would be raging about politics. This was after my father became a militant Reaganite. My mother had one foot out the door at that point. Babs was preoccupied; Lou, distant. Aunt Judith, those years, usually remained in Seattle during the holidays.

After dinner, but before dessert, Solly would stand up and say, "Well, it's getting late early."

Then he'd go outside and stuff himself into his Gremlin, the matchbox he drove those years, and drive south, back to the city.

SOLLY LIKED TO drive, even that crappy little car made him happy, but what he loved above all else was to walk. He'd walk for hours. On weekends, he walked all day. He once told Lucy—if he confided in anyone, it was Lucy—that if she wanted to know Chicago, she had to walk it.

"Walk west," he told her. "Away from the lake."

He'd walk with a sandwich in his pocket. He never carried an umbrella. I hardly knew him, and yet lately, this rainy April, I keep having visions of Solly walking. If it started to drizzle, he'd put his coat over his head. A working-class pharaoh loping down the sidewalk along Irving Park Road in the rain. *M* streets. Meade, Moody, Melvina. There's a nice name, Melvina. He stops for a rest on a bench in Merrimac Park before heading south on Narragansett toward the entrance of Mount Olive Cemetery. He's drawn to cemeteries like Ishmael is drawn to the watery parts of the world. The headstones are a comfort. He runs his fingers in the grooves of the names. There are days he feels less alone among the dead than he does out on the streets.

Sometimes he walks even longer, farther west and farther south, to where his parents and my great-grandparents are buried at Waldheim in River Forest. There, he places the stones he's collected along the way on their graves, before turning and heading, once again, for home. It's already late.

In *Blue in Chicago,* Bette Howland writes, "Chicago isn't a city: just the raw materials for a city." This might describe any city, but this city is especially rich in raw materials. Solly Rosenthal might have understood this better than anybody. Block after block he walks, studying the raw materials. The cracks in the sidewalk. The cigarette butts. Broken glass. The places where people imprinted their own shoe prints in what was once fresh concrete. Temporary immortality. He stops at the corner of Lawrence and Harding. There's a check-cashing store. A chow mein place. A Kentucky Fried Chicken. At the Admiral Theater: *Flesh Gordon.* Lights begin to pop on in the apartments above the storefronts. He likes to catch this, the moment when people start to turn on the lights in their apartments.

SOLLY PAUSES HIS mopping. A book on a student's desk has caught his eye, a blue paperback. He squeezes his bulk into the miniature desk as if lowering himself into a cockpit, which strikes him as funny, since the book is *Catch-22*. He's not read it, but he knows it's about war and probably has a fair share of cockpits. He wonders for a moment about the etymology of the word *cockpit*. Like his brother, Lou, he's always been interested in the origin of words, a trait both brothers inherited from their mother who'd come to Chicago from a place called Shershev in Poland and taught herself English by pestering her neighbors with questions and writing down their answers in a small black notebook she carried with her everywhere.

Solly opens the book to a dog-eared page in the middle and reads a paragraph the student has underlined. It's about an army chaplain who has the sensation that he's seen this naked man in a tree before, at some other time, in some other existence.

I ought to read this one from the beginning.

* * *

Déjàvu. French, of course. He didn't need Pauline to tell him that. Still, what wouldn't he give to be able to ask her about it? Not call her up. He's got her number. He can call her.

To ask her in the kitchen.

Some nights he goes into the kitchen for a glass of water and sees Pauline at the table reading with her glasses on. She could read for an hour straight and not look up once. A hallucination? Or does the fact that she used to sit like that with a book in her hand and glasses nudged toward the end of her nose suggest that she's left behind some physical presence that is not entirely fantastical?

Can I ask you a question.

What is it?
Déjàvu? How do the French fit all that into one word?
It's two words.
Oh.

He's got three more classrooms to finish. Then the gym.

How It Was Done in Chicago

> Everybody has a little larceny in them.
> — *Sonny Capone, who ripped off the line
> from Bing Crosby*

NOT EVERYONE IS on the take in Chicago. The whole point of being on the take is there's people who aren't. A crooked city needs its straights to uphold its reputation. Lou Rosenthal had always been one of the do-gooders. A lawyer who played by the rules as laid down by men who didn't always follow them themselves.

He believed that laws were greater than the imperfect men who made them.

When it turned out that Lou himself was one of the imperfect men, it might have stunned us, but not Lou. True, as the guilty party, it couldn't have. But also this: Lou had never held himself up to be any more righteous than anybody else. When he tipped his imaginary hat to other lawyers on LaSalle Street, it wasn't from a position of higher moral authority.

Rosenthals, it goes without saying, don't have the height to look down on anybody. (My father would have if he could have.)

By the standards of today's white-collar crime, the allegations against my grandfather were almost quaint. As a probate attorney, he had unfettered access to trust accounts. What he did was move money from some of these accounts, beyond his regular fees, into a personal account.

An individual scheduled by law to become, in time, a beneficiary of one of these accounts noted some "discrepancies" in the accounting. This individual notified the Illinois Bar, which notified the state's attorney, which began an investigation.

This is my understanding of what happened. I've never been able to track down any records, though whatever evidence might still exist is probably hidden in the columns of numbers in Lou's files.

More than anything, I remember how he wore the trouble on his face. Lou got ruddier, maybe from rubbing his face so much, as if he was trying to erase himself. He may not have been self-righteous, but he was still Lou Rosenthal. To the family and to everybody else. He'd always had such a flawless reputation. In his business, any whiff of impropriety was enough to disgrace him. There didn't need to be an indictment. Yet. Lou, quietly, and with deliberation, closed up shop. He sold his half of the law firm to his partner. He announced to Babs and the rest of the family that he'd be selling Waverly Road. With all deliberate speed. That's the term he used.

All deliberate speed.

He needed ready cash to cover the "discrepancies," which were, according to my father, upward of at least a few hundred thousand dollars. And, as far as I know, he did cover those discrepancies. But the damage was done.

What had he been up to?

A girlfriend? Prostitutes? Gambling? I don't know. I'll never know.

Once, after Lou's death, I asked my father. He howled with fake laughter.

"A smoking gun? The old man loved money as much as the rest of us. You're still buying the old Robert Lincoln crap. What did Abe's kid say? 'I get drunk off math'? Here's the math. Money evaporates. Embezzled money vanishes even faster."

"Embezzled?"

"Go ahead, search for a milder term. That's what you want, right?"

"Borrowed?"

"That's fine. It's just not accurate."

MY CONJECTURE IS he was in the hole. He couldn't afford 1414 Waverly Road. In today's market, the house is valued by Redfin at $1.8 million. In 1983, it might have been worth half that, and in 1965 even less. Still serious Chicago money, and Lou never had serious Chicago money. Nobody in our family ever has, though my father used to make false claims.

Lou might have been in over his head from the beginning.

Here's what I think. In 1965, when Babs and Lou exiled themselves to Highland Park, Lou was determined to do it in some style, to leave the old life behind them. If it took multiple mortgages over the years, mortgages he could barely pay, so be it.

THE NEW HOUSE on Burton Avenue wasn't any happier than our house, but it was a lot quieter. By 1983, my mother was sleeping in the guest room with the door locked. My father would stand out in the hall and rattle the knob and shout in whispers and my mother would say, *Stop shouting,* and my father would shout, *I'm not shouting!*

No need to dwell on this. And the scenes in our house weren't any different from the scenes in who knows how many other houses. I was in eighth grade. Lucy was already gone to Middlebury. After school, since I didn't do any sports, I'd walk to Babs and Lou's.

Even before Lou's trouble, any expectation of mutual happiness between Lou and Babs, notwithstanding the good years on Waverly Road, had long since dimmed. But there was never hostility — the opposite. For as far back as I could remember, Babs and Lou had loved each other out of familiarity and routine. They led separate lives under one roof. It's not the worst kind of love. Don't a lot of people spend a significant portion of their lives getting by this way?

NOT QUIETER, BURTON Avenue was silent. Lou's trouble not only squeezed them into a much smaller space, it seemed to shrink the number of words they said to each other, which were never that many in the first place. It was like they were on a tiny island and they retreated to either side of it. Lou at the kitchen table going over his financial statements and talking to his lawyers, and Babs in their bedroom, either on the exercycle or sitting at her dressing table or reading in the big green leather chair in the room Babs and Lou always called the library on Waverly Road. Now he had no study, no library, and the entire house on Burton Avenue was crowded with furniture like that green leather chair, pieces that Babs and Lou were too nostalgic to sell. There was a spare bedroom you couldn't walk into, it was so packed with couches and chairs and stacked tables. Though neither ever said as much, I think both believed the move was only temporary.

I'd go over to Burton Avenue after school and Lou would be at the kitchen table, rubbing his face. And Babs, who'd rarely cooked for him, would stick something in the microwave for a late lunch.

THEY FOUND SOLLY floating facedown in the north branch of the Chicago River. They fished him out near Goose Island. What Solly was doing in the Chicago River should have been the subject of more speculation. Nobody swims in the Chicago River. If the fish had a choice and could opt out, they would. In any case, according to Lou, Solly had never learned to swim.

Either he put himself in that water with no intention of coming out of it, or someone else did.

July of 1983. Though Lou's legal trouble seemed to have passed, he and Babs were still struggling to adjust to their circumscribed lives. My parents were finally splitting up. I was thirteen, which itself is havoc. Nobody wanted to dwell on the past, and Solly, the idea of Solly, really, belonged to another time. Things were collapsing, for worse and better, and there wasn't a lot of space for mourning a man who'd become a ghost to us years earlier.

That summer, too, the entire city of Chicago was seething. A vicious race for mayor. Harold Washington versus Bernie Epton. No such thing as a general election in Chicago. Unless the Democrat is Black and suddenly a little Republican Jew isn't a joke.

Solly's death was essentially a distraction from everything else that was going on.

The police said they had no evidence of any foul play. It had been a hot day, mid-eighties. A simple explanation was arrived at. Solly had only wanted to cool off, and in the course of dousing his face with river water, he must have slipped.

Cool off? In that sludge?

That was the story.

Lou drove downtown to the Cook County morgue on Harrison Street. Solly's body was swollen beyond recognition. Still, he knew immediately who it was, as if in the back of his mind he'd already pictured Solly just like that, laid out on a table, bloated with river water.

I was at my grandparents' when Lou came home.

"There wasn't a sheet over him," he told Babs.

My head was in the refrigerator, but I was listening.

"Isn't there supposed to be a sheet? City of Chicago can't afford a sheet to pull over a man who was born here, died here?"

SATURDAY IN MAY, warm, sort of, when the wind lulls a little, and I pick up Snook and we go buy some bread and cheese and a Hershey bar with almonds, and we make a little picnic on the beach at Loyola Park. An impromptu picnic, we've got no blanket. Snook says she doesn't like almonds. Why did I get chocolate with almonds? There's an Andre Dubus story called "The Winter Father" where a recently divorced dad on a picnic with his two kids thinks, I've become a winter father. Being a winter father means something specific to the father in the story. I don't remember what exactly, but it must have to do with being the sort of father I've become, a more distant one. A Wednesday-night father? "You can eat the chocolate and spit the almonds out," I say. "Like this. See? The chocolate's still the chocolate." "That's disgusting," Snook says. I tickle her and she laughs, and I laugh. We've become good at pretending we're having a good time. We've become decent actors, the two of us. Technically, I'm not at all a winter father. I'm at least an every-other-day father. I drive Snook to pre-K. I pick Snook up from pre-K. Swimming. Art lessons. Gymnastics. The park. The beach. Ice cream. Pizza. Spaghetti. She sleeps at the apartment at least two nights a week, sometimes three. She plays with Rudy when he deigns to allow her to. She draws at the kitchen table. She watches *Minions*. She's got a legion of stuffies here. She brought them in a suitcase. The living room looks like a zoo gift shop.

Winter fathers.

In *Kup's Chicago,* Kup writes that when his son, Jerry, was born, he was at Toots Shor in Manhattan gathering copy for a column. He also says that though he doted on Cookie (and Jerry, Jerry is always in parentheses), when you're out six, seven nights a week, you miss a lot.

Lou, too. He spent much of my father's and Aunt Judith's childhoods away at the war. And even after, he was more distant from his children than he was from his grandchildren.

Solly?

Solly was never a father.

But isn't an uncle a kind of winter father?

Snook and I at the beach. She keeps telling me to stop scribbling and dig.

"Dig, Dadda, dig."

"One sec, honey. One sec."

A BRIEF FUNERAL at Pritzger's in Skokie. Lou found a young, unaffiliated rabbi just out of seminary (none of us belonged to a temple anymore) to officiate. Lucy called him a rent-a-rabbi. We were all waiting to see if Pauline would show up, and she did, a bit after the rabbi started to speak, with a small boy in tow. She wore a brown business suit and flat shoes. When she took off her glasses — a few prayers and the service was over — her eyes were wet. She wasn't crying. It was as if she was storing up her tears for later. Wishful thinking (we pretended not to notice the ring), but Lucy and I couldn't help but believe, if only for a few moments, that the boy might be Solly's son. A lost son we hadn't known was lost. The child was three, maybe four; the math didn't work out. Nobody asked any questions. Pauline hugged everyone, brief, efficient hugs, but they weren't without a genuine squeeze of affection. The little boy shook hands with everybody, one by one.

One of Pritzger's assistants, a pimpled kid that didn't look old enough to have a license, drove Solly out in the hearse to Waldheim Cemetery, unaccompanied.

Pauline and her son didn't come back to the little house on Burton Avenue for cold cuts.

HE WAS THERE. That's part of it. Maybe most of it. He was there in December of 1963 when Irv and Lou went to Los Angeles to bring Cookie's body home. Had Solly not joined them on that trip, it might have gone worse, if such a thing were possible. Lou, on his own, might not have managed to get Irv back on the plane to Chicago.

"Dadda."

"Be right there, honey. Just one more note about Cookie—"

"What cookie? Where are the cookies?"

"No, Cookie's a person."

"You're making it up."

"No, Cookie's real, I mean—"

"Where is he then?"

"No, Cookie's a she. Not that it. Hang on."

Cookie and Solly. Now, in my mind at least, they've joined the same long, sad parade.

In life they hardly knew each other. Solly might have remembered Cookie as a laughing little girl. Cookie, of course, would have recognized his face from those times the two families got together. And his size. He would have been hard to miss even if she'd only barely glanced at him. Uncle Lou's brother. His name? It might have gone in one ear and out the other.

The Gossip Columnist's Daughter

This was a kid who'd ridden on Gary Cooper's shoulders. Mae West read her "The Three Little Pigs." James Cagney, Katharine Hepburn, W. C. Fields, Wallace Beery, Marlene Dietrich, Jean Harlow, Harpo Marx— Enough with these fucking lists already.

Solly Rosenthal?

It occurs to me now that he was the single person in our family who never made it into "Kup's Column." *What a way to shine,* **Solomon Rosenthal** *was named custodian of the year at the National Conclave of Custodians held biannually in Wichita...* **Sonny Bono,** *blah, blah, blah...*

"Dadda—"

"Yeah, honey?"

"This is so boring and I'm hungry."

FOR A WHILE, I thought, without saying it out loud, that eventually Lou might be heading for some jail time. That either he'd go on trial or he'd plead guilty to at least one felony or another. Not to Stateville. Some minimum-security, white-collar place where he could wear his own clothes and garden.

I'd call Lucy up at school, but she didn't want to talk about it. She told me to get my head out of my ass. "The sun doesn't rise and set with our damn family. We're descending into barbarism. What kind of superpower invades Grenada? Talk about imperialist dick wagging."

And then poof. Nothing happened.

I only learned later that Lou had quietly, without fanfare, voluntarily surrendered his license to practice law. But the trouble itself seemed to vanish. All the whispers of impending charges. The sale of the house, the constant talking to lawyers. The stacks of files on the kitchen table of the little house on Burton Avenue.

Nothing. No indictment was ever handed down.

Lou was still broke. But the threat was over. Lou carried the files down to the basement.

The following month, my grandfather swallowed whatever pride he might have had left and went to work for my father as a file clerk.

He needed the money.

IN THE SOVEREIGN on North Broadway, there's a bulletin board on the south wall with photographs pinned to it. The pictures are all faded and curling at the edges. Even so, the faces are alive with laughter, as if the past was all camaraderie and hilarious romp. Arms around each other, hoisting high cans of Pabst.

It's a place you want to be, back in the 1990s with these effortlessly happy people.

I imagine all those connections have long since been severed by death or moving away or betrayal or the ordinary exhaustion of just working and living. I've never seen any of these faces at the bar, or maybe I just don't recognize them because it was all so long ago and everybody's older now and looks different. I sit at the table closest to the bulletin board and look at a group picture of a motley softball team — a woman sitting in front holds an eighteen-inch softball in two hands like an offering.

With this oversize softball I bestow upon you eternal life.

SOLLY WAS THE last of us to be buried at Waldheim.

Lou, Babs, my father, and Aunt Judith are all buried north — at Memorial Park in Skokie.

Chicago Jews equate the north with progress. To go west is to go backward.

Waldheim is directly west of the Loop. Shortly before his death in 1945, my great-grandfather Max was worried that by the time Solly, the surprise child of his old age, passed away, there might not be anybody around to make the arrangements.

Maybe Maxie had a vision of a Rosenthal in a pauper's grave.

He bought Solly a plot and gave the deed and plot number to Lou for safekeeping.

To get to Waldheim you can take the Eisenhower Expressway to Harlem Avenue. Or you can go the long way and simply drive west on Madison, away from the lake, the direction Solly used to head on his solitary walks, for eleven miles of stop-and-go traffic, until you reach a vast, flat expanse, a throwback to the prairie that was once this city. It's a land of forgotten Jews, of headstones flush with the grass. The stones are arranged in small ghettos, often enclosed by a sagging, dilapidated fence. Every Jewish enclave in Chicago used to have multiple burial societies, sometimes there were three or four on the same block. For a small monthly fee that built up principal over time, you'd receive a plot and perpetual care. Waldheim isn't one cemetery, it's hundreds.

A few years ago, I went out there, but the office was closed and I didn't have a map. I thought I knew roughly where Solly was, on the south side near the wall that separates the cemetery grounds from a shopping center parking lot. It was March. There'd been a thaw. The snow had mostly melted. Headstones flush with the grass. No trees. Soggy, uneven ground. Name after name after name after name stretching up a small rise that wasn't quite a hillside. All the graves that weren't Solly's.

WE WERE NEVER a picture-taking family, and whenever we did take pictures on Thanksgiving at the house on Waverly Road, Solly either fled to the bathroom or, at the last second, managed to step out of the frame.

So, no, there aren't any photographs of Solly Rosenthal, and aside from the degree from Roosevelt and his grave (which I still can't find), there doesn't seem to be any other trace of his name anywhere. At the Cook County Clerk's Office, I did manage to unearth Solly's birth certificate. No first name. It says only: Baby Rosenthal. My great-grandparents hadn't chosen his name yet. Maybe they were still getting over the shock of his arrival and how big he was.

I've noticed something about certain physically large people. How sometimes they are abashed about how much space they occupy. Solly was one of these people. When he'd duck through a doorway, he'd apologize, as if he'd offended the doorway. We must have seemed so Lilliputian to him, and yet he moved among us deferentially. He left early, but he arrived early, too, and in his unobtrusive way would always help Babs set the table for Thanksgiving.

ABOUT A YEAR and a half ago, I tracked down Pauline. It took less than four seconds. She's since retired but at the time she taught in the French department at Johns Hopkins. I called her office and left a voice mail. About three hours later, she called me back.

"Little Jeddy!"

"Auntie Pauline!"

"I bought one of your books. I haven't gotten around to reading it yet. You know how it is. You teach, too, right?"

"I make a pretense."

"That's half of it anyway. Good god, it's been, what, forty years?"

"Something like that."

"Not possible."

We both took a breath.

I had an image of her rubbing Solly's forearm in a house that's long since been sold.

Now her voice? Her laughter? Eons away.

She asked about the family. I told her Babs and Lou were both gone. Babs just a couple of years ago at one hundred and one. My father, too.

"A hundred and one! Tough that woman. Always kept things close."

"I've got a daughter."

"Mazel tov."

"And your son?"

"Anthony's in New Zealand. Couldn't get far enough away from me. A programmer, but isn't everybody? Unmarried, still playing the field. He's having a fine time. I'm heading over there for a long visit, three weeks. He says he's looking forward to it, but we'll put that to the test."

When I asked her about Solly, she said she'd rather not talk about him, if I didn't mind.

Of course I didn't. Not knowing what else to say, I said, "It's nice to hear your voice, Auntie Pauline."

She laughed again, and four decades vaporized. Maybe that second "Auntie" shook something loose.

"You know Sol never wanted children. He loved them. He loved you and Lucy, but underfoot all the time? No chance."

"Is that why you two —"

"No."

"I don't mean to be invasive."

"You don't? But I'm the one who said I wouldn't and then — Do I think of him? Yes, I do. I do think of Sol."

We talked for a little while longer, neither of us wanting to be the one to hang up first. We both knew, even though we said otherwise, we probably wouldn't talk again.

Like a dolt, I repeated, "Nice to hear your voice, it really — "

Times you only say what you mean the second time you say it?

"Nice to hear yours, Little Jeddy."

In the Cold

I WOKE UP this morning thinking about *The Book of Laughter and Forgetting*. Milan Kundera died yesterday. The only thing I remember is the beginning. That's not a knock.

How many books do we forget completely? Pages upon pages that once held our attention, maybe our emotions, and not a shred remains?

The premier of the Czechoslovak Communist Party is giving a speech to a large throng of the party faithful. It's the anniversary of something or other. It's also the dead of winter, and the premier, whatever his forgettable name was, is hatless. A devoted underling is standing behind him. His name I do remember.

Clementis.

Here, boss, take my hat.

Clementis hands over his own hat in order to protect the far more important head from getting a chill. In the official photograph that marked the occasion, a picture widely distributed to the public, the premier is wearing a hat, while Clementis stands behind him, beaming, proudly bareheaded.

A few years later, Clementis is tried, convicted, and shot for being an enemy of the state. Spy for the West. Traitorous dog. Capitalist pig wallowing in shit.

The photo has to be corrected and redistributed. Clementis is edited out of history. Only his hat remains.

IN *A MAN, AN ERA, A CITY,* Kup writes that he and Essee would never have survived their darkest days if not for "the constant love of our real friends." He goes on to say that what he remembered best from that agonizing time was what Sidney Poitier said when he first phoned after hearing of the tragedy.

Even in this context, Kup can't look away from the opportunity to brag about knowing Sidney Poitier.

And the Rosenthals? Excised out of the public record. And the tens of thousands of words of "Kup's Column" and the two bloviating books that comprise his oeuvre, to use a dumbass English department word, are a public record.

In the years I've been trying, in fits and starts, to tell this, whatever this is, missing deadline after deadline, filling one notebook after another with stray notes, I've often thought there has to be a reason this isn't going anywhere. The culprit can't possibly be (only) my obvious lack of skill.

A conscience? Any conscience I've got left is roadkill.

I've said it already. I've never had much of a problem exploiting family wounds for a story.

Kup was a lightweight, especially as a friend; Essee a caricature of a Midwestern Marie Antoinette. They were also two parents with holes blown through their hearts.

I've got a daughter. She's asleep in the next room on a cot. Or she will be? What day is it?

But answer this: Who comforted Irv and Essee Kupcinet in real time, between November 30 and December 3, 1963?

It wasn't, with all respect to a noble man, Sidney fucking Poitier.

We write for all kinds of reasons, don't we, including out of anger, revenge, to settle an old score. My grandmother sprained her ankle rushing into 257 East Lake Shore Drive on the evening of November 30, 1963.

I'll ask it again. Who comforted the comforters?

Services for Miss Kupcinet will be held at 2 p.m. today at Temple Sholom, 3480 Lake Shore Dr., with private burial in Memorial Park Cemetery, Skokie. Her father asked that, in lieu of flowers, donations be sent to La Rabida Children's Sanatorium, Jackson Park, or to the Actors Fund of America, 612 N. Michigan Ave. There will be no visitation.

RABBI BINSTOCK HAS been droning on for at least the last forty minutes. For a while now he's just been talking to talk, to fill the space. He's forgotten the other woman's name. It's as if with her big eyes she's beseeching him to say something even remotely useful. But after a certain point, what can a rabbi say? Also, it's close to time.

He rises and says, "Take as long as you need, Essee."

"As long as I need?"

Binstock knows better than to respond. He's in the business. There are days when he conducts three funerals. Temple Sholom has twenty-five hundred members. Sometimes he has to hustle along mourners at one funeral to make room for the fresh ones coming in for the next. When his own mother died, he rushed the service. You can't clog the pipeline.

Tomorrow and tomorrow and tomorrow.

Anguish centers in the eyes. In some, like Essee's, there's undiluted hate.

The other woman clings to her.

The rabbi nods, says nothing, withdraws.

LOU DRAPES HIS overcoat on the seat next to him. He's in the second row, directly behind Irv, who's also sitting next to a vacant chair. Jerry Kupcinet is one seat away.

Irv's gasping for breath he can't catch. For Lou, the sound of Irv trying to squelch his sobs is worse than the sobs themselves. Jerry, nineteen and gangly and pimpled, numbed by his sister's death, reaches a hand toward his father across the vacant chair. He reaches, but not all the way. He wants his father to reach for him, too. Irv can't do it, and his inability to simply clasp his son's hand intensifies his sobs.

Lou watches, his own hands twitching uselessly inside his suit jacket pockets. What he'd give to reach over himself and gently squeeze the back of Jerry's neck.

The crowd is dense, there's hardly a free seat left in the house. All these people but so few voices. Nobody speaks. Only the noise of shuffling feet. Irv's sobs are amplified by the sanctuary's acoustics. Lou thinks: Why should this most private of experiences be such a public spectacle? Not all ritual is rational. He wonders about the origin of the funeral. Must have to do with those braggy pharaohs.

The hush tightens. Anxious feet are stilled.

Essee is making her way down the center aisle slowly,

each small step unsteady. Babs walks beside her, but slightly behind, one hand cupping Essee's left elbow.

A few times Essee stumbles.

Babs, if not for Babs.

People stare straight ahead but they all watch Essee out of the edges of their eyes as she passes row after row.

THE PAPERS WILL write about who attended. Mayor Daley, and Otto Kerner, the governor. Bob Hope and his wife, Dolores. Was Sinatra present? There were reports, never confirmed, that his private jet landed at Meigs Field earlier in the day and he might have been one of a number of men wearing a dark suit and dark glasses, standing in the back. No reporter ever got close enough to make sure.

Elizabeth Taylor was out of the country.

Neither Jerry Lewis nor Sidney Poitier attended.

Sidney Korshak was present. He was another of the men in dark glasses standing by the exits. His presence wasn't noted by reporters, at least in print.

What people who were in the synagogue that day would remember, including my parents, who were somewhere deep in that crowd, was how long it took for Essee to reach her seat. All eyes had been upon her.

IF IT IS cruel to say that Essee was performing at Temple Sholom, so be it. But isn't all mourning on some level a performance? How are we supposed to know how to behave? There's so little time to figure it out. One moment you're at a forgettable function at a Sara Lee plant, the next —

We can't rehearse. In the moment, we act. We have to do something. We've seen other people act it out before. It's not that we don't feel anything, it's that we don't know what to do with our eyes, our hands. Even if we're by ourselves, alone in a room, we act.

Public grief? On some level isn't it always a spectacle?

Everybody's watching.

Think of Abraham and Isaac. Isn't Abraham posturing before the ultimate audience?

Check me out, Yahweh. I've got a bad back, bad knees. I'm wearing these crappy sandals. Yeah and I'm, as you know, at least a hundred and ten goddamn years old, but I'm doing it, I'm trudging up Mount Moriah for you, big guy, for you. And look, my kid, he's right here by my side.

HOW FAR IT is, how far, the green carpet unscrolls endlessly beneath her shoes. Babs grips the ball of her elbow. The mourners, the stars, the mayors, the governors hold their breath and watch. Who's the woman with her? Essee has a sister?

AND THEN IT'S over and a horde surges forward toward Irv and Essee. "Turkey vultures," my grandfather mutters. "They want their meat."

Together, Babs and Lou move toward the center aisle and methodically work their way around the perimeter of the crowd to where Irv and Essee are standing. With patience and confidence in their position as insiders, they wait for an opening so they, too, can lean over and pull their friends close, but they won't say anything, because what is there left to say?

All these people with nothing to say and such a savage need to say it.

Something happens. After about ten minutes or so, as the cluster of VIP mourners, including the mayor and Governor Kerner, begins to fall away, a new circle, one of intimates, begins to form around Irv and Essee.

Bob and Dolores Hope, Sidney and Bea Korshak, Russ and Millie Stewart, and a few others, close Chicago friends, the Zelniks, the Feldmans, the Poskowitzes, the Baumgartens, close but no couple as close as —

And still Lou and Babs Rosenthal wait for a gap to allow them to move toward their friends. It never forms. The encircling holds, and the whole of the group begins to move as one, an amoeba-like cell with Irv and Essee making up the nucleus, toward the center aisle and the exit. Lou and Babs follow the amoeba but there's no penetrating this wall of other intimates. Finally, Lou looks at Babs, for what he isn't sure. Affirmation of what's happening? Commiseration? She provides neither. It's as if Babs saw this coming a long way away. The resignation in her eyes is serene. Not a gloat, just a fact. What's happened hasn't caught her unawares. The expression on her face is one I remember from when I was a kid. Babs always had this unperturbable calmness. Never raised her voice. Never exclaimed when she was surprised, because nothing ever surprised her, especially bad news. She didn't seem capable of being blindsided.

She had a way of knowing anything before you told her. I'd flunk a test. Lose a game. A girlfriend. Years later, a family. Babs is gone and I still see the expression on her face. Eyes wide, mouth gripped tight. You didn't see this coming? Really?

"Let's go to Skokie," Babs says.

Because, whether the circle opens or not, it isn't as if they can skip the burial. Weren't they Cookie's godparents? Yet for the next couple of minutes, neither moves, and I think of Babs and Lou standing together as the synagogue empties out. Together but separate, like two near strangers waiting for a bus in the cold.

LONELINESS FUCKS WITH time, and the seasons, like the days and the weeks, tumble together, and it's January 13, 2024, the morning after a major snowstorm, the city pummeled into silence. All so white. Like somebody's pulled a clean sheet over the streets. A white, white stillness. The other day I overheard a docent at the Art Institute talking about a painting called *Brilliant Yellow #9*. The painting is white, and the docent explained that the color white encompasses all colors. *We just don't know we're seeing them. It's a difficult concept that has to do* — She caught me edging in on her group, a jackass who didn't pay extra for the tour. I backed away.

This morning, I take her word for it. Lot of colors in this white.

I leave the apartment and defile the unplowed streets by making tracks straight down the center. The cars lumpish sculptures of cars. There's this muffling. As if the entire city has gone into sudden hibernation. Chicago as Moominvalley.

When I reach Jarvis, Hanna and Snook are already outside. Hanna's shoveling the walk. She's wearing an old blue hat of mine. Wilmot Mountain, circa 1978. Big blue-and-white pom-pom bobs as she dumps a pile of snow. Snook, in her one-piece snowsuit and little moon boots, is doing half angels, arms only, on the sidewalk, or where the sidewalk would be. I'm a cameo. I stand in the street and wait for one of them to notice.

EASIER AT THE cemetery. Weird, here you feel less like an outcast. Who's more left out than the dead? Lou imagines hands rising out of the ground and trying to grab the ankle of a mourner walking past.

Stop a moment. Wouldn't you at least read my name?

Theodore H. Spinner.

Emma Rubin.

Isaac Feldberg.

And mine?

And mine?

Lou and Babs at the graveside. They can't see past all the people in front of them. It's cold, gusty. The pale sky can't be distinguished from the color of the old snow on the ground. The little tent they've set up for the family is flapping. Nobody can hear the rabbi as he shouts the ancient prayers into the wind.

When the time comes, Lou joins the line of other men and takes up the shovel, digs a bit, and drains the half shovelful of dirt and stones onto the casket.

Describe this sound, the stones.

They don't wait around for Irv and Essee this time. Instead, Lou and Babs walk a couple of rows west, to the plot

Lou purchased only a few years back. A treeless spot about thirty yards away from Cookie's still-open grave.

Irv and Lou bought plots at the same time. As close as they could get. Kupcinets and Rosenthals were going to be near neighbors for all time. Rosenthal is already chiseled on the family stone.

They use machines now, Lou thinks. Have for a century, probably. It's why all the names look alike.

THE MORNING AFTER Cookie's funeral, December 4, 1963, Essee called down to the doorman on the intercom.

"Puck."

"Yes, Mrs. Kupcinet?"

"Please tell Barbara I don't live here anymore."

When Babs arrived at 8:15, Puck, standing in front of the Kups' private elevator, delivered the line verbatim. Puck was like that. You asked him to do something, he did it.

"Please tell Barbara I don't live here anymore."

He said it so fast, Babs didn't catch the meaning at first.

"What? She's not home?"

Now Puck only looked at her. The old man, his uniform, his elegant white mustache with the little twists on the ends. Lou always said he looked like an old Prussian general from the Great War. Puck stood by the private elevator as if he was guarding it, and in a way he was. He was guarding the elevator from Babs.

How many years had Puck waved her through the lobby (white marble floor, a row of small chandeliers, a black leather couch nobody ever sat on) with a whoosh of both his arms like he was ushering her onto a stage?

Barbara? Even calling her Barbara was a deep cut. Nobody called Babs Barbara. Just as nobody called Essee Esther.

Puck, standing between Babs and the elevator, tried to be kind.

"It's an aftershock," he said. "It's likely an aftershock."

BABS AND ESSEE never spoke to each other again.

Essee died in 2001.

IN THE FIRST column he published in the *Sun-Times* after Cookie's death, Kup writes about how a few weeks earlier he'd groped for words to describe the majesty of Jackie Kennedy at her husband's funeral. Now he's groping for words again, this time to describe the majesty of another young —

    The whole city mourned with him. There's not any question.

The other day, the medievalist across the hall said something that cut to the bone.

    There is no medievalist across the hall.

    What?

    He's a fiction, an imaginary friend —

    Professor O'Connor? Frank?

    — barely even a friend since you usually forget he even exists, which makes sense given that he doesn't —

    True, I've never seen his face in person, but that's because he still wears a mask all the time. We hired him over Zoom during the pandemic. He calls me the Unabomber, I call him the Lone Ranger. Maybe he's got an autoimmune issue. Imaginary friend? What are you if he's —

I'm all you've got. I'm Lou to your Irv, circa 1963.

Can I go on?

I'm stopping you? I weigh twelve pounds.

Frank asked me what I was working on. We were talking in the hall, this was last spring. Or fall. Or — So I told him about the rift, again. He'd heard it all already. He indulged me, as he does. But this time he tugged at the bottom of his mask like it was a beard (maybe he's got one under there) and said, "Your grandparents were with these people in the very worst moment of their lives. Wouldn't Irv and Essee have been reminded of it every time they saw them? Doesn't it make absolute sense that they'd drop them like old shoes?"

I'VE ALSO HEARD it said that friendships do not survive the death of a child. After a loss like that, what's a lesser loss? I can also see the inconsolable need for Irv and Essee to believe (whether either one of them ever believed it or not) it was murder. Even a violent death at the hands of a lover or a stranger would have been preferable to suicide. What could it possibly have mattered that other people, even people they loved, got hurt?

IN "KUP'S COLUMN" dated January 31, 1964, Kup quotes a rival columnist, Mike Connolly, who wrote in the *Hollywood Reporter* that Elizabeth Taylor and Richard Burton had been spotted chatting up Irv Kupcinet and his wife, Essee, the other night at Chasen's. Taylor and Burton had, according to Connolly, SOS'd them over to their table. "Please join us, we're the friendless ones..."

Kup sets the record straight. Taylor and Burton had extended the invitation not because they were the friendless ones, but in order to express their condolences. He goes on to explain that the two stars had been on the set of *The Night of the Iguana* when they heard the news about Cookie. The cast was so distraught they called off filming for the day.

The night the Kupcinets were at Chasen's, Babs and Lou were in Rogers Park, getting ready to go out. Babs was sitting at her dressing table finishing her makeup. Lou, already dressed, was in what Lou's mother had always called the parlor, reading John Galsworthy's *The Forsyte Saga*. They had dinner plans that night with some friends. The L. Woods Tap in

Lincolnwood. It wasn't Chasen's but it was somewhere. Best baby back ribs in Chicago.

Babs had been making a point of them going out lately.

"Lou?" she called out.

"Yes?"

"Are you ready?"

"Who are we meeting?"

"The Nussbaums."

"Again?"

Even if they'd still been in their good graces, they wouldn't have been at Chasen's in Hollywood. But Babs would have been in the know. That's what would weigh on her over the years. How they'd talk. How they'd gabble on for hours. Essee would have called her the next morning, or maybe even that night, to tell her what Liz was wearing and how much she'd had to drink and what she'd eaten and how much of it and how heavy she looked or didn't look.

THE ANNUAL FISHING trip to Bimini. Before Kup and his friends departed, he'd always publish a column trumpeting the fact that he and some select fellow sailors had just received orders from Combinex to ship out at 0800 hours tomorrow. Combinex, he'd explain, was navy talk for the commander of the Bimini Expedition. And Combinex himself was none other than *esteemed Loop solicitor* **Lou Rosenthal,** *an ex-war hero who still lapses into the lingo from his days as a captain of an LST in the Pacific theater...*

And the impending mission was always, every year, so fraught with danger that Combinex ordered his shipmates to undertake it without the accompaniment of any member of the opposite sex, or children. No exceptions! When one of the men objected, as every year someone tried to, Combinex was hard, Combinex would not relent.

Achtung! Orders are orders in the military!

By July of 1964, there was a new Combinex, and he gave the same orders and refused to relent on the women-and-children rule in the same corny way.

Lou never missed having his name in the paper. But it must have galled him to be replaced so blithely as commander. And he had to have muttered, if only to himself: *What in God's name does Lenny Goldstrich know about navigation? The man couldn't pilot a Sunfish out of Montrose Harbor.*

GIVEN THAT THEY both worked downtown, Irv and Lou couldn't avoid running into each other from time to time. At the Morrison Hotel, the Berghoff, the Cape Cod Room, Café Bonaparte, the Glass Hat, or, as sometimes happened, in the locker room of the Standard Club.

Hiya, Lou.

Hiya, Irv.

They'd try and edge away after that. But in the small locker room this wasn't easy, and invariably, as they tried to get out of each other's way, they'd touch, and this led to a flicker of eye contact, during which they'd have a slightly longer conversation.

Things good, Lou?

Oh, I wouldn't complain.

That's good.

And you, Irv?

And Irv would grin a kind of wordless apology. Because how to answer? He was Kup. Of course, he was good.

They'd turn away from each other then and move on to the showers or the urinals or Kup would see someone else he knew.

Nort!

Irv! Terrific column on George Halas.

The old coot's a national treasure.

Yeah, but this Armstrong? Maybe time for the old coot to get back down on the field?

Or one or the other would head to the gym to lift a few weights. Or to the pool to take a swim. Into the 1980s men still swam naked at the Standard Club. I used to watch my grandfather and my father swim with the old Jewish judges whose skin sagged off their bodies like drapery. When they finally allowed women to swim and mandated suits for everybody, Lou thought it was yet another harbinger of the demise of civilization.

No, you can't relitigate the old hurts and sorrows every time you run into a former friend in the locker room at the Standard Club. But there must have been moments when Lou, wearing only a towel, would sit on the bench after one of these brief reunions and pause before he pulled on his pants. Amid the laughs and backslapping and locker room hoopla, Lou, who never enjoyed the unnecessary loudness of glad-handing, might remember a quieter time, like when the four of them would drive to Michigan City for the weekend.

Lou at the wheel of his old Nash Ambassador. He and Irv up front. Essee and Babs cackling like pheasants in the back seat.

The back seat of the old Nash folded out into a bed.

Irv used to kid him about it. How the Nash was a mattress on wheels, no need to get a room.

Funny, Babs and I never once used it. We always left the kids at home with my mother. Why'd we never unfold that bed?

The windows open, wind in their ears. This would have been before the war, in '38 or '39, and they were all still so young. That bloated boat of a sedan lurching toward the Indiana border.

Irv points toward a swamp to the west of the road.

Out there, he says. See it? They call it Wolf Lake.

What about it?

It's where they dumped Bobby Franks in a culvert.

Oh, Lou says and feels it in his chest. Good god, I remember.

Little Bobby Franks in his little gray suit.

To be a Jew in Chicago at that time. It was as if every Jew in the city took turns clubbing Bobby Franks on the head with a chisel.

Wasn't the kid Leopold's cousin?

Let's go for a walk, Irv says. Cain said to Abel.

You said it.

Did you know they stopped for sandwiches? While the kid was dead in the car. They stopped for sandwiches.

Sandwiches?

They didn't say anything after that. That way Irv and Lou used to have of talking without talking.

The Nash hurtles forward, wives in the back seat, giggling. A weekend at the beach without the children.

Lou sits on his damp towel.

Men dressing, men undressing.

Irv's voice: Honorable Judge Holzer! How's business, Reggie?

Splendid, Kup! Yourself?

I BOUGHT A reprint of the UPI telephoto for twenty-five dollars.

Some outfit called historicimages.com.

The catalogue description: *Irv Kupcinet walks down the stairs of Karyn Kupcinet's apartment at 1227½ North Sweetzer.*

The half address still gives a stab. A starter apartment. A stop on the way somewhere else.

Kup's wearing dark glasses. He's slouching. His chin seems as if it's resting on his tie. His hands are in his pockets.

Behind him, in a side view, half in the picture, half out of it, is a man who resembles my grandfather. He's looking up at a man who's standing at the door of the apartment. I don't know who this other man is. A detective?

Uncle Solly isn't in the picture.

Descending the stairs ahead of Kup and dominating the scene is Sidney Korshak. He's dapper, and wearing a jacket my dead father would have described as herringbone tweed. There's his large head and heavy jowls. Under his left arm he's holding a small purse with a single handle, the type a woman might carry on a formal occasion. In both his hands he clutches what seems to be another small pocketbook.

Korshak's eyes are closed as if he's praying. Something

serene about him. A calmness. He's got this. He's going to make certain his old buddy from Lawndale makes it through. Battered, but he'll make it through. Whatever Korshak needs to do, he'll do. If this includes quashing the stories about Cookie's personal life that are killing Essee back in Chicago, he'll have the stories quashed. In the next few hours, Korshak will make a number of calls. And soon enough, the stories will stop and the murder story, limp as it is — will stick.

The caption that accompanied the photograph when it was originally published in the *Los Angeles Times* read:

> *Newspaper columnist Irv Kupcinet (second from the left, dark glasses) descends the stairs after visiting his strangled daughter's apartment on 12/1. The other men in the photograph were not identified.*

Now, not identifying Lou Rosenthal is one thing.
But Korshak?
It's well known that he shunned photographs. Dominick Dunne used to tell a story about the time he snapped a picture of Korshak at a holiday party, and the party immediately went dead silent. Another about how Frank Sinatra once had to fire a publicist because she included Korshak's name on a guest list.
Listen, Sidney Korshak. He doesn't exist.
And yet it does strain believability that United Press International wouldn't have known the man in the herringbone jacket.

Unless they, too, had their marching orders. Never print his name. Korshak doesn't exist —

But there he is, right in the middle of the photograph that was seen at the time by hundreds of thousands of people.

IN *BLUE NIGHTS,* Joan Didion tells a story about the day she and her husband and their newly adopted baby went to the Bistro in Beverly Hills to celebrate the adoption being made official. The maître d' granted them the honor of sitting at Sidney Korshak's table. Korshak wasn't in that day, but that didn't mean anybody could sit at his table. If it sat empty, it sat empty. Didion quotes what Robert Evans, the studio exec (*Love Story, Chinatown, The Godfather, Rosemary's Baby*), had to say about Korshak. A nod from Sidney Korshak and the Teamsters change management. A nod from Korshak and Vegas shuts down. A nod from Korshak and all of a sudden the LA Dodgers can play night baseball.

You get the idea.

Sidney Korshak understood that the perception of power, power as abstraction, itself is power: tangible, deployable power. A four-part investigation by Seymour Hersh in the *New York Times* connected Korshak to labor racketeering, bribery, fraud, extortion, payoffs to judges, kickbacks, blackmail. And, sure, the occasional murder. According to Hersh, Korshak never received a parking ticket, let alone an indictment.* I like to imagine the meter maid with the gumption to slap a ticket under the wiper blades of Korshak's baby-blue Eldorado.

---

* It's been suggested that the only plausible explanation for the lack of any prosecution is that Korshak must have been a federal informant. The man's been dead since 1996, and still he's got me wondering if even passing on the thought that the man was a rat will get somebody somewhere pissed enough to stuff me into a trunk and toss my body over the Indiana state line in a Hefty bag.

SID?

Irv! How's your bird?

My feet, my back, my blood pressure, my gums are bleeding. You want me to stop?

You and me both.

Listen, Sid.

Go ahead.

Remember Lou Rosenthal? Probate attorney. Little guy? Navy?

Didn't I meet him when—

Yes.

I remember the hairless yid. What about him?

He's got a toe in some warm water.

Yeah?

Client trust funds. He's got the Illinois Bar and Dick Devine sniffing around. Look, Sid, it's not like he wasn't intending to shift the funds back.

Of course he was. Now that the state's attorney—

Sid.

I'll look into it.

You will?

Honey, you're asking me again?

The Gossip Columnist's Daughter

Will you be in Palm Springs in February?
Could be.
Buy you a steak at Melvyn's?
I'll like that.
Can I thank you?
No.
Give a fat, wet kiss to Beanie, will you?
Done. Love to Essee.

Dear Unsolved Unit (Bulldogs), Los Angeles County Sheriff's Department,

I'm writing in reference to Homicide File #2-961-651. I'm a professor of creative writing but I seem to have developed a modest knack for private investigation. I believe I have information (okay, call it a well-informed hunch) that could lead the Bulldogs to close yet another cold case and further enhance your reputation of never...

"LUCE."

"Yeah?"

"Got a minute?"

"No."

"I have a theory."

"Another one?"

"You remember how Lou's trouble just disappeared in 1983? One minute it was there and then it wasn't?"

"Not really."

"You don't?"

"I remember the trouble."

"And then what happened to it?"

"I guess you're right. It went away."

"Did you ever wonder why?"

"Not really. I mean, I was relieved. What's your point?"

"It was Kup."

"What about him?"

"I think Dad went to Kup, and Kup — "

"Can you text this?"

"You don't have thirty seconds?"

"Go on."

"You know how Dad always stayed in touch with Kup. Remember? Sometimes he'd bring me with him to the *Sun-Times*?"

"The sailor suit! You have to admit the sailor suit was pretty cute on you. Maybe you should go to an army-navy and buy a pea coat. Bring back that look."

"Would you listen?"

"What makes you think that old faker still had any clout in 1983? By then he was a serious joke, he'd always been a joke, but by then—"

"What if nostalgic clout was still clout."

"So what are you saying?"

"I'm saying Kup made a call."

"To who?"

"Sidney Korshak."

"Ah, the bogeyman!"

"If Kup had run out of clout in '83, Korshak certainly hadn't. In '83 Korshak was still turning tricks for Joe Batters. When the Hotel and Restaurant Union—"

"Okay, so then what happened?"

"How much time do you have?"

"Give it to me in a nutshell."

"Dad reached out to Kup. Kup reached out to Korshak. Lou's problem: gone."

"Interesting. Listen, Rachel's calling me on the other line, I've got to go."

"Rachel hates me."

"She doesn't hate you, she's just filled her quota of cis men in her life. It's not personal."

"It's not personal?"

"A spot might open up. Someone could die or — Listen, I'll call you back in five."

IN 1996, THE same year Sidney Korshak died in bed in Beverly Hills, Lou Rosenthal had a fatal stroke in his seat on the Chicago and North Western, the 5:32 northbound. He was still commuting back and forth to work at my father's office. Nobody noticed that he didn't get off at the Ravinia station. Most of his friends were either dead or retired.

An old guy, slumped. Who'd notice?

At the end of the line, in Kenosha, a cleaner discovered him. She called the paramedics, but by then it was a formality.

TONIGHT WE WATCHED *The Night of the Iguana*. A priest, played by Richard Burton, is on the lam from a statutory rape charge, and so he reinvents himself as a tour guide in Mexico. You roll with the plot. It's Richard Burton. There are comic scenes where Burton tries to interest a group of church ladies in Aztec architecture but all the ladies want to do is go back to the hotel and take a shower. All this heat and dust! There's one scene where Burton speaks with one of the women, Hannah (with an *h*), played by Deborah Kerr. Hannah's not at all the spinster she's been pretending to be. She's got her own despair. She calls it the blue devil and she wrestles with it every day. Burton's curious. How does she fight it?

I breathe, Hannah says. And sure, I drink, too. Rum-cocos. And then she says, turning away from him, I also take lovers [pause], even beach boys.
    Beach boys!
    The line should be funny, or at least a little seductive. But it's not. Deborah Kerr says "beach boys" like they are the bitterest pill anybody could possibly swallow. I can't explain it, but the line made tonight even darker.
    Rudy? Rudy? Where'd you go?

"GOOD SISTER ROSENTHAL."
"You have the wrong number."
"You didn't call me back in five minutes."
"Wasn't that three days ago?"
"Four."
"Sorry."
"There's more to it."
"More to what?"
"Sidney Korshak killed Uncle Solly."
"You've crossed the Rubicon."
"Hear me out."
"Pure, unadulterated bonkers."
"Lou knew something."
"Yeah? What?"
"That Korshak paid off the coroner to rule Cookie's death a homicide."
"How do you know that?"
"Deduction."
"So, you don't."
"I've let the sheriff's office in Los Angeles know I have information."
"About Solly?"

"No, Cookie."
"And?"
"They haven't called."
"Why am I not surprised?"
"Lou insulted Korshak. So there's a personal dimension, too."
"I'm getting dizzy, Jed."
"Basically, Lou dissed him."
"The standoff in the coat closet?"
"Right!"
"I always thought Dad made that story up."
"Why? To make Lou look tough? All Dad ever wanted was to tear Lou down."
"You got a point. But it makes no sense."
"What?"
"First, Kup asks Korshak to help Lou out of a jam — "
"Yes, and he does it. Why does he do it?"
"Jed, that's what I'm fucking asking."
"As a favor to Kup, most definitely. But also to make Lou Rosenthal beholden. Remember, he's the Fixer."
"I thought it was to keep Lou quiet about him paying off the coroner to rule it a homicide."
"That, too."
"And then Korshak turns around and drowns Lou's innocent brother?"
"Orders him drowned. But yes, you're getting it now."
"Even for you, this is beyond — "
"Shot across the bow, Lucy. Brushback pitch. Take out the brother. What would it have cost him? Look what I can still do.

Easy. You think Korshak forgot an insult? Ask Jimmy Hoffa. You know he once booked himself into Korshak's suite at the Riviera in Vegas. Nobody, I mean nobody, stayed in Korshak's suite at the Riviera."

"I fear for you, Jed—"

"Call me Marlow. Call me Encyclopedia Brown."

"And look at this place. When was the last time you made the bed? There's dirty laundry in the kitchen sink. If I wanted to live with a pig, I'd have signed up to be the feline representative at the Farm-in-the-Zoo. "

"Rudy?"

"The cat or your sister, does it even matter at this point?"

"But what about these quotation marks?"

"Little marks at the beginnings and the ends of sentences? Two doodads determine your sense of reality?"

"I clean up when Snook's here."

"Barely."

IT'S NOT LIKE I don't get it. The desire for another version. A couple of ex-cons materialize from another life and push the big lug into the river. Nice to imagine an alternative.

Odds are Solly died, like the rest of us, of a broken heart — whether we're dead or not.

v.

Us

Why does one feel so different at night?
— *Katherine Mansfield*

MY MOTHER TOLD me once that there was a rumor going around in the early sixties that Babs and Kup had had some sort of fling.

"Kup had a reputation with the ladies," my mother said. "All you had to do was ask him. He used to love to tell this story about himself and Joan Crawford on the night of the Oscars—"

"But Babs? Babs and Kup?"

"You know how things go around," she said.

"No," I said. "Tell me how things go around."

My mother looked at me in the dark of the car. I was driving. We were on our way back to Highland Park from a play at the Goodman. This was years ago. I'm trying to remember what play it was and I can't. Let's say it was *The Cherry Orchard*—though it wasn't—because that play always puts me in a questioning mood.

"You want me to spell it out for you? How rumors have a beating heart of their own?"

"Even though you were a generation younger, you moved in the same circles as Kup and Essee?"

"Don't you ever get bored of them?"

"I'm just wondering how you heard that Kup and Babs had a thing."

"Yes, we were younger, of course, your father and I, but we'd see them out. The Pump Room, the Buttery at the Ambassador East. Chez Paul. There wasn't an event, a party, an opening —"

"I know, I know."

"They'd come sweeping in, those two, to rescue any gathering. Because at last they'd arrived."

We were quiet for a while. I thought about cocktail parties in the late fifties. An apartment on the Gold Coast. The roaring chatter, the dim light, all those bodies clustered together, the conversations more like jousting than talking. The laughter rising and falling.

And the man-about-town and his wife would circulate.

"Essee had this cackle," my mother said. "She'd say something and then she'd cackle at whatever she'd just said. That's how you knew she was in the vicinity."

It was raining. We were on the Edens. That thump of the windshield wipers, like a metronome. We were tired from the play, whatever we'd seen.

"It was Babs," my mother said.

"What about her?"

"It was the way she acted around Kup. When she was in his physical presence. She avoided getting too close, you know? And he, too, he always kept his distance from her. Just something I picked up on. Went on a couple of years. And then it stopped. After Cookie died, everything stopped."

"So you didn't hear it."

"Hear what?"

"The rumor about Kup and Babs. You saw it firsthand."

"Maybe I did, Jed. I don't know."

"Sounds like you were the source."

"You pump and pump for information. Haven't you got your own problems?"

"You want me to answer that?"

"Look, Jed, Irv and Lou and Essee and Babs. It's all water under a bridge that doesn't even exist anymore."

The Cherry Orchard. All that fluttering around, all that useless hand-wringing. Such beautiful inertia. David Mamet (talk about a writer who's gone bananas) says somewhere that nobody in the play gives a damn about the cherry orchard. He's right. All the characters want to do is talk about the past. To wallow in what's already happened. The future is a dull abstraction. And the present? Forget the present.

"You think that was the source of the rift?"

"What?"

"Babs and Kup. An affair?"

"Don't be stupid."

"So no?"

"A rift doesn't last forty years because of some fling that probably didn't happen anyway. It was between the two of them."

"Which two?"

"Do I need to write this thing for you?"

My mother was silent for a while. The rain pounded the roof of the car. I turned off the expressway onto Lake Cook and headed east.

"Who knows? There was no drama that I know of. No recriminations. After Cookie's death it was like they simply hadn't known each other, as if a lifelong friendship had simply been expunged. After, Babs — it's hard to describe — she was heavier on her feet. I'd hardly have noticed, but she was a woman who'd always been so light on her feet."

SPRING (?) 2019. There's Chicago April that's colder than any February. Snowless and bleak and the wind bellows off the lake. We'd been up half the night already. The radiator clanging like a troll trying to get our attention from a dungeon. Our bedroom on Jarvis. The lights were out, but the shades were up, and the streetlight on the corner of Jarvis and Clark, though dim, illuminated the room. Baby supplies scattered like drug paraphernalia. Bottles, diapers, wipes, crusty jars of food, wooden toys because Hanna didn't believe in plastic ones. Hanna's books and papers and sketchpads. My books and notes and (ungraded) papers. Our laptops. Old coffee cups growing a lunar-looking mold.

"It's because I'm mopey," I said.

She shook her head. She stood by the door, holding a pillow to her chest. She was leaving to spend what was left of the night on the floor in Snook's room.

"You are mopey, but that's not — "

"I'm preoccupied with my failures."

"You do love your failures."

"I'm bitter I'm not famous."

"Jed, I'm tired."

"I'm annoying. I live in the past."

"Check, check."

"I'm sexually needy."

She came back and sat down on the bed, knowing the conversation, if that's what this was, wasn't over, that I wasn't going to let it be over. She looked at me in the half dark. Her hair was down, and a few curly strands dangled in front of her eyes. She wasn't wearing her glasses, and I know I must have looked blurry to her.

"I've never minded your horniness. You think I'm not horny? I know after Snook, I've been less — "

"Are you horny now?"

"No."

She turned away. I stared at her lower back. She always slept in a tank top. It was too short and there were her obliques, I think they're called, muscles of hers I especially loved.

"You're seeing somebody else."

"If I had time to sleep around, I'd sleep."

"Okay, so — "

"We're a lot. And we became a lot so fast after we met up again. A lot, a lot. You know?"

"You want more space? How about Skokie? Skokie's becoming sort of hip."

"Skokie's hip?"

"What about Evanston?"

"Never."

She began kneading the bedspread, something I remember my mother doing when she was trying to think of what to say to get me to sleep. She'd sit on my bed and knead the comforter.

"It's not space. But you do fill every inch of this house, even when you aren't here, and between Snook and my clients and you, I'm squeezed—"

"My foot's asleep. You're never more aware that you're just a piece of meat than when your foot's asleep."

"See?"

"What?"

"What does this have to do with how you feel about your feet?"

"Go on."

"A parting. For a while. A trial."

"A separation?"

"I said parting."

"What's the difference?"

She stood up. Her bare feet on the cold floor. She stood on her toes and stretched.

"I've always loved your toes."

"Jesus. Look, do you want me to move out and you stay here with Snook?"

"I'll move," I said.

"You think you couldn't handle it?"

"I know I couldn't handle it. Also, Snook—"

"She'd get used to it. We'd figure it out together."

"I'll move," I said.

"Sure?"

"Yes."

"Okay."

"You can take Rudy."

"Great. Where is that predator?"

"Snook's room. He got bored of us hours ago."
"You want to screw around?"
"Now?"
"He's not here to glower."
"Yes."
"Really?"
"I said yes."
"Wow."
"It doesn't change."
"I know."

She lay down again next to me and yawned and stretched. A siren, an ambulance going by on North Clark. Block by block, it faded out of earshot. I wished I knew a thing about how sound traveled through space and time.

"Music?"
"Not tonight."
"The Pogues?"
"No."
"Silver Jews?"
"No."
"Wilco?"
"Please, no."

I waited. Our room on Jarvis. The light from the corner.
Hanna: "Let's get this show on the road."

I'VE NEVER BEEN able to find a picture of Essee and Babs, just the two of them. It must have been one of those alliances that's so cemented that to take a picture and memorialize it seems redundant.

Lucy and me. We can talk across dimensions, and yet over our entire lives we've taken only a handful of pictures together.

The two weren't just inseparable, my mother says. They were almost interchangeable. The laughter. The whispering. And when they weren't in the same room, they were always, always linked by the phone.

But the long distance—

Oh, damn the long distance. The Sun-Times *pays all the phone bills, including the ones from the hotel.*

I do have a picture of Kup and Babs. It was taken at one of the testimonial dinners given in Kup's honor in the early sixties, maybe when he was given the Heart Award by the Variety Club, and in it my grandmother is standing between Irv and Lenny Goldstrich, the guy who took over from Lou as Combinex.

Irv and Lenny are chortling about something. Babs is looking straight at the camera. Irv's honker of a nose is blocking my grandmother's right eye. There's something sly and

knowing about her smile. As if she's signaling to the photographer, This may all seem frivolous to you, yet another testimonial dinner, some stupid chitchat. And it's true, there's nothing memorable about this. Another night of conversations that won't be remembered in the morning. But consider this, it's also life itself, and while these two jokers may not know it, I know it, that all the nights, all the forgettable nights make up whatever time we're granted, and if you think this is nothing, then life itself isn't anything.

HANNA IS A board-certified Lacanian psychotherapist, one of only four Lacanians in Chicago. Before the pandemic she had an office on East Van Buren, but now she mostly does telehealth out of what used to be my upstairs closet study in the place on West Jarvis.

In the months when Hanna was pregnant with Snook, we used to roam around Rosehill Cemetery and talk amid the graves and the oak trees and the stone obelisks pointing skyward. There are few quieter parks in the city. I'd point out highlights. Oscar Mayer's grave. Ignaz Schwinn's, the dude who bestowed the banana seat upon the world. Lulu Fellows: the girl in the glass box. There's a book on her lap, but she's not reading it. Lulu stares right at you from behind the rain-smudged glass. She died at sixteen, in 1883. People leave gifts. Dolls, flags, a Mountain Dew bottle with a flower in it.

"And look, see the mausoleum? Bobby Franks. First, Richard hit him with a tire iron, and then Nathan, or maybe it was the other way—"

"Can we for once skip Bobby Franks?"

"It's our original sin. Every Jewish Chicagoan carries the burden of the taint—"

"That's ridiculous. Two twisted freaks."

"That's your diagnosis?"

"I'm not a psychiatrist."

"What would Jacques Lacan think?"

"Lacan? Of Loeb and Leopold? He'd think a lot of things. He'd have had a field day with those two."

"And?"

"Oh, I don't know. He'd have said something like, They broke past the constraint of language. For Lacan, Language is a construct, it's symbolic. That doesn't mean it isn't all-powerful. Because we believe in it. Language says it's not okay to kill a little boy on his way home from school. Loeb and Leopold were like, *Language? We're not going to let little old language stop us.* Perverse, but not irrational. Utterly logical. I'm dumbing this way down, but that's the idea— Forget it, you're not listening."

It was fall, Hanna was pregnant, we were walking through the piles of leaves.

From a distance Hanna looks taller than she is. Sometimes I see a woman in a crowd walking down the steps of the Thorndale L station—and I follow her with my eyes for a while before I realize it's her.

THERE WAS A point, in the early sixties, when Essee and Babs were no longer, as Essee would say, chickadees. Without Babs waiting at home for news, Essee might not have mustered the energy to go out at all. It had always been work, but at the same time it used to be so exhilarating. Now it was only work. But you couldn't be married to the man about town if you didn't leave the house.

"You know what Sammy said to me?"
"Sammy who?"
"Oh, Babs, Sammy who!"
"What did he say?"
"He said, 'Essee, baby,' you know that smoky voice Sammy has. 'Essee, baby, you still have the sweetest icy eyes,' and I said, 'Still, Sammy? Still? What do you mean by still?' For once that little man was at a loss for words. Oh, Babsy, most nights I just want to scream, I want to crawl under the table and scream. Irv says stay home if I'm so miserable. And you know the only thing worse than having to get dressed again is — "
" — not having to get dressed again."
"Are you laughing at me?"

"Yes."

"I can't see your face with my sweet icy eyes, but I could swear you're laughing."

"I just told you I am."

"Lunch?"

"I'm teaching all day. Three ballet classes. Introductory, intermediate — "

"Rats. It's not like you need the money. Lunch?"

"I've got an hour between one fifteen and two fifteen."

"The WAC?"

"Not enough time."

"I'll come north," Essee says. "Ann Sather's?"

"One fifteen? You'll be there?"

"Since when am I late?"

"Ess."

"I'll start getting ready."

WE THOUGHT OF ourselves like the couple in *Love in the Time of Cholera*. Fated to find each other again. Those times in your life when time no longer weighs anything. We tried not to gloat about it, even to ourselves.

What if Hanna and her friends hadn't wandered into the Sovereign on a Tuesday night? Who goes out on a Tuesday?

What if they'd gone to Cunneen's or Moody's? Or the Public House? Or Ricky G's? It's not like the Sovereign has much to offer, aside from the fact that the music is always good, it's never crowded, and they allow dogs. One night I brought Rudy, which wasn't a hit with Rudy or the regulars. A cat in a bar is terrifying for everybody. Above the bar there's a map of Ireland. A lot of nights I study it. County Sligo. Any place called Sligo is worth my time. Once, I overheard a woman say, *I'm an emotional procrastinator.* I've been loyal to the place ever since. Some darknesses become yours.

Those first few weeks, we'd spend long mornings in bed. I canceled classes. Hanna moved some of her appointments around. I'd prop the sheet with a broom, bristles up, to make a tent, and we'd climb all over each other and the tent would collapse and we'd sleep and then climb some more. We resurrected a joke from college. We used to say we dwelled in the country of us. Back then we'd made a pact never to utter a word of this schmaltz to anybody. We renewed that pact. Who wants to hear about other people's delirious happiness?

And what's easier, in hindsight, to lampoon?

SATURDAY NIGHT BLEEDS into the morning of Sunday, December 1, and the two of them are tangled in sheets and blankets on the floor of Essee's bedroom. Essee still won't get up and lie on her bed. As if to lie on a bed would do Cookie some dishonor. Babs holds her. Essee's skin boils. The lights are all on. Essee wants them on, all of them, the overheads, the lamps, all that blazing wattage. From the street, all night long, the rest of the windows of 257 dark, the bedroom must have looked like it was on fire.

Outside the door, the dog pitter-patters.

Essee demands that Babs bring her the papers.

"Shoplifting? Arrested? I'll kill her."

"Ess."

"I will, I will, I will."

Babs hushes in her ear, "Lie down, darling. Won't you lie down before you collapse?"

"No."

Again, Babs holds her until the short day begins to darken and at last Essee goes slack and Babs gently lowers her head onto one of the gathered pillows, and yet Essee, after only a few minutes or so, wakes. Her head shoots up from the pillow. She shouts, "Coffee! Coffee!"

Babs hustles to the kitchen, makes the coffee, feeds the dog. Three times she runs back to the bedroom to check on Essee while the coffee brews. When it's done, she brings it back to the bedroom and hands the steaming cup to Essee.

Her eyes tightened shut, Essee whispers now, "Can't you make it hotter, B?"

And Babs carries the cup back to the kitchen and reheats the coffee in a saucepan and runs it back to the bedroom but now it's not coffee Essee wants. She's torn her nightdress off.

Eyes still closed. "Where are you?"

"I'm here, I'm right here."

IN LOU'S PAPERS there's a file marked simply "KK." Inside is half a piece of sky-blue paper, perforated and torn, as if someone had ripped it off a pad. About the weight and texture of a piece of airmail paper.

> CORONER'S PROPERTY RECEIPT BOOK (OUTGOING)
> #9776
> 12/2/63
> RECEIVED FROM CORONER, COUNTY OF LOS ANGELES, STATE OF CALIFORNIA. The following described property found on the body of Karyn Kupcinet:
> 1-4 Ring Band

It must have been Lou who retrieved her personal effects.

He would have given the ring to Irv. But why did he hold on to the receipt? Did he want to spare a father the starkness of the language? *The following property...* Or maybe he hadn't thought about it at all. Maybe he just stuffed it into his pocket and later, back home in Chicago, he found it.

Then he filed it, as he filed everything.

I once asked Hanna about the ring size. She said Cookie must have had pretty small hands, or at least very thin fingers.

SENIOR YEAR, FOR her thesis project, Hanna rented an empty storefront in a little town outside Champaign called Rantoul. She'd asked a doctor how many Benadryls she could take at one time without them killing her. At first the doctor wouldn't answer. Hanna said she was going to do it anyway, so he might as well give his professional opinion. The doctor said, *I never said this. No more than five at a time. Now get out of here.* We bought a mattress at the Goodwill in Urbana and drove it back to Rantoul. Then she put up a single sign on the door:

> *Woman Sleeps*
> A Performance by H. Abrams
> Thursday, Friday, and Saturday, 7 p.m. to 10 p.m.

That Thursday around 6:15, she swallowed six pills and lay down on the mattress. She read poetry for a while, and, after about fifteen or twenty minutes, passed out.

I handled security. I sat in a folding chair by the door and read the paper like a museum guard. We'd bought me a uniform, also at the Goodwill, a Cub Scout den leader's shirt with a stitched patch that said Dan.

There weren't many problems. We didn't publicize it. Aside from the sign, there were no flyers, no explanatory material of any kind. It was Midwestern guerrilla art. Nothing remotely like this was happening downstate in the early nineties. If more people had known about it, they'd have run us out of Champaign County.

One guy came in eating a gas-station hot dog. A bit of relish plopped onto the floor every time he took a bite. He stood there chewing, watching Hanna. My job was to enforce the only rule: no one was to touch her.

It wasn't that Hanna's performances lacked action. Even in that deep Benadryl-induced sleep, she'd still toss and turn. On a few occasions she talked in her sleep, though I could never make out what she was saying. There was something dangerous about how beautiful and defenseless she was. Something cherubic about it, and Hanna's never been cherubic. Maybe any sleeping person looks angelic? She was what, twenty-two that year?

(Even now I struggle to describe her face, and I saw her yesterday. How can she be so imprinted on my brain and the best I can do tonight is greenish hazel eyes, high cheekbones, and slightly upturned nostrils like tiny pistol barrels?)

Another time an old woman wandered in and knelt beside the mattress and touched her cheek so tenderly I didn't have the heart to enforce the no-touch rule.

On Saturday, the last night of the performance, Hanna's adviser attended, a flamboyant woman in a dress printed with huge sunflowers. Professor Margarite raved about the success of the project, pacing around the room talking as if she was talking to Hanna. I think she thought Hanna was acting. *I wish John Cage were here to see this...*

All three nights, after I locked the door at ten, I'd take a few pills myself. Then I'd lie down on the mattress and wrap my arms around her and we'd both sleep long past noon.

THERE ARE CRIME scene photographs, including one of the couch after they removed Cookie's body. Cigarettes are scattered around the carpet. On her door is a wreath. A little bell hangs from it.

But the image that keeps coming to mind is from before the Goddards found her.

Her agitation dissipates as her breathing slows, the pale light of the black-and-white television washing out the color of her face. She shifts around to get more comfortable. And maybe, like Hanna on her mattress in Rantoul, she murmurs a few unintelligible words.

Then she's out, she's drifting.

"IT'S LATE."

"Asleep?"

"No."

"What are you doing?"

"Reading."

"What?"

"The new Colson Whitehead."

"Oh."

Pause.

"Aren't we set for tomorrow? You've got to meet the other moms at Tumbletown at — "

"I know, I love those special nonslip socks they give you."

"Okay. So — "

"Can I ask you something in your professional capacity?"

"No."

"It's not about me."

"Still no."

"Can I anyway?"

"Fine."

"It's about Cookie."

"Who?"

"You know, she's the subject of my, you know, you know."

"What?"

"The actress. Kup's daughter."

"The one your mom says took pills?"

"That's right. But that's not what I — "

"What, then?"

"The night she died she told her ex-boyfriend about a ghost baby. She said somebody left a baby at the door of her apartment."

"A ghost baby or a real baby?"

"She said it was a real baby."

"So why'd you say ghost baby?"

"Because the baby didn't exist."

"How do you know?"

"Well, I don't. I mean, there was no record of it. She'd had an abortion earlier that year."

"Was the ex-boyfriend the father?"

"Of the aborted baby or the doorstep baby?"

"Either one."

"The aborted one."

"What did he say about the doorstep baby?"

"He told her to call the police."

"That's all he said?"

"He wasn't exactly a scholar of human self-deception. He was a TV cowboy."

"Did she call the police?"

"There's no record of it."

"And so you think the baby wasn't real?"

"I think it's unlikely."

"But not impossible?"

"That somebody left a baby on her doorstep? No, not impossible. So what do you think?"

"In terms of what?"

"Like, you know, in terms of what was wrong with her."

"How long has she been dead?"

"Sixty-one years."

"I'd say she deserved better."

"Yeah."

"Listen, it's late."

"All right."

She didn't hang up.

"Do you still do that thing with your feet?" I asked.

"What?"

"When you raise your feet and rub your feet together? Just when you get into bed to get the dust off? That cricket thing, you still do it?"

"Why wouldn't I?"

"bring me the baby."

"I can't, Ess. She's in an incubator. She's got these tubes. For a while they thought she might not — "

"And now?"

"With the machines, she's breathing."

"What's her name?"

"Lucille."

"Lucille? After that red-haired giraffe?"

Babs shrugs. "I've no idea."

"Bring me the child."

"Ess."

"I want to see that baby."

LUCY CALLED. SHE remembered something. In 1983, when everything was going to such shit all over the place, she'd gone over to Waverly Road. It must have been around Thanksgiving because she was home from Middlebury. Babs and Lou had been packing the house up for weeks, and when Lucy let herself in through the back door, the kitchen was strewn with open boxes and all the cabinets and drawers were open. Babs was sitting at the big round table in the corner of the kitchen weeping. Lucy had never seen Babs tear up, much less all-out cry.

We used to call that big round table in the kitchen of the house on Waverly Road the Knights of the Round Table, and we'd all sit around it for Lou's breakfast feasts. Lou would make heaps and heaps of pancakes and Lucy and I would gorge ourselves to the point where we'd be about to puke and Lou would stand before us with a frying pan and a spatula and say, *Room for one more?*

"She was bawling," Lucy said. "She'd stop and blow her nose and then start again. Remember? How when Babs blew her nose she always sounded like a goose?"

"I remember."

"I always assumed it was the house, and that Lou might be

going to jail and all that. Now I wonder. There's only one thing that could make somebody cry like that."

"But after twenty years?"

"Sometimes it takes that long."

THE AFTERNOON OF December 2. Soot-gray sky. The lake lurks, vast beyond the windows.

At last, Essee's asleep. Together, they're still on the floor.

And still all the blazing light. When Babs tries to close her eyes, whatever time of the morning it is, her eyelids are nothing against all that light.

A few small bump bump bumps on the door. Not the dog. She locked Cleopatra in the broom closet.

Babs edges slowly away from Essee and opens the door.

"Judy, Judy, Judy."

She closes the door behind her and squeezes her daughter.

"The doorman almost wouldn't let me up," Judith says.

"Oh, honey, I forgot to tell Puck."

"Can I make some sandwiches or something?"

"Please, there's tuna. I haven't — leave them outside the door, all right?"

"Mom?"

"Yes?"

"How's it going in there?"

"Hard to say."

AND DON'T WE carry around certain names like talismans?

Uncle Solly. Auntie Pauline. Even Sidney Korshak.

But Aunt Judith isn't even a minor character. She's only got a cameo in all this. Lucy and I never knew her much at all. In my finite wisdom, I tell my students that a reader can't establish an emotional connection to a character they know little about. Another one of those bogus things I say to kill time. On the street, on the L, in a coffee shop, aren't there moments when we're nearly floored by a single passing look into a stranger's eyes? And then? They vanish...

After she earned her MBA at Wisconsin, Aunt Judith took off for Seattle. If Chicago is the center of the universe, something any astronomer on this city's payroll will attest, then Seattle is a Neptunian outpost. She didn't come home often. When she did, because she feared flying, she always drove her VW Bug convertible halfway across the country. When I asked my mother to tell me more about her the other day, she said, Judy kept her distance, a lot of distance. She was the free spirit of the Rosenthals. Lord knows you all needed one. She worked in a bank but wrote poetry. Baked her own bread. And, horror of horrors, even out in Seattle, she patently refused to marry anybody, and it wasn't like she didn't have offers.

My mother said that Judith once told her that when she was a girl, Essee Kupcinet used to kneel down and get really close to her, nose to nose, to inspect her for signs that she might become pretty.

Your eyes, Judy, I think they could be hazel.

They're brown, Aunt Essee. They've always been brown.

"I JUST REMEMBERED something else."

"What?"

"She stole Essee's egg."

"Who?"

"Judith."

"Mom, you're like Lucy—remembering things at the last minute."

"Our memories have to adjust to your timeline?"

"What egg?"

"Well, she thought it was a Fabergé egg."

"I'm lost."

"You know those Fabergés can go for tens of thousands, and a lot more, actually. Who knows why. What do you do with them? This one was a small one, so even if it had been real, it wouldn't have been worth so much. Anyway, Judith didn't steal it because she thought it was valuable. She just thought it was pretty. And she wanted to steal something, anything, from Essee. On her way out the door to the bus station, she stuffed it into her bag. Turned out it was a knockoff, worth at most a couple of hundred dollars. Still, a month later, when Essee noticed it was missing, she fired the new Japanese maid."

WHEN JUDITH DIED of pancreatic cancer in 1997, Babs and Lou flew out to Seattle and brought her body home. Always, always, the return to Chicago. She'd asked that there be no funeral. My mother planted some flowers in the yard in her honor. Violets because Judith had loved violets.

BABS DIDN'T WILT. She never walked around as if she was wounded. She put her head down and lived. Tooled around town in her powder-blue Cadillac Seville, blowing off stop signs because she was late to class. For years and years and years, she continued — deep into her nineties — to teach dance and exercise classes at the rec center. A life lived in a hurry. Always on her way somewhere. What was the alternative? After the temporary hullabaloo of losing Waverly Road and Lou's troubles, she was right back at it.

On Tuesday afternoon, she played bridge. On Wednesdays, canasta. On Saturdays she and Lou would drive out to Long Grove and play golf. The hairdresser. Getting her nails done. But mostly, as I say, she worked at the rec center, the one that used to be behind Sunset Foods until they moved it to Park Avenue.

"YOU?"

"Were you expecting someone else?"

"Those days are over, remember? Your name comes up on the screen."

"It's okay if you were."

"I wasn't."

"What about the Pilates teacher you said was hot."

"I only went twice. Why would she call me?"

"I'm just saying."

"What are you doing?"

"Reading."

"Who?"

"Colson Whitehead."

"Still?"

"He really is amazing. The characterizations, the momentum — "

"I'll have to get a copy."

Pause.

"Jed?"

"Yeah?"

"You want to come home? Just for the night? Come home?"

"Yes."

"Just for tonight."

"I heard you."

"You think I'm cruel?"

"You're not cruel."

"Because if you think I'm cruel—"

"I said you're not cruel."

"Will you?"

"Snook?"

"Three consecutive play dates, from ten a.m. to five. The kid's out, out—"

"Rudy?"

"What about him?"

"He doesn't like to be alone at night."

"Bring the cat."

"I'll come, you know I'll come."

"I'm not begging."

BUT THE ACHE remains. I say it does reach across the generations. Somebody had to love Essee Kupcinet. Turned out it was Babs Rosenthal. Who you love becomes your lot. This can't be an original thought. Still, this morning it thunders like some divine revelation. Essee was my grandmother's lot. Destiny sounds too puffed up. Lot's better. Like a parking lot.

It was Babs who followed her, holding up her train, as Essee walked down the aisle in the ballroom of the Belmont Hotel. It was Babs who gripped her elbow as she walked down another aisle twenty-five years later. There were times, throughout the rest of her life, even at Sunrise or Sunset, when Babs would look up from whatever she'd been doing and expect to see Essee bolt through the doorway.

AFTER MIDNIGHT ON December 3, the day they will bury Cookie. For hours there's been no sound at all from the master bedroom. Judith opens the door and peeps in. The two women are on the floor beside the bed. All that light and the windows reflect even more of it. Now it's her mother who's finally asleep. Essee sits bolt upright. Babs's head rests on Essee's bare thigh. A long moment passes before she notices Judith at the door. Essee cringes and begins to claw her own face. Judith is about to shout No!, when she sees that Essee's long nails aren't touching her skin. It's a pantomime. Grief will not disfigure. The woman's shredding air. Essee turns to her own reflection mirrored in the windows. And that's when she watches herself deliver her line, the line my sister and I repeat to each other, sometimes as a joke, sometimes out of awe for the inspired malice of it.

"You? You're the one that survives?"

Acknowledgments

The frontispiece photograph is used by permission of the Associated Press. The photograph of Karyn Kupcinet on page 208 is used by permission of the Los Angeles Public Library. All other photos by @apaniaguaphoto. Many thanks to the Chicago History Museum and its kind, supportive staff for providing access to the Irv Kupcinet Papers.

Immense gratitude to the following: Rhoda Pierce (Mom), Eric Orner, Ellen Levine, Josh Kendall, Yvette Benavides (cohost of *The Lonely Voice* podcast from Texas Public Radio), Maya Guthrie, Ben George, Pat Strachan, Betsy Uhrig, Caitlin Van Dusen, Alberto Rodriguez, Nick Regiacorte, Alex Gordon, Julie Gordon, Matt Goshko, David Krause, Melissa Kirsch, Donal McLaughlin, Stuart Dybek, Marisa Silver, Andre Dubus III, Dominic Pacyga, Dave Eggers, Rob Preskill, Ricardo Siri, Angie Del Campo, Elizabeth Garriga, Darcy Glastonbury, Sarah Jean Grimm, and Kimberly Burns.

And to the Tuckerboxers: Vievee Francis, Sally Brady,

Acknowledgments

John Griesemer, Bill Craig, as well as Robin Weigert, Richard Schiff, and the Sunday group.

To Riccardo Duranti, Italian translator and dear friend.

I'd also like to thank Wendel Cox and Shawn Martin of the Dartmouth College Library for their expertise; the Vermont Studio Center and Sarah Audsley; and the Hawthornden Foundation of Lasswade, Scotland, and Hamish Robinson for the gift of fellowship, time, and space.

In memory of Rudy, 1998–2012.

About the Author

Born in Chicago, Peter Orner is the author of seven acclaimed books, including *Maggie Brown & Others; Love and Shame and Love; Esther Stories,* finalist for the PEN/Hemingway Award; *Am I Alone Here?,* finalist for the National Book Critics Circle Award; and *Still No Word from You,* finalist for the PEN/Diamonstein-Spielvogel Award for the Art of the Essay. His work has appeared in *The New Yorker,* the *Paris Review, The Believer,* and *The Best American Short Stories* and has received four Pushcart Prizes. A Guggenheim Fellow and recipient of the Rome Prize from the American Academy of Arts and Letters, Orner is chair of the Department of English and Creative Writing at Dartmouth College. He lives with his family in Vermont, where he's also a volunteer firefighter.